DOUBLE KISS

By Ronnie O'Sullivan

Fiction
FRAMED

Non-Fiction
RUNNING

RONNIE

RONNIE O'SULLIVAN

DOUBLE KISS

MACMILLAN

First published 2017 by Macmillan
an imprint of Pan Macmillan
20 New Wharf Road, London N1 9RR
Associated companies throughout the world
www.panmacmillan.com

ISBN 978-1-5098-6397-6

1 3 5 7 9 8 6 4 2

A CIP catalogue record for this book is available from the British Library.

Typeset by Palimpsest Book Production Ltd, Falkirk, Stirlingshire
Printed and bound by CPI Group (UK) Ltd, Croydon, CRO 4YY

Visit www.panmacmillan.com to read more about all our books
and to buy them. You will also find features, author interviews and
news of any author events, and you can sign up for e-newsletters
so that you're always first to hear about our new releases.

To Steve Peters and Keno Fu

– you both know why you mean so much to me.

Acknowledgements

Thanks to everyone involved in making
Double Kiss a reality, from my agent, Jonny Geller,
and all the team at Curtis Brown to my editors
Emlyn Rees and Victoria Hughes-Williams,
and all the team at Pan Macmillan.

1

'It's coming home . . . It's coming home . . . It's coming . . . Football's coming home . . .'

The Ambassador Club was packed tighter than a tube carriage during rush hour. The owner, Frankie James, reckoned there had to be 150 punters in here. Maybe more. Pumping their fists in the air, with their England flags draped down their backs, looking like a bunch of pissed-up, wannabe superheroes all trying and failing to take off.

The hulking, great silhouette of Spartak Sidarov stood wedged in the open doorway, bright sunlight pouring in through the tiny gaps that his massive shoulders hadn't quite blocked out. Frankie's old mate was more used to bossing Oxford Street night club queues, but it was good to have him here today, seeing as how many people had turned up this afternoon to watch the match and how hammered most of them already were.

A good job too that Frankie and Xandra had put the hardboard covers on the club's twelve snooker tables that morning, while Dave the Shock had been installing the two big wall TV projectors he'd picked up from the Rumbelows clearance sale. Because none of this crowd were here to play. The whole room stank of smoke and spilt booze. There wasn't a ball or a cue in sight.

The tabletops were littered instead with overflowing ashtrays and pint glasses, and a young woman called Shazza was now curled up on table six and snoring like a drain – Frankie kept half an eye on her.

Everyone else's eyes were glued to the screens. England one, Switzerland nil, with just ten minutes to go. It was the first match of Euro 96 and the action was taking place right here in London, just up the road at Wembley. With the whole world watching. Or at least that's how it felt.

'Come on, boys. Keep the bastards out,' Frankie muttered under his breath, swilling dirty pint glasses one after the other through the glass-washing machine behind the bar, his shoulders tightening up as the Swiss surged forward again.

He'd put a hundred quid down at Ladbrokes on England to win. But not just this match, the whole tournament, three weeks from now, at odds of 7-1. A win would mean Frankie could escape Soho for a nice little holiday.

He hadn't had a day off since Christmas, not once in the last six months.

He glanced back at the photo montage his mum had stuck up here on the wall between the optics. Back when her and the Old Man had still been together, and they'd all used to head off down the Costa del Sol along with a bunch of other families from round here. His mum was right there in the middle, her beautiful smile suspended in time, as she hugged her two precious boys – Jack and Frankie. Frankie couldn't have been more than thirteen.

2

Frankie was rudely brought back to the here and now by loud cheers and shouts of encouragement. Up on the screen, the clock ticked over to the eighty-three-minute mark. The crowd started belting out the Lightning Seeds' anthem again, even louder this time.

'Three Lions on a shirt . . . neeeeeever stopped me dreaming . . .'

Frankie joined in. It was hard not to. This sodding tune was that damned catchy and the stakes were that bloody high. He grinned across at Doc Slim and Xandra. Both working the bar beside him. Doc doffed his worn leather cowboy hat, looking more and more like Colonel Sanders by the day now that he'd upgraded his grisly grey moustache to a full-blown beard.

Xandra was sporting her new, that-girl-from-the-Cranberries, cropped barnet, along with the panther tattoo on her bulging right bicep that Frankie had sprung for on her nineteenth birthday last month.

Bloody kids. She was only five years younger than him, but he still felt like her dad. He'd even insisted on meeting the tattooist and checking he was properly licensed before he'd let him set to work. But then Frankie had always been older than his years. He remembered his mum always saying that about him, even when he was a nipper.

'Don't give up the day job,' Xandra laughed, mock grimacing and sticking her fingers in her heavily studded ears. She'd already told him she'd heard cows in labour singing better than him on the County Antrim farm where she'd grown up. The bloody cheek.

Then *booooooooo*. The crowd's choral antics switched to jeers. Frankie's ice-blue eyes locked back on the screen. Bollocks, double bollocks, Stuart Pearce! He'd only just been bloody penalized, hadn't he? For handball. In the box. Shit-a-brick. This was all Frankie needed. England starting off their campaign with a draw.

Pearce's nickname – 'Psycho, psycho, psycho!' – rumbled through the crowd. The Swiss striker, Türkyilmaz – 'Wanker, wanker, wanker!' – stepped up for the kick. Seaman stared him down from the English goal, his dodgy 'tache and slick-back glistening in the blazing hot sun, making him look more like he was planning on selling his opponent some double glazing than blocking an actual shot.

Frankie couldn't watch. It was the same as whenever he watched Tim frigging Henman on the box, tightening up on his second serve at set point. Frankie sometimes felt that maybe he was capable of jinxing it all personally, just by wanting it so much.

He looked the opposite way down the bar instead, at Ash Crowther and Sea Breeze Strinati, who were both hunkered down on their usual stools, with their bent backs squarely to the room, totally wrapped up in the same game of chess they'd been playing since last Tuesday. Or was it the Tuesday before?

Then the whole crowd groaned, '*Noooooooo!*' And Frankie forced himself to look back at the telly. Arse flaps. The Swiss players were celebrating all over the pitch. Practically cartwheeling, the cuckoo clock-fiddling bastards. Gritting his teeth, he watched the replay. Türkyilmaz went left. Seaman right. Leaving it one all now, with less than four minutes to go.

'Bloody England,' he groaned.

'Aye,' Slim grumbled, bumping his hat on the ceiling light as he reached up to fill a tumbler from the optics. 'It's at parlous times like this that one almost wishes one had been born a Kraut.'

'Oi, mate, two pints of Guinness,' some bumfluff-chinned, pumped-up teenage lump in a white Umbro tracksuit yelled across at Frankie. 'Er, please?' he quickly added, clocking Frankie's glare, along with his black suit and tie, and no doubt wisely hazarding a guess that he was the boss man round here.

Dress smart. That's what Frankie's Old Man had always told him. Look like the man and most people will treat you like him too.

He'd not been wrong. Frankie served the lad, who was all smiles and friendliness now. Even gave Frankie a tip, which he bunged in the communal Heinz baked beans can by the till, safely out of reach of any tea-leafing bastards in here. Today's event had transformed the whole of Soho into a pickpockets' paradise, bursting with pissed-up punters, all flashing their cash.

He risked another glance at the screen. Two minutes left, before injury time. With England nowhere bleeding near the Swiss bloody goal. He obviously wasn't the only one getting that sinking, Tim Henman feeling. The cheering and chant-ing had all but tailed off, an uneasy, muttering half-silence taking its place.

The drinks queue had finally dried up, with the whole

crowd now transfixed by the screens. Maybe that was no bad thing either: the Ambassador Club had been non-stop for the last two hours and Frankie was knackered and Xandra and Slim's eyes looked like they were being held open with matchsticks. But, on the upside, at least the till was overflowing for a change. The takings were even better than Frankie had hoped for and he allowed himself a little smile. But, Christ, would he sleep heavy tonight.

'Another drink, boys?' he asked Ash and Sea Breeze.

Ash looked up and scowled. Sea Breeze just scowled.

'Fine, suit yourselves.' Frankie walked back over to Xandra. 'Miserable old gits,' he said.

'Still not talking to you then?'

'No.'

She shot him an awkward half-smile.

'It's not funny,' he grumbled. 'In fact, it's downright bloody rude. I've known them both since I was a kid.'

'And that, old chap, is precisely their point,' said Slim, fixing himself his usual whiskey and soda. 'They've been coming here longer than you. It's like a second home to them.'

'More like the opposite of home,' Frankie said. 'Half the time the only reason they're here at all is to get away from their bloody wives.'

'*And* for my erudite and loquacious company,' Slim said.

'Yeah, I do actually know what those words mean,' Frankie said. Which was at least half true.

'They just feel like they should have been consulted, that's all,' said Slim.

6

He was talking about the TVs. The Sky Sports signs outside. The new customers.

'This is a business,' Frankie said, 'and a business –'

'Needs to make a profit,' Xandra and Slim parroted, both of them rolling their eyes.

Frankie felt himself flush. Christ, had he really been saying it that much? A half-cheer went up from the crowd, then died down. Tony Adams. But the shot went nowhere. Then more muttering and shuffling started up. It felt like no one else in here really reckoned that England were going to score again either. The whole atmosphere was winding right down.

'You two taking the piss doesn't make it any less true,' he told Xandra and Slim. 'We've got to move with the times –' *If we don't want to get left behind* . . . He nearly said that too, but stopped himself just in time. Could already see them starting to roll their eyes again. 'Anyhow,' he said, 'it's not like we're doing anything else that every other bar in town hasn't already done.'

'I think that's rather their point,' said Slim, lighting up a B&H. 'This is an oasis of culture and tradition. Or rather' – he glanced distastefully up the screens – 'it *was* . . .'

Frankie had had enough. 'Yeah? Well, bad luck. This isn't a charity or a museum. The TVs ain't going anywhere. At least until the final. Especially if England get through.'

'Ah, so there *is* a chance this'll turn back to a proper club after that, then?' Slim said. 'You should have just said. I'll let the boys know.'

A *proper* club? By which he meant a snooker club, which is exactly what the Ambassador Club had been since

7

1964. And, yeah, a big part of Frankie wanted that too, to keep the tradition alive, but for that he needed money and the plain fact of the matter was that all his usual punters like Ash and Sea Breeze just didn't bring in enough cash.

'It all depends on how the tournament goes,' he said. He meant *his* tournament, not this one. Snooker, not footy – the Soho Open. The tournament he'd spent every second of his free time these last six months trying to set up. 'If that starts to make money, then fine. We'll go back to how it was. But until it does, the TVs stay and this lovely lot' – he pointed at the crowd – 'they stay too. Because it's their wonga that's currently keeping this place alive. And, anyhow, I don't see what your problem is with any of them, they all seem perfectly bloody nice people to me –'

A sudden burst of shouting. A goal? Nah, nothing doing on the screens. Frankie's eyes flicked right. More yelling. Shit. Trouble. A surge of bodies over there in the corner. The sound of breaking glass.

Bollocks! Here we go again. Frankie gritted his teeth in anticipation of more trouble coming his way, just when he didn't need it. The story of his fucking life.

2

Frankie reached for 'Old Faithful', the heavy, lead-lined cue he kept under the bar, but decided against it. No, not yet. He knew half the bastards in here, so best not to panic. After all, things still might not get out of hand.

But then more shouting flared up and the crowd of punters surged. Hell's tits. It was time to get a shift on, so he barged his way out from behind the bar and started forcing his way through the crowd.

Yeah, plenty of people in here he knew. Soho faces. Regulars. Berwick Street market traders like the tattooed twins, Tate and Lyle, whose dad was a stand-up comic who worked the pubs round here. Low-level gangsters like Mickey Flynn, who'd taken a beating off Terence Hamilton's boys last year and now only had one eye. Most of them were smart enough to get out of Frankie's way. Some of them might even back him up if push came to shove.

But plenty of others too. Hoolies. Hoodies. Caners. Casuals. Half of them total strangers, looking like they belonged more in some dingy, after-hours club than here in the daylight.

'Spartak!' he shouted.

But the man mountain from Russia had already bundled through from his sentry point at the door. His red Mohawk cut through the crowd like a fin.

Frankie hauled his way through the knot of writhing bodies, squeezing past the jukebox and the filthy old cigarette machine.

Right, what the hell's going on, then? He looked for someone to grab, then stopped, because, typical – who else would it bloody be, but his sodding little brother, Jack? Right here in the middle of it all, squaring up to some rotten little scrote.

People said Frankie and his brother looked alike – what with their Sicilian black hair, square jaws and boxer's fists – but all Frankie ever saw when he looked at Jack these days was hassle.

Jack had come here today all dressed up like he was expecting a call from Terry Venables himself. Only now his England shirt was ripped and covered with Guinness. And its collar was being pinned to the wall by some wiry, pock-marked headcase who clearly had designs on knocking his teeth into the middle of next week.

'Let him go,' Frankie snapped, stepping right into the ferrety little bastard's line of sight. 'Right. Bloody. Now.'

All eyes on him, waiting to see what would happen next. The final whistle blew up there on the screens, but no one even looked up.

'You, get lost, or you're next,' said the scrote, twisting his grip on Jack's collar even tighter, bringing the blood right up into his cheeks.

Frankie's fingers curled into fists. He'd shifted automatically into a fighting stance. 'I'm not going to tell you again. Let go of him now.'

The kid flashed Frankie another filthy glare, then looked round sharply, trying to suss out what he was up against. Frankie did likewise, because there was no way this little wanker would be acting out like this if he was on his own.

And there they were, over the kid's right shoulder. His three mates, all kitted out in shiny white trainers and new tracksuits – like they'd just lifted them all from the same sodding shop. Pints in their fists like they were planning on ramming them into someone's, anyone's, face – but most likely of all, of course, his.

The scrote's wolfish grin stretched wider. Reckoned he had this nailed. Had the odds on his side. Hadn't spotted Spartak edging stealthily in behind his pals – or as stealthily as it was possible for an eighteen-stone ex-special forces soldier with a twelve-inch Mohawk to move.

'And who the hell are you? Eh?' The scrote gave Jack's collar another violent twist, just to let them all know who was in charge.

The way he said it. Not a local. A Scouser. Frankie normally got on with them just fine, but this one didn't look like he wanted to be friends.

Over the kid's other shoulder, Frankie clocked Tam Jackson, box-jawed and concrete-browed, cracking a broken smile. The only bloke apart from Frankie in here in a suit. One big enough to fit a fridge.

Tam was the biggest face in here. He worked for Tommy Riley himself, the local gangster *numero uno*. He'd arrived with Jack and five or six of Riley's other boys, most of them just street soldiers, dealers, enforcers – all half Tam's age. But that's how Tam rolled, wasn't it? Shelling out for drinks from his croc skin wallet, being the big man. Only he didn't much look like he was planning on flexing his muscles to help Frankie today. More like this was just another piece of sport he was planning to watch.

'Me?' Frankie switched his attention back to the Scouser. 'I'm the bloke whose face you're going to be thinking about in hospital for the next six months, if you don't get the hell off of him and get the hell out of my club.'

Frankie's eyes locked on him. Come on, then, bring it. Because here, in the thick of it, with his blood now well up, Frankie didn't care. This was his place and no one was in charge here but him. Fists up, he was ready. No way was he going to back down.

The kid's eyes flickered. The cogs behind them whirred as a sense of doubt crept in. As he took in Frankie's frame and all the time he'd spent in the kickboxing gym the last six months.

The scrote's other three little tracksuit bastard mates started crowding in then, all well coked up. Maybe they fancied their chances too. Well, fine. So be it. Frankie braced himself. Had already decided which one he was going to hit first. His eyes caught Spartak's. The big man was right there behind them in position now too, licking his lips.

'I believe that you boys should be using your ears and listening good to this man,' his voice then boomed out, causing two out of the three of these peasants to look round – and then up. 'Yes, that is right. And you know why?

Because I have not even been fed today and I particularly enjoy eating little weasels like you for my tea.'

Spartak's gold tooth flashed and he smiled down on the hoodies. Tam clearly liked the way this show was shaping up, but the scrote's three mates were now having serious second thoughts. One started slowly shaking his head, another hooked his thumb at the door.

For a second Frankie thought the ferrety kid, who still had hold of Jack, was going to have a crack, but then he wobbled too.

'All right. All right,' he said, slowly releasing Jack's collar and stepping back, not taking his eyes off Frankie for a second. Yeah, definitely not as stupid as he looked.

Jack spluttered and coughed, doubling up, heaving air down into his lungs.

'Go on, have him,' said some buck-toothed bastard on Tam Jackson's right. Some geezer who Jack had been knocking scotches back at the bar with earlier. He was all designer black shirt and jeans and gold chains and attitude – a right little oik, but one Frankie could do without getting involved. A smudged prison tattoo showed on the knuckles of his clenched right fist. No doubt this kid would like nothing more than for the whole bloody place to kick off.

Jack took half a step forward and pointed a finger at the Scouser. 'You wanker,' he wheezed.

What the hell? Frankie's glare practically pinned his little brother to the wall. All Billy Big Bollocks now, was he? Well, he could bloody well forget it. Jack had never been a fighter, not unless he had plenty of backup around him. But maybe that was the problem now, he did.

13

'Leave it,' Frankie warned him, stepping in between the two of them. No way was he having this whole situation blowing up again because of Jack. Not now that he'd nearly got it under control. 'Out,' he warned the Scouser. 'I'm not telling you again.'

Ferret face took another step back. Then another. The crowd slowly parted, then, to let him and his three mates get through. Slowly, slowly, they went. All the way to the door. Then 'Fuck off!' one of them shouted and hurled his pint hard into the crowd. It smashed against a pillar, showering broken glass and lager down all over Tam Jackson and his mates.

Frankie's turn to smile then. Did Tam see him? Hard to tell? Because already his boys were running out shouting after the Scousers. All apart from Jack, who Frankie held back.

And then it was over, as quick as it had started. Then, as the eyes of the crowd focused back on the TV screens, the chant kicked off again.

'Three Lions on a shirt . . . Juuuuules Rimet still gleaming . . . thiiiiirrrty years of hurt . . . neeeeeever stopped me dreaming . . .'

3

Frankie switched on the telly upstairs in the living room of his flat up above the Ambassador Club while Jack flopped down on the sofa. Post-match analysis. John Motson banging on about how England could have done better. How they'd need to up their game against the Jocks on Saturday.

'So what *was* that all about then?' Frankie said. 'You and him, downstairs?'

'Seaman,' Jack slurred.

'I take it you don't mean what's inside your knackers?'

'Ha ha. No. Piss off. I mean as in David. Holiest of holy goalies. When that Swiss prick fired that ball past him, that Scouse wanker down there cracked some gag about Seaman never keeping clean sheets.'

Frankie smiled. 'An old one, but a good one. But so what?' he said.

'So he then announced that anyone dumb enough to support Arsenal needed their head examined.'

'The tosser.'

'What I told him. Only then he went one further. He spat on the flag on the wall.'

He meant the Old Man's flag. The club flag. The Gunners flag. The one the Old Man had nailed up there the first day he had taken over the Ambassador, back in '84.

'And that's when I hit him,' Jack said.

'*Hit* him?'

'Well, pushed him,' Jack admitted. 'And don't tell me you wouldn't have done the same. Or the Old Man.'

Frankie said nothing. No point in denying it. Because, yeah, the Old Man would have done something, all right. Had always liked a brawl, word was. Probably came from all that hanging out with them bad boys back in his murky youth here in Soho. People like Riley, who the Old Man had leased this building off. And Terence Hamilton too. Before Hamilton and Riley had grown up into rival gang lords and had ended up at each other's throats.

Jack was right about Frankie too. Years gone by, he would have more than likely got involved as well. But not any more.

'I want this place kept off the cops' blacklist, not on it,' he said. 'I'm having enough trouble trying to find sponsorship for this tournament without us getting any worse of a rep than what we've already got.'

'What?' Jack said sourly. 'You mean, thanks to me?'

'Look, what happened last year . . . I know it was none of your fault,' Frankie said. 'You got set up.'

For murder . . . for the murder of Susan Tilley, who was bludgeoned to death the night before she was due to marry Dougie Hamilton, the son of Terence Hamilton. Frankie would never forget Jack coming running in here the morning after the poor girl had been killed, all covered in her blood and with no memory of where he'd been for the previous twelve hours.

'I was set up because of who I was,' said Jack, 'because of who I was hanging out with . . . I know that's what you think.'

Only partly true. Jack had been unlucky too. There were any number of other petty crims like him who could have been picked to take the rap instead. But there was no point in getting into any of that now.

'We'll never know why that sick bastard chose you to pin it on,' Frankie said. 'He was crazy. That was obvious from his confession.'

The real murderer's body had eventually been found with a signed, typed letter by his side, detailing how he'd killed Susan Tilley and why.

'I still dragged the club's name through the mud, didn't I?' Jack slurred. 'And our family name. All over again. Just the same as with the Old Man.'

And, oh yeah, the press had loved that, hadn't they? The parasitical bastards. Jack James, the son of convicted armed robber Bernie James, who was currently still a resident of HM Prison Brixton, with nine years of his sentence left to run.

'But you were proved innocent,' Frankie said. 'The same as Dad will be one day. The cops, the press . . . and that poor girl's family. Everyone now knows that what happened to her that night had nothing to do with you.'

Not that this had stopped Jack trading off his brief brush with notoriety, which had boosted his rep and earned

17

him a whole heap of kudos in the criminal fraternity he was still hanging out in.

Frankie caught his own reflection in the darkened glass of his computer screen on the desk. There were only two people left alive who knew what had really happened to Susan Tilley that night. Frankie and the father of the groom-to-be, Terence Hamilton. Frankie, because he'd worked out who the real killer was. And Terence Hamilton, because . . . well, because he'd taken matters into his own hands after that. Leaving the two of them now with enough dirt on each other to land either one of them in jail if the other ever spoke out.

'Anyhow, it's all history now,' Frankie said. 'Let's just leave it in the past.'

'Just like everything else, eh?'

Jack meant their mum. Their dad. The whole shit parade that had got them to where they were today.

'Yeah,' said Frankie, 'just like that. End of.'

Jack sighed, rubbing at his eyes.

'When did you last eat?' Frankie said.

He fixed them both beans on toast and sat down next to his brother to eat. Jack got stuck in, clearly ravenous. Those first few months last year after he'd been let out of prison, Frankie had made sure to check in on him regular, like. To get some decent grub inside him and see that all was well. But Frankie had let it slide, with him then getting back on the booze himself, and forgetting his priorities. Until here the two of them were, back to hardly seeing each other. And all his own piggin' fault.

Jack burped and let out a long, contented sigh. Frankie

smiled. It was good to see him like this. Letting himself be taken care of for once.

'I can't believe you still live here,' Jack said.

He and Frankie had been flatmates here until two years back, when Jack had upped sticks and told Frankie he was moving in with some one-night stand. Of course, that had all gone tits up pretty fast, but he'd then found somewhere else to crash, and then somewhere else after that, before finally getting his own flat sorted over on Warren Street. A right shithole.

'Your place so much better, is it?' Frankie said. He was fishing, really. Still couldn't help thinking Jack would be better off here, where he could keep an eye on him.

'It will be come Monday,' Jack said.

'And why's that?'

'I'm moving.'

'Where?'

'Ladbroke Grove.'

Nearer to people like Stav Christoforou and Mo Bishara – dealers, pimps and lowlifes. 'You sure that's the best place for you?' Stav was one of the bastards Frankie reckoned had helped set Jack up last summer. Not that he'd been able to prove it. Yet.

'I'm not moving there for the company,' Jack said. 'More an investment.'

'You thinking about *buying* somewhere?' Frankie couldn't keep the surprise from his voice.

'Not just thinking, bruv. Doing.'

'You do know you need a deposit, right?'

'Already got one.'

'From where? And don't tell me you and your mates are making that sort of cash from that bleedin' techno night you're running over at Shepherd's Bush.'

'Techno?' Jack laughed. 'Get with it, bruv. That shit died out with the dodo.'

'Yeah, jungle, triphop, whatever.' Truth was Frankie didn't think much of any of that kind of crap. He'd ducked in on Jack and his mates a couple of months back. A bunch of nutters doing pills, bouncing round off walls, hugging each other like they were all in love. And as for the music. Repetitive bollocks. He'd not known how to dance to it at all. Playing Dad to Jack all these years meant he'd never really got into clubbing the way a lot of guys his age had. Granddad, that's what Spartak sometimes teasingly called him. Old before his years.

'Riley,' Jack said.

Meaning who'd given him the money. Tommy Riley. The boss man himself.

'For what?'

Frankie knew Jack was still doing a bit of work for him, but low-level stuff. Like driving his dolly birds round, running errands, but nothing that would add up to a flat. Nothing that could get him in too much trouble either, he'd been hoping.

'Just the usual. This and that.'

Frankie wasn't buying it. 'You swore to me that working for Riley was just temporary. That you are still looking for proper work.'

'Yeah, and it's not like I haven't tried.'

'But what? Not any more? Now you've given up? Because that's what this sounds like, you taking a deposit off Riley to buy a flat. Like you're now just planning on getting deeper and deeper into his world, right up to your neck.'

'And what else am I meant to do?' Jack snapped. 'It's not like there's a million other legit jobs out there with my name on them, is it? Not after me being in the papers last year. And not with my qualifications either. Or lack of them. Or maybe you've forgotten about how I didn't exactly get much of an education, what with Mum skipping out and Dad getting done for armed robbery.'

'She *didn't* skip out,' Frankie said. '*Something* happened to her and the Old Man wasn't *done* for armed robbery, he was stitched up.'

'Anyway, what makes you so different?' Jack snapped. 'You're taking Riley's money too.'

'Every penny I have, I've earned,' said Frankie. 'Out of the club. Dad's club. Our club. And I've told you a hundred times before, you can come here and help me run it too. All you've got to do is say the word.'

Jack sneered. Actually sneered. It was all Frankie could do not to grab him by the throat.

'Work here? There's hardly enough to pay the wages of them two downstairs . . . Anyway, it's not Dad's place. Or ours. Not really, is it? Because Riley still owns the building, doesn't he? You just pay him rent. Just the same as you had to give to Tam today.'

He was right. Jackson hadn't been here just for the

sport, but collecting the monthly payment Frankie owed on the lease.

'And any time he wants to pull the rug on you, he can,' Jack said. 'Because he's still the bloody man.'

More truth. Frankie stared at the wall. Riley owned every brick of it. Which was why he had to make this tournament work. To get out from under him. To maybe buy this place outright off of him. Or to set something else up.

'I do my best. I do what I can.'

'And so do I,' said Jack. 'And, right now, that means working for Riley. Not doing anything stupid. Not like what I promised you I wouldn't.' He meant front-line shit. Dealing. Enforcing.

But it still left him working for a gangster. One engaged in a turf war with Terence Hamilton. Out there. On the streets. And with no intention, by the sounds of it, of even trying any more to get out.

'Anyway,' said Jack, sparking up a fag and taking a jittery drag, 'the money I've put down on the flat isn't from that. Not wages.'

Wages? Jesus. He wasn't even trying to hide it now. He really was full-time on Riley's books.

'Then what?'

'Tommy told me to think of it like a bonus.'

'What, like you're some kind of merchant banker?' Frankie scoffed.

'For keeping my mouth shut,' Jack said. 'About him. And his operations. For not telling the pigs anything about him that whole time they had me banged up last year.' He flicked ash onto his plate.

Frankie snatched the plate off him and marched through to the kitchen.

'Jesus,' Jack shouted, 'why can't you just be happy for me for once?'

4

Frankie was up and at 'em bright and early the next morning. One of the big advantages of being on the wagon for as long as he had been this time round was that he'd started waking up feeling like he'd used to as a kid. He felt alert, with bags of energy and piss like Evian. Instead of the usual sick feeling, with a mouth like the bottom of a parrot's cage and piss like golden syrup.

He had a quick shower and got dressed in his running gear – a Rolling Stones T-shirt, trackie bottom shorts, Adidas trainers. He preferred to keep things old school, none of that Umbro or Reebok crap. He was out the door by eight fifteen: pounding the pavement was part of his new routine – a 10k run three days a week with kickboxing training on the days in between.

He'd come a long way since December, when he'd been back to his worst following the pressure of everything that had happened last year. Sneaky snifters by day, pints behind the bar come evening. Staying out all night drinking with whoever. Gambling. Coke. Nights alone back in the flat. But that had always been his problem, hadn't it? He never could just have a couple of pints, or the odd cheeky fag or line when he was out with his mates. He was either off it altogether, or on it like a bonnet till he crashed.

And crashed he had. On New Year's Eve. That incident with that girl he'd picked up in the Atlantic. Picked up and had done a bottle of Wild Turkey and two grams of gack with. Picked up and hadn't worn a condom with. Picked up and had then found out she had a boyfriend, who'd tipped up sober from the hospital where he'd been working his night shift and had leathered ten bells out of his sorry, drunken self, before slinging him out on his arse.

Incidents. Yeah, that's what he called them. The shit you did to yourself that you wish you hadn't. The shit that made you realize you weren't in control at all and had to sort yourself out.

As he headed off along Poland Street, he tried not to think about his chat yesterday with Jack. It was hard though, as he'd been up half the night, worrying himself sick, trying to think of ways to get him away from Riley's gang. But how? Only by having something better to offer him. And the only way he could do that was by making this bloody tournament work – something he was already busting his gut to achieve.

He tried to focus on his running instead, as he headed down Broadwick Street and on towards Shepherd Market. He tried to picture himself as a real athlete like Linford Christie, going for gold. Not so easy, mind, what with all these smashed bottles and Burger King and Wendy's wrappers he was having to skirt around. There wasn't much of a crowd cheering him on round here either. Hardly a soul out, in fact. Apart from a couple of street sweepers and some chatty smackhead flirting with his own reflection in a porn shop window.

But that was Soho on a Sunday morning for you, wasn't it? Everyone sleeping off their excesses from the night before. Either that or they'd all suddenly got religion and were kneeling in church, repenting their sins. As-bloody-if.

He called in at Bar Italia on Frith Street on his way back home and picked up a double espresso to go. Not even half nine yet and already the place was packed. A mix of tourists and locals. A smattering of Italian speakers among them, something that always left Frankie regretting he'd never learned to speak it himself. His granddad, Tadeo Balistreri, was Sicilian. Not that Frankie had ever had the pleasure. He'd died in a road accident after going back there for a funeral, leaving Frankie's gran here in London to bring Frankie's mum up on her own.

Doc Slim was making out like a lizard in the sun with a table and two chairs set up on the pavement when Frankie got back to the Ambassador, sucking on a cheroot and cradling his first whiskey and soda of the day, a concoction Frankie knew would get progressively darker as evening approached until the need for soda was dispensed with altogether. Spotting Frankie, he blew a lazy plume of smoke in his general direction and tilted the brim of his busted old straw panama hat.

'Morning, boss. And how the devil are you, this fine morning?' he said.

'Pretty good.'

'Glad to hear it. Kind Regards just popped round. He left that.' Slim nodded at a stack of files on the table.

Frankie opened the envelope on the top. 'Your dad's case notes, as promised,' it said in Kind Regards' familiar scrawl.

The Old Man's best mate and cousin, Kind Regards, had represented the Old Man in his original trial for armed robbery. Not the glory boy barrister stuff in the actual court (not that there'd been much glory at all once they'd lost), but most of the grunt work behind the scenes. And that's what was in here. The graft. The details. Including maybe something that all the lawyers had overlooked?

Kind Regards had tried putting Frankie off looking into it further. Repeatedly. He'd already explained how he'd tried arguing with the powers that be that the fifteen-year sentence was unreasonably excessive, but it had fallen on deaf ears. And now, in the absence of any new and compelling evidence, he was still struggling to get solid grounds to mount an appeal.

But Frankie couldn't just leave it there. He picked up the files. Maybe all it needed was a fresh set of eyes.

'Anything important?' asked Slim.

'Nah.' Frankie didn't want to get into it. Slim and the Old Man went way back, with Slim still visiting him each Wednesday down the nick like clockwork. If Frankie told him he was planning on looking into ways of helping get him out, then Slim would want to help too. And what was the point in getting his hopes up, until he knew if any of this was going to lead anywhere at all?

'Mr Listerman was also kind enough to pay us a call . . .' Slim said.

Daniel Listerman. Tommy Riley's lawyer. His *consigliere*

too, not that he'd ever get his own hands dirty. Left that to Riley's other boys. The Tam Jacksons of this world.

'What did he want?'

'He'd got wind of that trouble yesterday with those lads from Liverpool.'

'News travels fast.' Especially bad news. 'What did you tell him?'

'That you sorted it all out. The same as you always do.'

Same as the Old Man always had as well. Prior to him taking over the club in '84, the bloke who'd leased the club off Riley had paid him protection on top of his rent. But Frankie's dad had put a stop to that when he took over. Had come to some sort of arrangement with Riley. Frankie didn't know what. Didn't want to either. Just so long as Riley didn't try winding back the clock and stinging him any more than he already was.

'And how was he with that?' asked Frankie.

'Sweet as a nut. At least, I think.'

'Nice. Thanks.' Maybe Listerman had just been passing by then. Had just wanted to check there'd not been any damage to what, as Jack had annoyingly but rightly pointed out, was still his boss's gaff.

'He did say see you next Friday, mind,' Slim said.

'Yeah?' Meaning he'd obviously got wind of the Soho Open's launch night too. Again, hardly surprising. But not good news either, because Frankie was still keen on keeping the tournament well out of the local firm's reach. And had been doing pretty well on that score too, hooking up instead with a contact of Kind Regards called Andy Topper, a sports agent based over in Haymarket. 'The Topster', as he liked to be called, knew everyone in the industry and had taken a 20 per cent stake in The Soho Open Ltd, the company Kind Regards had helped Frankie set up. Friday night the plan was to get as many potential investors and partners into the Ambassador Club as possible and to sign them up with a view to launching the actual tournament next year.

'Listerman said Tommy would be coming too,' Slim said, 'as well as a few of their lads.'

Frankie felt his skin prickle, liking the sound of this less and less. The last time Riley had set foot in the Ambassador was after Jack had been released last year. But otherwise he never came here to play and didn't seem much interested apart from the rent – so why the show of force now?

'You thinking maybe it's just a friendly visit?' Slim asked.

Frankie doubted Riley knew the meaning of the phrase. 'Dunno, but I guess we'll find out soon enough.'

Heading for the doorway, Frankie told himself not to be paranoid. So what if Riley was planning on tipping up? Was that really so weird? He knew everyone with a finger in every pie this side of Watford. Including probably half the bookies and promoters Frankie had invited along for the night. Chances were he'd use any opportunity to flex his muscles and remind anyone visiting that he still ran this part of town.

'Oh, and I've loaded up the Breville for you,' Slim called out. 'Organic honey-roasted Devon ham. From my second-favourite corner shop, no less. You just need to switch it on.'

'Cheers,' Frankie shouted back, his stomach starting to growl.

Toasted sarnies. Food of the gods, that's what Slim always said. Him and Frankie's mum had always used to compete with each other for the most sophisticated fillings when she'd worked at the bar here before her and the Old Man had separated. Brie and grape. Pesto and crab. Christ, the eighties had a lot to answer for.

Frankie ditched the files on the bar top and flipped the Breville on, before going down into the basement and getting changed into his tatty old overalls, and picking up the painting gear.

The club didn't open for another hour. Meaning he might as well get busy finishing off the decorating, before heading up to the flat for a shower. He grabbed his toastie and went back outside, nodding his thanks to Slim.

'Lush,' he said. 'It's got a lovely tang to it.'

'That'll be the Fortnum's Piccadilly piccalilli.' As in Fortnum & Mason's, his second-favourite shop after only Harrods itself. 'I've left you a jar in the fridge.'

'Good man.'

Frankie jammed in his earphones and hit play on the Sony Discman clipped to his belt. Small Faces. 'Itchycoo Park'. One of his favourites. He set to with the brush on the last of the brickwork that needed doing, nice and steady, wanting it to look good and professional, like.

He'd been tarting the place up himself in time for Friday to save money. The effing prices decorating firms charged round here were a bloody disgrace. Xandra had been helping out too. She'd done such a good job on her living quarters at the back of the club when she'd moved in here off the streets that he'd been happy for her to pretty much boss this new phase of the club's renovation herself. She'd used to work for a building firm back in Northern Ireland, before she'd run away and had ended up here in the big smoke down on her luck and living on the streets.

As well as giving the whole club a fresh lick of paint inside, he'd already given the external wall and front doors a new coat. White for the walls. Green for the door. Was meant to be lucky, according to Beijing Barry, who ran the Chinese medicine shop round the corner. Said it was good *feng shui*, whatever the hell that was.

Frankie finished up round the back of the guttering. Leaving just the door frame to do. He covered the hinges and locks with masking tape first, just like Xandra had taught him. Then washed the wood down with sugar soap and got cracking with some serious sanding.

'What the –' Flinching, turning, Frankie jerked his earphones out.

'Whoah! Steady on now, Chuck Norris. I was just saying good morning to you there, all right?'

Xandra was grinning, arms up. Meanwhile Frankie had his own arms up in a cover-up guard position as if he was expecting a fight.

'Shit, sorry,' he said.

He noticed she wasn't alone. The girl standing next to her had sparkly blue eyes, a great big beamer of a smile, and jet-black hair that matched the little black cocktail dress she was wearing. Or not so little, just little on her. Because the girl herself was a couple of inches taller than Frankie, leaving her a whole head higher than Xandra. Not that this

31

seemed to be bothering them much. The two of them were holding hands.

'And you must be Frankie,' the tall girl said. 'Xandra's landlord and boss.'

Landlord. He'd never really thought of himself as that. Probably on account of never having actually charged Xandra any rent for living in the bunch of rooms at the back of the club that he'd helped her fix up into what was now her own little flat.

'And mate,' said Xandra.

'Yes, quite,' said Frankie. 'I wouldn't want your friend here thinking I was some sort of evil overlord.'

'Maxine,' Xandra said, shyly introducing her companion. 'She, er . . . we, er . . .'

'We met each other last night. In Mescalitos.'

The tequila bar round the corner. Where Xandra and Slim and a few others had headed off after Frankie had shut up shop here.

'And got on well enough to end up back here,' Maxine said.

'And after how many shots was that?' asked Frankie. He meant it as a joke, but it came out all Dad-ish and Xandra rolled her eyes and Maxine smiled awkwardly, both of them clearly big enough and street-wise enough to take care of themselves.

'Oops,' said Xandra in the silence that followed.

'What?'

'You missed a bit. Over there.' She took the paintbrush from where he'd left it on the pot lid and stretched up on tiptoes to fill in a patch on the brickwork he'd not seen. 'But otherwise not bad at all,' she said, putting the brush back down. 'You wouldn't think it to look at him, but he's quite a quick learner,' she went on. 'Not just a pretty face.'

'Very funny,' said Frankie. 'Now if you don't mind *fecking orf*, some of us have work to do.'

'A quick learner, but a terrible mimic.' Xandra smiled. 'We're off down Berwick Street for a coffee. Do you want us to bring you anything back?'

'Nah,' said Frankie. 'Thanks, but I'm all right Nice meeting you,' he told Maxine.

'You too,' she said, and her and Xandra wandered off down the street hand in hand.

'Ah, love's young dream,' Slim said wistfully.

He was right. They could have been together for years. Well, good for them. Just so long as this Maxine took good care of Xandra, Frankie was happy. Because, just like Slim, Xandra was family now.

Crossing the street, he made a square with his fingers and thumbs to look through. Yeah, the old club didn't look half bad with its new lick of paint. His dad's old mate, Dickie Bird, was due over this afternoon to photograph the outside of the club for the little leaflet he was doing for the weekend to hand out to his potential sponsors and business partners. He'd already done the inside last week. Dickie normally just did porn, but he was the only bloke Frankie knew with a decent camera and he'd agreed to do it along with the printing too for a knock-down price. He had a neat little computer program of his he used for knocking out posh, bespoke porn mags for Mayfair toffs and City boys who liked whacking off over pictures of themselves on the job.

'You all right to hold the fort?' Frankie asked Slim, crossing back over. 'I need to get that copy I've been writing for the tournament leaflet over to Dickie this morning.'

'Sure,' said Slim. 'Ah, and before I forget, I put yesterday's post upstairs outside the flat. Oh, and you owe me two quid.'

'What for?'

'Some postcard from Spain. Whoever sent it hadn't put enough stamps on. I had to pay the postie before he'd hand it over.'

'Spain?' Who was that from, then? Frankie didn't know anyone living there. Couldn't think of anyone on holiday out there at the moment either. 'Right then. Thanks. I'll catch you later,' he said. 'Anyone needs me, just give me a bell.'

'Or,' an unpleasantly familiar voice interrupted, 'I could just save us all the time and effort and have a little word with you now.'

5

Frankie felt the hairs standing up on the back of his neck, even before he turned round. DI Bloody Snaresby. The same bastard who this time last year had tried and failed to put Jack away for good.

And, yep, sure enough, here he was. All lanky, spidery six foot six of him. Flashing his cheddar rind of a grin at Frankie, as the sun beat down on his balding grey scalp. Suited and booted, even on a Sunday. For church? Frankie doubted it. The second he'd step inside he'd have gone up in flames.

Frankie said nothing. But he didn't like it. He'd not seen this wanker in nearly a year. So what in the name of buggery bollocks was he doing here now? He walked slowly forward until his gaunt, angular face was barely inches from Frankie's, so close Frankie could smell the stale Juicy Fruit gum on his breath.

The phone started ringing inside.

'Do you want me to get it?' asked Slim.

'Yeah. Can you? Thanks.'

Snaresby watched him go, then turned back to Frankie and flashed him another short smile.

'I'm sure you're familiar with the history of the Kray brothers?' he said, 'Ronnie and Reggie? The Brothers Grim?'

'What about them?'

'It's just that I've been thinking, about how they started their – how shall I put it? – *careers*? Managing a run-down little billiard hall not entirely dissimilar to this.'

He meant the Regent. Over Mile End. And, yeah, Frankie had heard of it and plenty of not so nice stories about what had gone down there. But so what?

'What's your point?'

'That sometimes even the mightiest of empires can rise up from the humblest of beginnings . . .' Snaresby waved his hand expansively across the front of the Ambassador Club, giving Frankie a blast of his Old Spice deodorant as he did so.

'Fascinating,' said Frankie, resisting the urge to take a step back, knowing that Snaresby would only see it as weakness.

'And pertinent,' said Snaresby. 'Because the way I hear it, you're planning on starting building a little empire of your own as well.'

'I don't know what you're talking about.'

'Oh, but I think you do. This snooker tournament you're setting up. The Soho Open.'

'Which is completely above board.'

'As I would very much hope.'

'If you don't believe me, you can go check with the council. Or Companies House too for all I care.'

'Oh, I already have.'

'Good, then you'll see I've dotted every "i" and crossed every "t". Everything I've got planned, it's totally legal.'

'And very impressive it is too. Although I have to say not entirely surprising. Because, as I think I've mentioned to you before, I never did have you down as being quite as . . . *impulsive* as the rest of your family.'

Impulsive. A euphemism. Crooked, he meant. But no way was Frankie getting into that now. He knew better than to let this bastard wind him up when he'd done nothing bloody wrong.

'So why're you here bothering me at all then?' Because Snaresby might be many things, but stupid wasn't one of them. Meaning that if he'd come here on his day off, there had to be something in it for him.

'No reason.' Snaresby picked at something caught in his teeth. 'Or perhaps every reason. I suppose that just depends.'

'On what?'

'On whether your snooker tournament attracts any, er, trouble.'

'Like what?'

Snaresby poked his tongue into his cheek, still irritated by whatever it was he'd got caught. 'Well, as I'm quite sure you remember, there was that incident last year, when person or persons unknown threatened to burn down your club.'

He meant the break-in, when someone had poured petrol all over one of the tables and a photo of Frankie's parents, and had left a message telling Frankie to back off from looking into his brother's case. Not that it had worked, but it had certainly given him a fair few sleepless nights.

Snaresby smiled thinly, clearly enjoying reminding Frankie of the fact. 'And then only yesterday afternoon,' he went on, 'during our nation's predictably disappointing draw with the Swiss, I hear there was some kind of an altercation here again. With some young gentlemen of the Liverpudlian persuasion, or so I understand.'

'One that got resolved without anyone getting hurt.'

'And very glad I am to hear it,' said Snaresby. 'You see, the last thing I'd want, or would indeed tolerate, is any kind of trouble or criminal activity here on my manor.'

Snaresby whipped out a brass Zippo and a pack of cigarettes from his jacket pocket. He sparked one up, surprisingly fast, his watch glinting in the sun. A Breitling. Pricey. Looked as nicked on this bloke as his suit.

'I mean, I'm sure you'd agree,' he said, taking a long, thoughtful drag, 'it would be a great shame to see a noble and innovative venture like your tournament falter and fail at a prematurely early hurdle for reasons of violence and criminality outside your control.'

What was this? A shakedown? 'Are you threatening me?' The words were out before Frankie could stop them. Because surely not even Snaresby would have the bollocks to try something this blatant in broad daylight?

'Who? Little old me?' Snaresby laughed a short, high-pitched laugh, but then his smile flattened. 'Oh no, Frankie – I mean, *Mr* James – I'm just here to give you a little advice, that's all. To ask you to keep your venture on the right side of the law. To keep in with the right people. To

38

make absolutely sure that you protect both their interests and yours.'

Frankie just stared. Because what the hell? Was he hearing this right? Was Snaresby here as some kind of a messenger? But for *who*? Who *were* the *right people*? Riley? Was Snaresby really in his pocket, like Frankie had started to suspect last year? Or Hamilton? Because he'd wondered that too. And because with all them lot growing up round here together, along with his mum and dad too, anything was possible. Whatever screwed-up relationships they had, they went back for years.

'You seem to have run out of your usually amusing comebacks,' Snaresby said.

Frankie wanted to hit him then. To wipe that superior smile off his face. That same smile that said, no matter what Frankie thought he knew, Snaresby always knew better, Snaresby always knew more.

But, no. He wouldn't give him that. The satisfaction of having baited him. Or the moral high ground that went with it and the chance to get his claws into Frankie's life.

No point in asking the prick, either, who might have sent him here. Or whose interests he meant Frankie to protect. Snaresby was old school and knowledge was power. He'd not give up anything he didn't have to, anything that might not serve him first.

Instead Frankie just stared right back at him, unblinking, into those shark-grey eyes. Let the tosser know he had the measure of him. Let him know he didn't trust him. Let him know he wasn't afraid.

'You once told me to keep out of your business,' Frankie said. 'I'm now telling you the same.'

'Ah, but you *are* my business.' Snaresby stared hard back into Frankie's eyes. '*This* . . .' He stretched his spidery arms out wide. '. . . *is* my business. All of it . . . Soho. Mayfair. Green Park. Piccadilly. Haymarket. Fitzrovia. And St James's . . . All parts of my little kingdom, every square inch. As well as every good or bad beating little heart that resides inside . . .'

Frankie had heard enough. Turning his back on Snaresby, he marched back into the club. Snaresby called out something after him, but he didn't turn round. Fuck him. And his kingdom. What Frankie was trying to build here was his. And would stay his.

No matter what Snaresby or any other bastard he might be working for thought.

6

Frankie grabbed the post Slim had left for him on his way into the flat and stuck it on the little hallway table inside, in between the Old Man's golf bag and the antique hat-stand where his favourite straw trilby still hung. He tried not to think about that bastard Snaresby and focused on the tournament instead.

He still half regretted taking on the job of writing the copy for the brochure himself. Had got a quote from one of the little media agencies round the corner. But it had been way too steep and he'd decided to save the money. He'd almost got an A level in English before he'd dropped out. So he'd figured how hard could it be, writing a ten-page marketing document?

Answer. Quite hard. Quite bloody hard indeed. It had taken him nearly two weeks all in, every scrap of time he'd had in between getting up and work and hitting the sack at night. Turned out writing about *Macbeth* and the nature of evil was a piece of piss, next to bigging up an event upon which your entire future depended.

Still, at least it was done now and he'd even got a logo he'd designed, pinned here on the wall, which Dickie said he'd be able to use. A door with a bright neon bar sign above it, saying 'Soho Open', only done with snooker balls instead of light bulbs. And, yeah, it did look shit hot, even if Frankie did say so himself. Art was another A level he'd been halfway to getting when the Old Man had been arrested. He reckoned his old school mistress would be well proud of this.

He sat himself down at the computer in the living room and carefully went through the copy he'd written. Banging it onto a floppy disk, he hurried round to Dickie's grot shop over on Beak Street, where the legend 'PRIVATES ON PARADE' stood arched in glowing pink neon letters above its tinted, scuffed glass door.

'All right, Ed? Dickie around?' Frankie asked the heavily tattooed lad on reception.

Ed the Head, so called on account of a certain part of his anatomy that had frequently featured in Dickie's more under-the-counter productions, looked over from the lady he was boxing a pink dildo for, and waved Frankie towards the glass bead curtain at the back of the shop.

'Downstairs,' said Ed, who from the scowl on his face was clearly not enjoying the new Sunday Trading opening hours.

Frankie made his way along the aisle, weaving past a couple of blokes who were busy perusing the various filth mags, DVDs and sex toys on display. Beyond the curtain, he climbed down a rickety spiral staircase into the cramped basement.

The smell of joss sticks, lube and rubber was almost overpowering. Frankie checked the stockroom first, but there was nothing in there but stacks of mags and racks of gimp suits. No one in the little studio either, with its white reflective walls and big brass double bed. And thank God for that. Frankie was still getting over the time he'd popped down here unannounced to borrow some jump leads for the Capri a few months back, only to find Dickie busily pap-ping away at some posh old bloke dressed up as a Nazi with a dwarf whipping the shit out of him with a teacher's wooden cane whilst squirting whipped cream all over his bare buttocks.

'Fuck Off, I'm Busy', said the sign on the darkroom door at the end of the corridor, in red neon script.

'Oi, Dickie, you Welsh bastard,' Frankie shouted, knock-ing hard. 'It's Frankie. You in there?'

'Gimme a minute,' a deep, muffled voice came back.

The red sign clicked out thirty seconds later and Dickie emerged from the darkroom, shutting the door behind him. He was dressed in a pair of pink goggles, threadbare white Y-fronts, and one left sock. Frankie did his best not to laugh, but didn't quite make it.

'Aw, leave it out. It gets bloody hot in there, don't it?' said Dickie, his big bald face sweating as he scratched at the green Abertillery RFC badge tattooed across his hairy, ample gut. 'Anyhow, moving on. You'll be pleased to hear I got some cracking shots of inside the club last week for you. Was just in here developing them now.'

'Fantastic.'

'All a bit sterile, mind, for my taste, personally, but you say that's what you want . . .'

'Sterile?'

'Well, more corporate, I suppose. But, I mean, that was the vibe you were after, right?'

'Right.'

Dickie sighed.

'Why? Is that a problem?'

'No . . . not necessarily.'

'What?'

'Just that – and far be it for me to tell you your own business, like – but I just couldn't help thinking that the tables inside the club, well, they would have looked better a little bit more *adorned* . . .'

'Adorned?'

'Yeah, you know, with perhaps a couple of birds draped over the tables. Perhaps even playing, like – and, no, I don't mean with each other, or anything dirty like that . . .'

'Hmmm. I'm not sure that's quite the kind of image for the tournament that we're trying to project.'

'Seriously, though, I could do it quite tasteful. You wouldn't even need to see their nipples or minges or anything. Trust me, you'd be amazed at what you can conceal with a couple of well-placed balls.'

'Thanks for the idea, but, er, no thanks,' said Frankie. 'Just some straight-up photos of the club front and inside will be fine.'

'Right-ho, suit yourself, but if you do change your mind –'

'I won't. But are you still good for coming along on Friday to do a bit of papping for us? The Topster – that's the sports agent –' Frankie explained, 'he reckons it will be good to have a few crowd shots of the night, as well as of the two pros he's got coming in to play the exhibition matches, to be able to use further down the line. Should be good too. Both lads are just outside the world top hundred. And both local, so they're doing it mates' rates. All we've got to do is pay expenses.'

'No sweat.' Dickie had produced a half-eaten pasty from God only knew where and took a big bite. 'OK if I bring a date?' he asked, spitting flakes of pastry out all over his gut.

'Of course, whoever you like. And you are still going to be all right to have these leaflets ready for me in time?'

''Course. Consider it done.'

'Nice. Here's your wedge, then.' Frankie handed him an envelope with the cash they'd agreed. 'And here's the copy for the leaflets too.'

'Go, Chaucer,' Dickie said, taking the floppy disk off him and stuffing the last of his pasty into his mouth.

*

It was only when Frankie got back to the flat that he remembered the mail he'd left there on the table. He flipped quickly through it as he walked out to the kitchen to fix himself a cuppa. Bills, bills and more effing bills. This bloody club was like a bleedin' sieve. The more money he poured in, the faster it poured out.

He got to the postcard last of all. From Spain, just like Slim had said. Palma, Mallorca, to be more precise, although he'd always thought the latter was spelt with a 'j'. The image on the front showed a strip of touristy restaurants and bars. All smiling, tanned punters and blue skies and jugs of sangria. Like someone had taken a snapshot of heaven.

But who was it for? He flipped it over, thinking it couldn't be him. Had probably been delivered here by mistake. But no, there his name was. Frankie James. In block capitals. Along with this address. Written in black biro. Something about the writing he recognized. Something that gave him this weird feeling right in the pit of his gut.

He read what was written below:

YOU WERE THERE FOR HIM. JUST LIKE I ALWAYS KNEW YOU WOULD BE.

That was it. No signature. Nothing else apart from a smudged lipstick kiss.

But Frankie had heard the phrase before. Almost word for word. Eight years ago now. Right from her own pink-painted lips. The same day his mum had disappeared.

7

Monday morning and Frankie couldn't get his mum out of his mind as he drove his black Capri over to Festive Al's warehouse in Clerkenwell Green to haggle him down on the seating for Friday night.

Question after question kept running through his mind. Could it really be her? And if it was her, why now, and why not in person?

What did *You were there for him* mean? If the *you* was Frankie, then surely the *him* had to be Jack, right? Because Frankie *had* been there for him last year when he'd needed him most, just like his mum had made him promise her all those years ago.

'He thinks he can take care of himself, but he can't.' That's what she'd said that day she'd disappeared, as his little brother had cycled off down the road in a strop. 'You know that. And promise me, *promise me,*' she'd said, grabbing his wrist so hard it had hurt, 'you'll always be there for him. No matter what happens.'

He remembered every word. Had played them back through his mind a million times. Had she known she'd be leaving them both behind that day? Had she not just been asking him to step up, but had actually been saying good-bye?

But an even bigger question than these was *how* could she have found out about him helping Jack last summer? Sure, what had happened to Jack was public knowledge. Splashed all over the papers. But Frankie's name hadn't appeared in any of that. Nor what he'd done.

In fact, there were only four people left alive who knew anything about Frankie's involvement in clearing Jack's name. The Old Man, who'd told him to do whatever it took. Tommy Riley, whose tip-off had helped Frankie work out who the real killer was. Snaresby's deputy, Sharon Granger, who'd nearly pieced together just what Frankie might have done to help get Jack set free. And Terence Hamilton himself.

Was it really possible that one of them had spoken to his mother? Or talked to someone else who had? But who? And why? And *how*? How the hell could anyone have done that, unless they'd already been in touch?

It just didn't make any sense. Unless, of course, the post-card wasn't from his mother at all. And it was someone else entirely who'd written this. Someone who, for whatever reason, was intent on messing with Frankie's head. In which case, they were to be congratulated on doing a very fine job indeed.

Back in Soho, Frankie watched his old mate Taffy taking out the club's tables on a bunch of flatbed trucks, and then deliver the single pristine competition table that would be centre stage come Friday night.

He then called in on Dickie Bird to pick up the leaflets. Dickie was busy downstairs 'casting', but had left the leaflets in a box upstairs with Ed the Head. And good news

– he'd done a surprisingly professional job, with not an erect penis in sight. The logo on the front and the photos of the club inside looked great too. Even the words didn't read half bad.

Frankie stashed them safe and sound back in the flat and then went down into the club. Xandra was at the bar, listening to the answerphone, with Friday's guest-list folder spread out before her.

'All shaping up nicely,' she said as he joined her. 'That was that bloke from Ladbrokes head office. He's a yes.'

'Excellent.' Frankie allowed himself a smile. Christ, it really was all coming together, wasn't it?

'All right if I ask Maxine along too?' Xandra said. 'She's happy to muck in.'

'Sure.' Frankie smiled again. Good to see a little twinkle in her eyes. It was all well and good her hanging out with him and Slim all the time, but it was nice to see her putting down a few roots of her own.

'And what about yourself?' she said. 'You bringing anyone special?'

'Like who? Courteney Cox?'

'I was thinking more maybe Sharon. You do still mention her quite a lot.'

He blushed a little. 'Do I now?' He'd not noticed that he did.

She meant Sharon Granger, Snaresby's deputy, who Frankie had been at school with back in the day and who he'd had a fling with last year while all that stuff with Jack had been going on. A fling that should never have happened, as Sharon had made perfectly clear at the time. Only then she'd changed her mind, hadn't she? Once Jack had been set

49

free. But it had been too late. Annoyed and rejected, Frankie had already moved on. And then she'd caught him kissing another girl and she hadn't spoken to him since.

'Probably not the best idea,' he said. 'Not with half the mob we've got coming.' Mob being the operative word. Listerman the lawyer had now put Tommy Riley down for ten tickets in all. Meaning more than likely ten faces Sharon would recognize from mugshots plastered across the investigation corkboards over at the West End nick.

He gazed across the cavernous room. It looked so strange in here with just the one competition table and nothing else. This really was it, wasn't it? His future. And who knew yet which way his luck might go?

'Hello, folks,' Slim said, making a beeline from the front door to the competition table.

Frankie smiled. He'd been hoping that Slim might turn up so he could have a go. It was obvious just from looking at the excited grin on his face that Slim was thinking the exact same thing.

'Rack 'em up, old timer,' he told him. 'A quid a frame. Let's see what you're made of, eh?'

'And you fix the drinks, the usual for me, old chap.'

Less than an hour later and Frankie was three quid up and zeroing in on the black. Slim was pretty useful himself, but Frankie had been getting better and better these last few months. Had been playing down here a lot on his own early mornings before anyone else showed up. Xandra said it had even got to the point where she'd bought earplugs to stop the incessant *clack-clack-clacking* from waking her up in her bedroom at the back of the club.

Frankie was hooked. Snooker kept his demons at bay and it seemed to take him fully over. It allowed him to stop thinking about anything else, to just *be* . . . Not even running did that for him. When he was in the zone, this was his total focus, where, for just a short while, nothing else outside this beautiful rectangle existed. On the green baize nothing else mattered, apart from this moment, this angle, this spin, this shot.

And *crack* – he took his shot now – and watched the pocket swallowing the black, and the cue ball rolling to a rest against the side cushion. And perfection. Just for a split second. That's what this was, when you got it just right. He knew nothing in the world that felt better than that.

'Well played,' Slim said, getting up from his seat, a whiskey and soda in one hand, the fingers of his other trailing along the burnished length of the table. 'You know, maybe you should consider playing one of these exhibition matches yourself.'

Frankie stood up, the spell of the last hour broken, the real world swamping back in on him again. 'Forget it,' he said. 'These lads we've got coming, they'd wipe the floor with me.'

Plus, it would hardly look right, him joining in trying to show off, would it? Not when he was meant to be running the show. Though no point in kidding himself, either. A part of him would love to have a crack.

'Maybe,' said Slim. 'Or maybe not. You never know with Lady Luck.' He raised his glass to her then, the photograph of Frankie's mum back there behind the bar.

Lady Luck: that's what he'd often teasingly called her when they'd both worked here together back in the day.

'Do you ever think about her?' Frankie asked.

'Of course.' Slim didn't look at him when he said it.

'I mean about what happened to her that day?' he said. 'About where she might have ended up?'

'Aye, but it never gets me anywhere.'

He'd been hit as hard as just about anyone by Priscilla James's disappearance. Almost as hard, Frankie reckoned, as him, Jack and the Old Man.

Frankie thought about the postcard. Should he show him it? He'd have seen her handwriting plenty working here with her. Enough to know if that card was really from her? But he couldn't bring himself to do it. Slim was as good as family, of course. But this was *family* family business. He needed to talk to Jack first. And, of course, the Old Man.

'Are you all right?' Slim said, looking at him strangely.

'Yeah.'

'Another frame?' Slim asked.

'Nah, you're good. There's some stuff I need to deal with upstairs.'

*

Back up in the flat, Frankie gave Jack a bell on his mobile. No answer. Of course, he was moving into that new flat of his. Today. So he left a message instead to say that he'd swing by there tomorrow.

Frankie went over to the desk and picked up the post-card from where he'd left it. Turning it over, he traced his fingertips over the lipstick kiss. He pushed his chair back and stared down at the desk drawers.

Locked. All the drawers were locked. Why? Because that's how the Old Man had left it. With no key. Because that was his private stuff in there. Paperwork, he'd said. But what sort? Maybe something Frankie's mum had signed? Frankie read the postcard's message again and studied the letters. He looked at the way the '*W*' of '*WERE*' sloped a little weirdly to the right and matched the '*W*' in '*WOULD*'. What if he could find some samples of her handwriting to compare it against? Maybe then he could prove it really was her?

He tried opening each of the locked drawers with plain brute strength to begin with. No luck. They all held firmly. He pulled the desk away from the wall and tried getting in from the back, but it was solid there too and underneath looked the same.

Sod it. Needs must. He went through into the airing cupboard, where the Old Man kept his tools. And not just tools either. He glanced warily back at that cavity there in the brickwork that the Old Man had tipped him off about last year. The one that had had the box with the pistol in it, that had already done Frankie way more harm than good. He dug out a couple of screwdrivers, a rasp file and a mallet from the Old Man's toolbox. Should do the trick just fine.

It took him less than two minutes to get into the first drawer. Another five and he'd busted open the lot.

8

'Well, it's definitely an improvement on your last place,' Frankie said to his brother the next day.

'Thanks for the vote of confidence, bruv.'

But Frankie wasn't kidding. Just like the proverbial cat with nine lives that he was, it seemed this Tuesday lunchtime that Jack had once again landed on his feet. The flat Tommy Riley had stumped up the deposit for was a onebedder on the corner of Bonchurch Road and Ladbroke Grove. Hardly what you might call a palace in terms of size, but it was clean and was in an area clearly on the up. Little bruv was going to make a few quid profit on this and that was for sure.

Not that Frankie hadn't still got his reservations, of course. About Riley having funded this. About Jack still working for Riley, even if he did say what he had him doing wasn't front line. But he had to admit it, standing here now, Riley stumping up the deposit for this certainly had its advantages too. And softly, softly, catchee monkey, as they said. Play his cards right, make a success of the tournament, and Frankie might even be able to winkle Jack out from under Riley's wing *and* have him keep this place.

'You going to be all right for keeping up the mortgage payments?' he asked.

'Yeah. Tommy put me in touch with this financial advisor bloke. He got me a good deal.'

'But all in your name, right?'

'Yeah. Just relax, OK? For once in my life, this is all totally and utterly above board.'

'The view's not bad either,' said Frankie, staring out of the kitchen window down at the little restaurant across the street. Brasserie du Marché. A young woman was standing out front talking into a mobile phone. In a white shirt and black apron.

'Pretty, isn't she?' Jack said.

'What?' Frankie pretended he hadn't seen.

'Her name's Tiffany. Part-time waitress. Part-time personal trainer. Full-time stunner.'

'Tiffany? Sounds expensive. A friend of yours?'

'No, not a close one. Or not *that* close. Not that I haven't tried . . .'

'But?'

'She reckons I'm too young for her. Cute, was the word she used.'

'Yeah, well, you've always been that, haven't you, you little git,' Frankie said, ruffling Jack's hair.

'Piss off,' Jack said, good-naturedly, pulling away.

Frankie grinned. 'You sure it wasn't this that put her off?' He flicked the little bunch of hair Jack had got tied up on the top of his head. 'Whatever the hell *this* is.'

'A topknot.'

'A what?'

'It's in right now.'

'In the barber's bin is where it should be.'

'Ha bloody ha. At least I don't go round looking like some extra out of *Reservoir Dogs*,' he said, flicking the lapel of Frankie's jacket. 'But you never know. *She* might like it.'

'Who?'

'Tiffany. Come on, let's pop across the road for a sherbet and a bit of scran and find out. It's French. All steak and *frites*, not chips.' He picked up his black trilby from on the back of the door. Not much of an improvement, it had to be said. But at least it hid that monstrosity on the top of his bonce.

'Fine,' said Frankie. It was a beautiful, sunny day. Why the hell not? The steak and *frites* bit anyhow. 'My shout, let's call it a house-warming present.'

'Bed-warming, more like, if you play your cards right.'

Frankie ignored him. Boys' talk. He'd been guilty of plenty of it himself over the years. Something he'd grown out of a bit more lately. You saw the nasty side of it, running a club. Not that Xandra couldn't handle herself, but it still amazed him how many punters still thought she was on the bar menu too.

The food over in the brasserie was as good as Jack had promised. The last place he'd taken Frankie to eat was his favourite dodgy doner van up in Islington, so this meal came as a relief. The waitress, Tiffany, was nice too. Even prettier close up. Funny with it. As in ha ha, rather than weird. She told them both this filthy joke about three blokes going skiing as they were paying their bill. It brought tears to Frankie's eyes.

'You not gonna even ask her for her phone number?' Jack said, as they stepped out into the sunshine.

'Nah, I'm good.'

Not that he didn't like her. He did and he reckoned the feeling might be mutual too. Because there she was, watching him. And no denying it. There was definitely a little spark there. He knew as well how useless he was at the moment. No good for a relationship at all. His head either still too messed up missing booze and missing Sharon, or too focused in on the tournament and the Old Man – not to even mention this bloody postcard that might as well have been burning a hole right in his suit jacket pocket.

'So what now?' Jack said. 'Hit the bars? Quaff a few lagers and tequilas?' He smiled, a little sadly, and flung his arm round Frankie, pulling him close. 'Only kidding, bruv. I know how hard it's been. But you've done well, you know. I'm proud.'

Jack . . . proud of *Frankie*? Blimey, how the world moved on. Who knew, maybe his little brother really was finally growing up after all?

'And, to be honest,' he added with a grin, 'you were getting to be a bit of prick lately, whenever you got drunk.'

Frankie had no comeback for that.

'So what say we go hit Lisboa instead?' Jack said.

'That still there, is it?'

'Part of the furniture. You could drop a ten megaton bomb round here and they'd still be serving the finest coffee this side of Bar Italia.'

But it wasn't just the coffee that was good, Frankie

remembered. The Portuguese pastries would give Bar Italia a run for its money too.

Their shadows stretched out ahead of them between the tat stalls either side of the street, as Jack steered them onto Portobello Road.

'Do you remember?' he said, sparking up a fag. 'That time we crawled right the way down from here into Notting Hill, stopping at every effin' bar on the way?'

How could he not? 'Yeah. Good times.' A couple of years back now, when Frankie had still been able to drink recreationally. Before it had become a lifestyle, and then a deathstyle after that. When he'd still been able to switch off.

His nostrils flared, catching a whiff of Jack's baccy. Something inside him swooned. A longing for all of it. The old days. The fags and the booze washing over him, carrying him along. He gazed down Portobello Road, bathed in sunshine. A street stretching as far as the eye could see with pubs nicely lined up either side, all lifted by the blue sky overhead. How easy would it be?

'But old times, eh?' said Jack, rounding the corner onto Golborne Road. 'Come on, let's go get you that coffee.'

They passed the fishmonger's, antique shops and furniture stores, and bagged themselves a nice sunny table outside Lisboa and ordered a couple of espressos. Jack took a final drag of his fag before stubbing it out. Smoke drifted across Frankie's face, but this time he just waved it away. The moment had passed. The temptation. He didn't want it any more. Not the fags or the drink.

Jack excused himself for a leak and Frankie took his opportunity to sweeten up his coffee even more. He was going to need it for what was coming next. Because the time had come. No point in putting it off any more. Even though he knew, just knew, that no matter what he said, no matter how he handled this, it was going to lead to a row.

He took the postcard from his jacket pocket and placed it image-up on the table. What he'd found in the drawers, after he'd gone through their contents, it had soon been enough to convince him that this was from her. No one else.

Letters and postcards by the score, that's what he'd uncovered amongst a bunch of other crap the Old Man had been keeping stashed away – old bills, cancelled insurance policies, maps.

All the letters and cards had been from her. From Mum to the Old Man. But there was no evidence of any that had come back. Was that because she'd kept them somewhere else? Maybe he'd chucked them out for some reason, or had never bothered sending any himself?

The correspondence went right back to when they'd first met. To some dance he'd walked her home from, to their first dinner. Even their first night together got a mention. Frankie's skin prickled with embarrassment even now at the thought. The letters brought to life when he met her mum, Frankie's gran, and when she'd stayed in Sicily with her distant relatives – each with unpronounceable names, like Vaccaro, Giordano and Ferrara. On one of them there'd even been a lipstick kiss, alongside the letters *SWALK* – sealed with a loving kiss. Shortly after they'd moved into their first flat together and the letters had stopped. Not much point in writing to each other when you lived under the same roof, Frankie guessed.

He'd compared the handwriting in all of them, all the capital letters that he could, with the ones on the postcard sent to him. He'd even bloody gone out down Menzies and bought tracing paper and put the different samples side-by-side on another piece of paper. Until he was as good as certain – or as good as he reckoned he was ever likely to be – that the handwriting matched.

It wasn't all he'd found in that drawer either. There'd been newspaper clippings too from '88, the year his mum went missing. Scraps from local papers, even a clipping from the *Standard* too and appeals for anyone who'd seen her, for her to get in touch with the police and let her family know she was well. But there were clippings about other women – unidentified female bodies. 'Jane Does', one of the clippings had said. Homeless people found dead. Drug overdoses. Drowning victims from the Thames. Each of them neatly crossed out whenever the poor woman in question had been identified. The victims weren't just London either, they were in Essex, Kent, even as far as Ireland and France. It seemed like the Old Man, no matter what he'd told Frankie to the contrary, had been carrying out a little investigation of his own.

'What you looking so serious about, bruv?' Jack asked, sitting back down.

9

'This,' Frankie said, tapping his finger firmly on the post-card and pushing it across the table towards Jack. 'I got sent it a couple of days ago.'

Jack picked it up and gazed down at the picture, baffled, before turning it over and reading it.

'I don't get it,' he said.

'What's written there. It's almost exactly the same as what Mum told me the day she went.'

'What do you mean?'

'She made me promise that I'd always be there for you. No matter what happened.'

Jack's expression crumpled. 'You mean, she knew she was actually going to be –'

'Leaving? No. I'm still not sure if that's what she actually meant.'

'But you only thought to tell me about it now anyway?' Jack couldn't keep the resentment from his face.

'Because she might have meant nothing by it. She might just have been doing what mums do. Just telling me to keep an eye out for you, that's all.'

'And now this postcard? Jesus.' Jack pushed back his

chair from the table, away from Frankie. 'You're telling me you think this is from her? That she's still alive and wants to –'

Jack couldn't even bring himself to say it. But Frankie knew damn well what he'd been about to say. *That she's still alive and wants to see us again.* Frankie already knew that Jack had blocked this possibility out a long time ago. Every time Frankie had ever raised their mum over the years, all Jack had done was look away. Like Frankie was some kind of a mug for even thinking about her at all. Only now did he see it, that glimmer of hope in his eyes.

'Well, who else can it be?' Frankie said.

Jack flipped the postcard over and stared at the image again. 'And, what? You expect me to believe that she's just out there? Living it up on Mallorca? And that, what, she's suddenly just decided to drop us a line? Out of the goodness of her own heart?'

'I know it's weird. And shouldn't make any sense. But think about it. What happened to you last year. Everything I did to . . . to help you, Jack. She must have somehow found out.'

Jack didn't know the half of it, what Frankie had done, the *things* he'd done, to prove Jack's innocence. Because Frankie had told him nothing the one and only time he'd asked. But he'd seen Frankie's face. How badly he'd been beaten. Whatever Frankie had done for him, Jack knew it had been no walk in the park.

'And what now?' Jack said.

'What do you mean?'

'Just that,' he hissed, trying to keep his voice down.

'What now? Because if you're right, if this really is her, then why the hell is she writing to you? What does she want?'

'*Want*? What do you mean, *want*? Can't you see? This might be brilliant. This might be the best news ever. This might mean that she –'

'That she *what*, bruv? Gives a shit?'

'No. Yes. That she's alive. That she's still out there.'

Jack shakily lit himself another cigarette – anger, fear, even hope? 'Or maybe this isn't even from her at all,' he said.

'Then who?'

'I don't know. Anyone. Some nutter.'

'What, just writing to me out of the blue?'

'Anyone,' he repeated. 'Someone who just doesn't like you. Doesn't like us. Someone who wants to wind us up.'

'But what's written there. What she said to me that day. How could someone else know? No one else was there when she said it. No one but me.'

'You could just be reading all that into it. It might just be what you want to believe. What's actually written here, it might not be about that at all.'

'But what if it is?'

Jack shoved the postcard back at Frankie. 'Even if this is from her, even if she's not dead like Dad says, and for some reason she's decided that it's suddenly OK now to get in touch . . . well, I don't want to know.' He stared unblinkingly at Frankie. 'I mean it. If she's been out there somewhere all this time, if she could have come back before, and *chose* not to . . .'

63

'She might have had a *reason*. Can't you see that? For keeping her distance till now.'

'There is no reason. Not good enough for that. No way. She skipped out on us, that's what she done. I don't know what happened to her after that, but that's how she left . . .'

There it was again, *skipped out*, the same phrase he always used. The thing he truly believed.

'She packed her bag, didn't she?' Jack went on. 'Don't you forget that.'

'Someone packed her bag,' Frankie said. 'Took her things. Doesn't mean it had to be her. Doesn't mean she went of her own choice.'

'Yeah, you tell yourself that, bruv. You tell yourself that like you always do. But what if you're wrong, eh, Frankie? What if she just left us because she wanted to? Because she didn't want to know us no more?'

Frankie stared at Jack's trembling fingers. Almost took the cigarette from him and stuck it in his own mouth. He wished he had a comeback for what he'd just said, but he didn't, because what if he was right?

'Even then, I've still got to know,' he said. 'One way or another. I've got to find out if this is from her.'

Jack stubbed out his cigarette. Frankie thought he was about to storm out, but instead he closed his eyes and rubbed at his brow.

'You shown it to the Old Man yet?' he finally asked.

'No.' He was booked in to visit him on Thursday, the day after tomorrow. It was the same day he visited him each week.

'But you will?'

'I don't know.' He really didn't. How would the Old Man react? Probably even worse than Jack. He'd hardly spoken about her for years.

'He might be able to tell better than us if it's her writing or not,' Jack said. 'I mean, they were together for nearly twenty years before he screwed that up too.'

Him. Or her. Frankie had never asked either of his parents why they'd split up. He remembered him and Jack being sat down together and told. By her. How sometimes people stopped being in love. How sometimes when they did they started arguing all the time. How they'd both decided that it would be best for everyone if they spent some time apart.

'Yeah,' he said. 'That's what I was thinking too.'

'And he's probably got a right to know an' all, hasn't he? I mean, if it really is her. And I'm not saying it is. I'm not saying that a-bloody-tall. But he's got a right all the same. In case she is actually, I don't know . . . reaching out, back into our lives, after all this time . . .'

Jack sucked on his cigarette, staring at the floor. Frankie knew he was panicked. That he was panicked. That he wanted this whole thing with their mum to go away. Back into the box he'd been keeping it in all these years. So he could get back on with his life.

'Come on, let's go,' Frankie said. This conversation was done. Frankie put the postcard back in his pocket and stuck down a fiver for the coffees. He wasn't in the mood for pastry any more. His appetite was shot.

They walked back to Jack's flat in silence. Tiffany was outside the restaurant again, and gave them a little wave and a smile. Frankie just nodded in reply, he felt wrung out and exhausted. Christ, if talking to his brother about his mum was this hard, how much worse was it going to be talking to his dad?

They heard the car before they saw it. Not a screech of tyres or the steady *dum-dum-dum* of bass, that was pretty much standard for this part of town, but jazz. A clarinet was playing, sweet and haunting. It felt like music from another age altogether. Frankie turned to look as the sound got louder and watched a top-of-the-range Merc pulling up alongside them.

The tinted windows glinted in the sun, so much so that Frankie had to cover his eyes, all the while trying to peer in at whoever was inside. The front passenger window nearest the kerb slowly wound down and a woman stared out. She must have been in her mid-thirties, with short, bobbed black hair and heavy kohl make-up – a diamond collar competing with the glare from the car.

'Frankie and Jack James?' she said.

'Yeah?' Frankie and his brother answered at exactly the same time, earning themselves another smile in reply.

'I've got a message for you.'

'What?' both the James boys answered at the same time again.

Frankie thought he heard another voice. Who else was sitting there inside? He tried peering in again, but couldn't see a thing. The Cleopatra woman was blocking his view of the driver and the tinted windows stopped him seeing into the back seats.

'It's not for everyone to hear,' she said, her eyes just on Jack now.

'No?' said Jack, smiling himself now, clearly enjoying this game.

'No. It's a secret. Come closer and I'll tell you.'

'Really?' Jack was half laughing now.

'Really.'

Jack stepped in closer. She held out her hand to him, like she was inviting him to kiss it. Expensive nails. Slender fingers. Something about her wrist, though, her arm, that didn't look right.

'Wait,' Frankie said, suddenly seeing what it was.

Too late. Her arm shot out, hooking round the back of Jack's neck as he leant in to hear what she had to say. Her other arm met it at his throat, pinning him tight in a lock.

The Merc's engine gunned. The vehicle shot forward with a hot screech of tyres. Jack went with it. Jerked clean off his feet. But he didn't just fall. Not like he should have. Because what Frankie had noticed about this woman, he'd been right – she might have the face of an angel, but she had the arms of a fighter, toned and strong enough to keep their grip on Jack as the Merc dragged him down the street, headfirst towards an electricity box right there – up ahead – on the kerb.

But Frankie was moving too – he'd taken off at the exact same time as the car and had grabbed hold of the girl's arms and was trying to tear them off Jack.

And he did. Just in time. Both he and Jack fell, their legs buckling and tangling. They missed the electricity box by less than in inch and stumbled, sprawling into a gasping heap on the pavement.

Motherfucker. Frankie stared after the car, its number plate a blur. Ten yards away already and disappearing round the corner of the block.

'Jack? Are you OK?'

Jack was flat on his back, gasping, rubbing at his red raw throat where she'd got a hold of him.

'Jack!' Frankie rolled over to help him. 'Can you breathe?'

'Yeah . . .' Jack curled up into a ball.

The waitress from across the road, Tiffany, came running over, dropping down beside Jack and cradling his head in her arms. Then, out of nowhere, a man jumped from his bike, leaving it skittering across the pavement, and ran towards them, shouting he was GP and asking if they were OK.

Frankie forced himself up. His suit trousers were ripped right through on both knees. One of his shoes was lying in the gutter six feet back. His knuckles were covered with blood from where he'd scraped them across the pavement as they'd rolled.

'Motherfucker!' he screamed, staring down the empty street at the corner where the Merc had vanished.

'Who the hell was that?' Jack panted, struggling, but managing to sit up. He was covered in dirt and dust and blood was dripping from his lip, but apart from that he looked miraculously all right.

But it wasn't the girl Frankie was thinking of at all as he kept on staring right down that road. It was the face he'd glimpsed in the back of the car, of the man who'd stared even harder back into Frankie's eyes as him and Jack were being dragged along. A man who Frankie was 90 per cent bleedin' sure he knew.

Dougie Hamilton, son of Terence Hamilton, who not only clearly now knew where Jack lived, but clearly still wanted him dead.

10

Frankie spent Tuesday evening and the whole of Wednesday burying himself in work, prepping for the tournament launch at the Ambassador Club. But he couldn't get that Cleopatra woman out of his mind. Or whoever had been sitting in the back. *Had* it been Dougie Hamilton? Frankie still couldn't be sure enough to tell anyone or do anything about it. He'd warned Jack to stay sharp and to call if anything happened. Frankie hoped that whoever it was had had their fun and would now leave Jack alone. He hoped, but he wasn't convinced.

*

Thursday morning and Frankie's blood was boiling as he picked up his Capri from the multi-storey where he kept it over by Raymond's Revue Bar a couple of hundred yards from the Ambassador.

Late last night he'd finally found some time to sit down and start reading through the Old Man's case files. But five minutes in and he'd gone apo-bloody-plectic, after reading the three names of the chief investigating officers who'd put the Old Man away.

Because Snaresby . . . Snaresby had been one of them – something that both Kind Regards and the Old Man had kept from Frankie, even while Snaresby had been trying to put Jack away last year.

Frankie had called Kind Regards up there and then to demand why. He'd kept it from him because he knew how Frankie would have reacted, because he'd have seen connections where there weren't any. Kind Regards genuinely believed that Snaresby had just doing his job, or at least said he couldn't prove that he hadn't.

Whereas Frankie now reckoned it was more like a vendetta.

Navigating his way round the clusterfuck of exits around Hyde Park Corner, he pictured the sheet of A4 in his jacket pocket, with all three of the cops' names written on it:

JOHN SPENSER SNARESBY

CRAIG STANLEY FENWICK

JAMES NICHOLLS

Frankie had never even heard of the last two. But he was planning on finding out as much about them as he could, and not just them, but Snaresby too. As well as any possible motive any of them might have to do Frankie's family harm. And where better to start than with a visit to the Old Man himself?

It was just as he was heading down Grosvenor Place

towards Victoria that he became aware of the white BMW 525 behind him. He lost sight of it round the dogleg at Buck Pal, but it wasn't long before he picked it up again in his rear-view mirror as he was hunting round the maze of little streets next to Brixton Prison for somewhere to park.

Could it really be the same car? And if it was, did that mean that whoever was inside was following him? Nah, he was just being paranoid, right? But even so, he slowed right down to get a dekko at the number plate and hopefully the driver too. Only, the second he did, the car sped off down a side street, and was gone.

The Old Man was already sitting waiting for him by the time Frankie got through to the Visitors' Room. He was nose-deep in *The Stand*, the latest Stephen King novel Frankie had brought him last week.

Frankie recognized one of the inmates on the table next to him too. Stanley Lomax. One of Riley's enforcers, who was in here on the tail end of a GBH charge. He'd kept an eye on Jack last year while he was on remand over in Wandsworth. Must have been transferred since. With him was a wizened, older guy with razor-sharp cheekbones, who looked like he'd been weaned on coke. Frankie nodded at Lomax, who nodded solidly back.

'You know Dolf and Lomax, do you?' said the Old Man, keeping his voice well low, as Frankie sat down opposite him.

'Lomax, yeah. He used to pop into the club from time to time. What did you say the other bloke's called?'

The Old Man leant on his hands to hide his lips from being read. 'Dolf. As in Adolf,' he said.

'You're kidding, right?'

'Let's just say his dad was a fan. And make sure you keep the hell out of his way. He's a dangerous fucker, all right?'

Frankie nodded. The Old Man stared hard into his eyes. 'So you want to talk about Snaresby,' he said.

'You what?' How could he know?

The Old Man smiled thinly. 'Kind Regards rang.'

Frankie swallowed. He hated this. The way it always felt like the Old Man had the upper hand in whatever conversation they had.

'Fine, so why didn't you tell me?' Frankie said. 'Last year, when I told you that Snaresby was the one who was bossing Jack's case, why didn't you tell me that he was the one who'd helped put you away an' all?'

'I warned you off him, didn't I? Told you he was a bastard. What else was I supposed to do?'

'Tell me he had it in for us. For our whole family.'

'I don't know that.'

'Yeah, you and Kind Regards both. But I bet you bloody well suspect it, don't you? I mean you must do. You grew up with him. You can't just think it's a coincidence that he –'

The Old Man's brow furrowed even deeper. 'I've got no proof. Don't you think that if I did, if I had one scrap of actual evidence that him or some other copper stitched me up, that I'd be sitting here talking to you in this shithole now?'

'Yeah, well, what if I can get proof?'

73

The Old Man grabbed his wrist, making him flinch. 'You keep your voice down,' he hissed.

There was something in the Old Man's eyes that Frankie had never seen before. Something that looked a lot like fear. He glanced across at Lomax and Dolf. Had they been listening too?

'There's something else,' Frankie said.

'What?' The Old Man still looked wary.

'No, not about your case,' Frankie said. 'This.' Digging into his jacket pocket, he pulled out the postcard and pushed it across the table, picture side up.

The Old Man put on his glasses. 'Majorca. Very nice. I always fancied having a little holiday there. Never did find the time.'

'Well, aren't you going to read it?'

He turned it over. 'Don't look like it's addressed to me.'

'Read it.'

Frankie had said it louder than he'd meant.

The Old Man did what he'd been told, then tossed it back down onto the table.

'Well?' Frankie said.

The Old Man shrugged. 'If you think that's meant to mean something to me, it doesn't.'

So Frankie told him. What he'd told Jack. What the last thing his mum had said to him on the day she'd vanished was. The Old Man listened, but he didn't look back down at the card.

'So that's it, is it?' Frankie said. 'Nothing? You've got nothing to say?'

'What do you want me to say? That it's her writing? That it could be?'

'Well? Could it?'

'I don't know. Maybe. In fact, no.'

'Why not?'

'Just because.' The Old Man growled, actually growled. 'Jesus, Frankie, I know you want to . . . for her to be . . .'

'Still alive.'

'Yes. But she ain't. She can't be.'

Jesus, it was like talking to his brother all over again. Why was he the only one who could see this for what it was?

'But why?'

'Because if she was alive, if she could come back home, she already would have. For you and Jack. Because she loved you. She'd never have abandoned you like that.'

The same dead end he'd hit with his brother. But what if it wasn't just him who still believed she might be out there? What if he was just the only one who was willing to say it out loud?

'You kept them,' he said.

'Kept what?'

'Her letters. Her postcards. Everything she wrote you. Even when you split up from her and moved into the flat, you never threw any of it away. After she vanished, you kept it all too. All those clippings about those women. Women who might have been her . . .'

'You been going through my stuff?' the Old Man flared. He spoke through gritted teeth, trying to keep his voice under control. 'You've got no right. That desk was locked.'

The Old Man's face was the colour of beetroot. For a second, Frankie thought he was going to lunge for him. But then, suddenly, the fight went right out of him.

'We were over, finished,' he said. 'But yeah, maybe a part of me did want it to go back to how it was, and maybe that's why I kept all those letters, to try and see where it all went wrong.'

'So why all the newspaper clippings?'

'Just because you break up from someone . . . just because that person doesn't love you any more . . .'

The way he said it. It was her not him who'd fallen out of love. *Mutual.* That was the word they'd always given him and Jack. But if it had been his mum who'd made the decision, then why? Because there'd been someone else? Or because of something the Old Man had done?

'. . . it doesn't mean you stop caring, about what had happened to them, about where they might be . . .'

'And that's just it,' Frankie said, stabbing his finger down onto the postcard, 'I do still care, I do still want to know.'

'Digging all this up, trying to find out what happened, you think you're going to find something good . . . her, still alive . . . You think there's going to be some happy ending to this, but I'm telling you now, there ain't.'

'The way you say it . . .'

'What?'

'The way you look . . . It's like you *know*, like you know what really happened to her. Or even if you don't know, it's like you *suspect.*'

The Old Man's eyes flicked across to Dolf and Lomax once more. And again Frankie thought he glimpsed it – that look of fear in his eyes. But even if they had just heard – so what? Why should he be afraid of them?

Back out on the street, Frankie clambered into the Capri. It was only when he started the engine that he saw the folded-up piece of paper that someone had tucked under the wiper. He got out and opened it and read the neat, looping writing:

Fear Lies in the Past

What the hell? Frankie looked quickly round, trying to catch sight of whoever had written it. But the street was empty. He thought straight away of that car. The white Beamer. *Had* he been followed? And if he had, *was* it them who'd written this?

He read the note again. But what did it mean? It was clearly trying to warn him off something, but what? Was it telling him to leave the past alone? But which past? His dad's case? His mum's disappearance? But who – apart from Jack, Kind Regards, Slim and the Old Man – even knew he was looking into either?

He pictured the Old Man again. That look in his eyes.

Dolf had left before Frankie, hadn't he? Quick enough to have got here first? But how would he even have known that this was Frankie's car? Unless he'd been the one following his Capri as well? But even if that was true, what possible beef could he have about the Old Man's

77

sentencing, or even less so Frankie's mum, to make him write something like this?

'Fear Lies in the Past'. He read it again. Because what if this note wasn't referring to either his dad's case or his mum at all? What if it was about Jack and what had happened last summer? Hamilton, Dougie Hamilton . . . Could his gang have followed Frankie all the way out here? But to warn him what? Was last year's nightmare never going to be over?

Frankie's face darkened. He felt the adrenalin rushing through his veins. He walked into the centre of the road and stared up and down the street. Was whoever had written this still watching? Well, fuck them, if they were. He wasn't afraid of them. Wasn't afraid of anyone. And if whoever this was thought they could mess with him, they had another think coming. And high time he let them know.

He tore the note in half, tossed it up into the air and watched it flutter down around him like snow.

He heard it then. A car engine starting up. Saw it too. The white Beamer 525, pulling out a hundred yards up ahead, and racing away, again before he'd a chance to clock its plates.

So much for being paranoid. Someone *had* followed him here. The only questions now were *who?* and *why?*

11

Frankie got the call from Paddington A&E late that night at just gone 3 a.m. He grabbed a cab from right outside the club and was by Jack's bedside less than ten minutes later.

'Bloody hell,' he said, taking Jack's hand and staring down at him. His face was a right bleeding mess. Literally.

'I'm all right,' Jack said. Or tried too. What actually came out of his cut and swollen mouth was something more like *ahgrawli*. Along with something small and white and wet with blood and spit.

Fuck. Frankie picked up a tooth. Someone had walloped Jack. And walloped him hard. Frankie had seen plenty worse down the gym. He'd been bashed up a couple of times this bad himself over the years, but seeing his brother like this made his skin crawl.

He listed what he reckoned he could see. A black eye. A split lip – or was that a *re-split* lip from the bounce he'd got off the pavement after getting dragged by that car? Broken teeth. As well as a nasty gash right across the top of forehead.

'*Dwunning . . .*'

'What?'

'*Dwoening . . .*'

'Drowning?'

'*Here . . .*' Looking round, Jack even managed half a smile.

And, Christ, yeah, Frankie got it now. The last time the two of them had been here. When Frankie had saved Jack from drowning after Jack had jumped off a bridge into the Regent's Canal for a bet when they were kids. Just after their mum had gone.

'What happened?' Frankie said, gritting his own teeth so hard they hurt.

'*Sumwuh juh muh.*'

'Jumma?'

'*Juhmmp muh.*'

Ah. Frankie got it. 'Someone jumped you? Who?'

'*Ah gu nu.*' I don't know.

Frankie stared into his eyes, or the one good one that wasn't puffed up anyway. But Jack just stared right back. Didn't flinch. Was sure of what he was saying then.

'Did you get a good look at them at all?' A name. That's all Frankie needed. Give him a name and he'd make whatever bastard had done this pay.

'*Nuh.*'

'Nothing at all?'

'*Nuh.*'

Bollocks. Whoever had jumped him had jumped him good.

'Are you in pain?'

'*Puills . . .*'

Good. They'd already dosed him up.

Someone started screaming at the end of the corridor. A female medic in blue scrubs hurried into the cubicle.

'Excuse me, sir,' she said. 'We're going to need to stitch him up.'

Jack didn't let go of Frankie's hand.

'Fine, but I'm staying right here,' Frankie said. 'Don't worry, kid,' he told him, moving his chair back to give the doc some room. 'We'll get you through this. Just you wait and see.'

'Very well,' said the doc. 'And you are family?'

'Frankie, his brother.'

She scribbled it down on her notes. 'I'm Indra from maxillofacial, I'm here to help clear him up.'

She peered down at the plastic label on Jack's wrist. 'Can you confirm your name and date of birth?' she asked him.

'*Jah jahm*,' Jack said.

'April second, seventy-six,' Frankie said.

Indra glanced at him, annoyed, but not big time, more like he'd just cheated at Monopoly or something at Christmas, but he guessed that's how it was here. Everything became normalized, the blood, bones, everything apart from the rules.

'Very well, then, Jack,' she said, focusing back on him. 'Now I understand from your notes that you've already been examined by my colleagues, and that you're scheduled to have a CT scan to check for any internal injuries and, in particular, your shoulder.'

'*Ig gign*.'

'It's fine,' Frankie translated.

'Yes, well, we'll still need to take a good look at it just

to be sure. And, regardless of the results, we're going to be keeping you in overnight as we're obliged to with any concussion.'

'*Ignot canthus.*'

'He says he's not –' Frankie started to say.

'That might be how he feels now,' she said, 'but the paramedics say he was semi-conscious when they reached him and very disorientated.'

'Does it say where they found him?'

'*The Grarfter.*'

The Grafton Arms. Warren Street. One of Jack's favourite drinking haunts. And the fact he could remember going there was probably good news too, at least as far as his head was concerned.

'I'm sure everything will be fine,' the doc said. 'And I don't know if my colleagues mentioned it? But there's going to be a delay before the scan, as London is keeping us even busier than usual tonight. Two helicopters already.'

Helicopters meant one thing, serious injuries. Hopefully the doctor didn't think Jack's injuries fell into that category yet, despite how mashed up he looked.

'Which means I've got time now to clean up your face and put some stitches in,' she went on. 'I hope that's OK? Do you understand?'

Jack nodded, as more screaming could be heard from down the corridor. Jack's functioning eye widened in alarm and the doc must have seen it too, because she gave him a reassuring smile.

'Don't worry, I'll be as gentle as I can,' she said. 'It says here on the notes from the ambulance and the police report that you were hit with . . . a baseball bat?'

A *what*? Frankie felt sick. She peeled back the sheet from Jack's torso. His white T-shirt was spattered with blood, his right shoulder horribly bruised and his arm already in a sling. Must have been done by paramedics on the way over. Jack reckoned it wasn't broken. What, then? Sprained? And how? Defending himself? That's what it looked like to Frankie. He pictured the bat swinging at him through the air.

The doc prepped a needle. Shit a brick. It was as long as a finger.

'Now this is a local anaesthetic,' she explained, 'and you will feel a little prick.'

'It won't be the first time, eh, bruv?' Frankie muttered.

'Yes, thank you, Mr James,' said the doc. 'Though if you are going to make jokes to cheer your brother up, perhaps you could make them a little more original?'

'Fair enough,' Frankie said. A twinkle in Jack's eye. Might even have been him smiling. Hard to tell. 'Right, you ready, bruv?' he said. Jack nodded. 'Then let's do this,' he told the doc.

She smiled grimly at him. But kindly too. They were a team now, the two of them. Frankie hated needles, but he didn't look away, not once during the next seven squirming injections she gave Jack in the head, before getting stuck in and clearing up his cut. And not once either during the fourteen stitches she put in after that.

*

Frankie ended up waiting there with Jack in A&E for another three hours, most of which, thankfully, Jack slept through thanks to whatever opiate painkiller they'd got him on. And, bless him, the sweet little bastard even had a smile on his face for most of it. Was probably having the time of his life.

Then he was off for the CT scan, before finally getting transferred onto a ward around 8 a.m. The ward sister told Frankie they'd be getting the scan back by ten. Not much point in Frankie going home then – though, God knew, he had enough to do. Tonight was launch night. Everything he'd been working towards all year.

He found a pay phone and called Xandra and The Topster and left messages to tell them what was happening and to ask them to hold the fort until he got back to the club. Which would be just as soon as he could. Once he knew Jack was OK.

He headed off into the depths of the hospital in search of a coffee and some grub, but the caffs weren't open yet and so he had to settle for a cup of instant from a machine instead, then found himself a bench in a concrete courtyard outside and sat down in the morning sun.

A *baseball bat*. Those two words. He couldn't get them out of his head. Them and a face. Douglas sodding Hamilton. Had that really been him in the back of the car that had dragged Frankie? And, if it had, was this down to him as well?

Dougie's fiancée had been killed with a baseball bat. Was that what this was all about? Could he still be refusing to believe that Jack had had nothing to do with it, was he still thirsting for revenge?

Frankie slowly shook his head. The second he'd read that note on the car he should have acted. Because that could have been another warning about this. He should have done anything he could to get Jack off the street.

But he hadn't. He'd been weak. He'd driven back telling himself he'd got no proof of anything. That he couldn't go asking Riley for help either, for the same reason.

Meaning all he'd actually done was call Jack up when he'd got home and told him to keep safe. He'd done nothing, in other words, except hope. That whoever had dragged Jack outside his flat had already had their penny's worth for whatever reason it had been. That that would be the end of it.

Well, he'd been bloody wrong. Because this didn't feel like the end of anything. It felt like the start.

And, just as bad, maybe all this was something he'd brought about himself. Because maybe it really was nothing to do with Dougie at all. Maybe what had happened to Jack had been because of what Frankie had done. Because he'd ripped that note up. Had tossed it into the air. And whoever had written it had decided to teach him a lesson. To stop him from looking into whatever it was they didn't want him to find.

Frankie remembered the look that had flashed across the Old Man's face when he'd grabbed Frankie's wrist and had told him to pipe down. And he wondered again who exactly he was afraid of. Dolf or Lomax? Or someone they knew? Or someone else entirely? Someone Frankie should be afraid of too?

'Good morning, Frankie, am I to assume that it just got lost in the post?'

Frankie recognized the voice and turned, his lip already curling. Snaresby. Blocking out his sun, looming over him like a bleedin' gravestone. Dressed in his regulation suit and tie, even at this hour, like he'd slept in it, which the bastard probably had.

'That what did?'

'My invite.'

'To what?'

'Why, your little party, of course. For your one day perhaps not so little tournament. I mean, it is still taking place tonight, isn't it? In spite of this little diversion you're currently caught up in? Or maybe you hadn't sent me an invite at all?' Snaresby smiled, waiting for an answer, but Frankie just shook his head. 'Ah, well, not to worry,' the Chief Inspector went on. 'It just so happens I'm busy this evening anyway.' He rolled his tongue slowly across his lips. 'It's Mrs Snaresby's birthday and she's on a promise, wouldn't you know, the lucky mare? Still, maybe next time, eh?'

'How did you find me?' Frankie said.

'That nice little sister running your brother's ward. You know, the one with the lovely, firm . . .' He cupped his hands over his chest, his little fingertips pointing out.

Frankie fought the urge to retch. 'No, I mean who told you about Jack? That he was even in here at all?'

'Oh, come come now, sunshine. Surely you must know by now that a good detective never reveals his sources.'

'What about a shit one?' Frankie smirked.

'Oh, very droll.' Snaresby pulled out his Zippo and sparked up a smoke.

'I'm serious. How did you know?'

'Oh, hadn't you heard, Frankie? The whole world's gone bloody computer crazy. Anything you want at the touch of a button.'

'What, and you really expect me to believe that? That of all the sodding assaults committed in this shitty city last night, his just happened to turn up on your desk?'

Snaresby smiled sourly. 'Nothing much gets past you, does it, sunshine? Fair enough. We like to keep a track of certain names down the nick. All you've got to do is programme them in.'

'And my brother's one of them?'

'Oh, not just your brother . . .'

Meaning Frankie was as well.

'Talk about fucking Big Brother.'

'Oh yes. Quite literally in this case.'

'That's police harassment.'

'Or police protection, depending on your point of view. Because, you've got to understand, the last thing I want is all that nastiness from last summer between Riley and Hamilton's mobs bubbling up again.'

'Who says it is?' Sure, Frankie reckoned Dougie might be behind all this, but he'd got no proof and he doubted the cops did either. Jack certainly couldn't have told them anything last night.

'Just a bit of a coincidence otherwise, wouldn't you say? Him getting attacked with a bat like that. The same as

Dougie Hamilton's fiancée was. Not to mention Danny Kale last summer as part of the little turf war too.'

So he'd made some of the same connections as him. Frankie said nothing. Snaresby trailed his long fingers over his buzz-cut, balding head.

'Trying to remember how it felt to still have hair?'

Snaresby ignored him. 'Do you know where we found him? Your little brother? Down an alley round the back of a pub. Honestly, I don't know why you bother with him. The only reason he'd probably gone down there at all was to get his little knob sucked or to score.'

'Why don't you just watch your bloody mouth?' Frankie said. No one here but them two, meaning he didn't have to watch his own. 'You're doing it again. Treating him like a villain, when he's the victim in all this. You think he's got himself neck deep in trouble again. Well, he hasn't. And this *is* harassment, you've got no right – my brother was proven innocent.'

'Well, proof's stretching it a bit, wouldn't you say?'

'Someone else confessed to the murder. What more bloody proof do you need?'

'Ah, but a confession's hardly rock solid, is it? Particularly from a dead guy.'

'It was enough to help you put my father away.' A local gang leader, Manny Thompson, had confessed to the Mayfair robbery shortly before he'd hanged himself in prison. After fingering the Old Man as his accomplice and telling the cops where the cases with the stolen wedge and jewels from the looted safety boxes were stashed, all covered in his and the Old Man's prints.

'Ah, so you've finally worked out I was on your father's case, have you? I was wondering how long it would take.'

'So my father wasn't good enough for you, was he? You had to come after my brother as well.'

'Just doing my job. The same as I keep telling you.'

'The same as Craig Fenwick and James Nicholls were?'

'Ooh, someone has been doing their homework.' Snaresby flashed him a half-moon smile. But what shocked Frankie was his lack of surprise. 'Yes, sunshine, just the same as them.'

'He's innocent.'

'I think you've already made that point.'

'I don't just mean Jack.'

Snaresby smiled. Wide, now. Like a wolf. 'Oh, ho-ho. Your father may be many things, Frankie James, but an innocent he is not.'

'I mean of that robbery. What he's in prison for.' Even if the Old Man hadn't exactly always lived a squeaky-clean life, he'd never consider anything like armed robbery. He'd sworn to Jack and that was good enough for him. 'He was stitched up.'

'By me? Well, go on, you might as well say it. It's fairly clear from the look on your face right now that you'd like to rip my guts out.'

'Either by you, or by Fenwick and Nicholls. Maybe it was someone else on your team?'

'That case, Mr James, is watertight. It's history. The same as your father until he gets out and there's nothing you can do that'll change that.'

'Yeah? Well, maybe I'll go talk to Fenwick and Nicholls and see what they've got to say.'

But Snaresby's grin just widened. 'Good for you and good luck with that. Because one of them's moved to Australia. And the other one's dead.'

12

The round of applause started on its own, with whooping and whistling as the black was potted by the winner of the two pro players who'd been laying on a demonstration for the crowd. Frankie's guests were having a cracking night out so far.

Festive Al had installed four blocks of tiered seating around the single snooker table in the centre of the room. A boxing ring formation, he'd called it, enough for five rows of seats per block. Two hundred in total. Each seat full.

Right, speech time. Frankie took a slug of water as he waited for the clapping to die down. His mouth felt like the bleeding Sahara. Christ, he could do with a proper drink to help calm his nerves.

Xandra had her arm around Maxine and beamed a huge grin across to him, nodding him on in encouragement. She was right, he could do this. And do it sober. And it'd be all the better for it but, Christ, he'd been gasping for a drink all night.

He'd already chatted to well over half the industry faces he'd invited here. Potential sponsors, promoters, managers, players and sports journos. Even the health and safety bloke from the council. But there was still plenty more jawing to do.

He stood up and cleared his throat. Jesus, even that seemed to echo round the room. Xandra nodded at him again, her eyes blazing. She'd made him practise this twenty times or more earlier this evening after he'd got back from dropping Jack home from the hospital.

Just don't rush it, she'd said. Look them all in the eye and smile, and only *then* do you start to talk. He could do this. Yep, come on. Time to give it his very best shot.

'First up, I want to say a big thanks to the players,' he said, nodding to the two lads, who'd both just given this audience a half-hour master class in long-potting and trick shots, 'who we'll no doubt be seeing a lot more of on our TV screens over the coming years and hopefully here in the Ambassador Club too.'

A smattering of applause broke out as the two lads bowed. Dickie Bird's camera flashed away, recording the moment for posterity. He was luckily wearing more than just a pair of pants tonight, even if the date that he'd brought with him – who'd insisted on helping out with the scoring – was wearing a black rubber dress that left very little to the imagination, and even less doubt about what she did for her day job.

'And next up to all of you lot,' Frankie said, 'old friends . . .' He nodded at Kind Regards and Slim, over at the bar. '. . . and new.' He held his glass out to Andy Topper, who was sat between a couple of managers from one of the London bookie chains in the front row opposite. 'And, of course, most important of all, all the industry people here who've kindly given up some of their precious time to check out what we're planning on doing here. Me and Andy are looking forward to talking to you all more as the evening goes on.'

More applause, a couple of cheers and catcalls and a nod from Andy. He didn't look flustered at all. After all, he lived and breathed this shit. He'd offered to do the speech, but Frankie had said no. No matter how queasy this made him, he knew he needed to do it. 'You've got to own it. Make it yours' was how Kind Regards had put it a few weeks back. 'Or one day someone else will take it away.' And he was right. No point in being a bit part in his own sodding opera, was there? Nah, he needed to be Pavarotti tonight.

'And, last of all, a toast,' Frankie said. 'To the tournament we're going to be launching properly next year – the Soho Open. We're determined to make it a permanent fixture on the snooker calendar, by bringing the best players and the best fans in the world together, right here, to the best city in the world.'

A big roar of approval met his speech and Frankie raised his glass of sparkling water up high and waited as silence descended.

'So, that's it from me,' he said, 'but do hang around, the night is yet young and the Ambassador has always been a home from home' – he grinned across at Ash and Sea Breeze as he said it, and was pleased to see even a little smile coming back his way from them both – 'so please do make it just that, your home, for tonight.'

Xandra and Maxine whooped good and loud, setting off another round of applause. Then everyone started getting up, heading for familiar faces or just the bar. Frankie suddenly felt the weight of it falling from him.

Had he said everything he needed to? His heart was still thumping in his ears. Part of him just wanted to sink right back down into his seat. Or duck upstairs to the flat and lock the bloody door.

But this was part of it too, being front of house. Being the man.

'Good work,' Andy said, coming over and giving him a firm slap on the back, 'that hit just the right note.'

Grinning a broad, pearly smile, he smoothed down his barbered, slicked-back blonde Aussie surfer hair. Flawless, he was. Like some fresh from the packet Ken doll. And only a few years older than Frankie too.

He was wearing a smart, fitted suit, so new it practically still had the labels on it. But that was The Topster all over. Sharp as you like and professional with it. Every single person he'd introduced Frankie to his evening, Andy had remembered not just their names, but their partners' and kids' names too to make them all feel like they weren't just here for business, but because they were friends.

'It wouldn't be happening without you, mate,' Frankie said, and it was true.

Another Mighty White smile. 'Good on you for saying it. But now let's keep working this room. Still plenty of people left for you to meet.'

*

It wasn't until half an hour, and a couple of dozen expertly steered conversations, later that Frankie had time to pause for breath. Not that he was complaining. The stacks of promotional leaflets Xandra had left around the room were already nicely low. As well as working the bar with Slim, she and Maxine been doing a great job of making sure that everyone walking out of here had one stuffed in their pocket.

Even more importantly, everyone seemed to have taken the end of his speech at face value and was having a whale of a time. Christ knew what the bar bill was going to be – he'd deal with that in the morning. But for now he just wanted a quick word with someone else who'd made all this possible – and to apologize to him an' all.

He found Kind Regards down the far end of the bar, nursing a Cuba Libre and halfway through a smoke. He was as dapper and neatly suited as ever. Frankie often wondered if he even wore a cravat to the beach.

'I just wanted to thank you,' he said.

'For what?' He scratched warily at his greying temple. They'd not spoken since Frankie had slammed the phone down on him.

'The advice you gave me a couple of weeks back.'

'Which bit?'

Frankie smiled. Because when wasn't Kind Regards giving him advice? 'About owning it, standing up and being counted. About being seen here tonight.'

'You did well.'

'Thanks and I just wanted to say sorry as well,' he said. 'For shouting at you. About Dad.'

'It's all right. I probably deserved it.' But, even so, he looked relieved.

'No, you've only ever tried to look out for me. I know that. But all that stuff with Snaresby, with Dad, it's just . . . I don't know, just something that's going to always make me see red, until I've sorted it out . . .'

'And you still think you might be able to?'

'I don't know. We'll see.'

Snaresby. Frankie cringed at the thought of him about with his poor wife tonight. He was still reeling from his run-in with him this morning. All that shit he'd said. And what he'd told Frankie too, about there only being one other copper left alive who might be able to tell him the truth about the Old Man's conviction.

'How's Jack?' Kind Regards asked. Frankie had left a message for him earlier, telling him what had happened. 'I'm going to pop by and see him tomorrow.'

'All right. No permanent damage as they say. Better than all right, actually.' Frankie smiled, couldn't help himself. 'He's being waited on hand and foot.'

'By who?'

'His friendly neighbourhood waitress, actually. This girl called Tiffany. Seems she took a bit of a shine to him after watching him nearly get run over Tuesday and then seeing me drop him off back home this evening in a sling. Told him she'd bring him round a tray of food, after she'd finished her shift.'

Funny, wasn't it, how things worked out? Frankie didn't think that Jack had clocked it yet, just quite how sweet this

Tiffany was on him. Must be all the fresh stitches and dried blood. Maybe stopped him looking so cute.

Kind Regards smiled too. 'He could do with someone decent in his life.' His expression hardened. 'You told Bernie yet?'

Bernie . . . the Old Man. 'No,' Frankie said.

Kind Regards looked shocked, the kind of shocked that meant that if Frankie didn't tell him soon, then he'd have to instead.

'There's someone else I've got to speak to first,' Frankie said. 'Someone who might sort things out.' Frankie spotted him, Tommy Riley, holding court down the other end of the bar with his entourage. Excellent, Tommy was top of his 'To Do' list tonight.

'If you say . . .' Kind Regards didn't look convinced, small surprise there. The Old Man hated being kept out of the loop where his kids were concerned.

'A quick question, though, while I've got you to myself.'

'What?'

'Those files you gave me . . . is it possible that anyone else apart from you could have found out we're looking at them again?'

'I can't see how. Other than the copies of the trial transcripts I requested from the court itself, there'll be a record there of them being sent out to me . . .'

Meaning if someone was keeping an eye on things there, then they'd know there was new interest in the case. *Anything you want at the touch of a button*. Wasn't that what Snaresby had said? No wonder he'd not shown so much as a flicker of surprise when Frankie had mentioned his two ex-colleagues' names.

Frankie noticed one of Riley's minders was staring daggers at him. A tall, slim, athletic-looking geezer. Dressed in a powder-blue suit. With cropped blonde hair and a nose so hooked you could hang him up on it. Tanned like he'd been left under the grill too long. Did Frankie know him? Nah. Someone with that kind of chippy attitude, he'd have remembered.

'Get yourself another drink,' he told Kind Regards, 'and I'll see you back here in a mo.'

13

Proper villains like Tommy Riley didn't need VIP areas as anyone important enough ended up next to them anyway. Everyone else, well, they could just sod off.

Four of Tommy's boys were standing round him now, muscle harder than any wall. Tam Jackson was the gateway and he didn't waste any time letting Frankie know. He stepped right into his path as he tried to walk past.

'Do you fucking mind, son? This might be your club, but if you want to get to Tommy, you've still got to go through me.'

Son. The cheeky sod. What, like Frankie was just some stupid kid? Frankie squared up to him, the pair were the same height, same build. So how little did he think he was now?

'All right, easy, Rover,' Tommy Riley called out, waving Tam aside and beckoning Frankie through.

Rover. Frankie liked that. He failed to keep the smile off his face, something that wasn't lost on Tam.

'Find something funny, do you?' he asked, moving aside slower than a fucking glacier.

Tommy Riley had the arms and torso of a professional

wrestler. In fact, he'd always been like that, according to Frankie's dad, even back when they'd been kids. His glistening brown eyes, almost as dark as his thick, slicked-back hair, were fixed steadfastly on Frankie. The guy had the assured confidence that he was still the top dog round here. He shook Frankie's hand firmly with a fist the size of a house brick. The geezer had bite.

'Frankie James, meet Ritz Aziz,' he said, nodding at the man he was with, a smart-looking business type in a posh-as-fuck white suit. 'A personal friend of mine.'

'Good to meet you, Mr Aziz,' Frankie said, shaking his hand. 'And thanks for coming along.' He already knew the name. An 'investor', of whatever multiple of sins that might entail.

'Nice place you've got here,' said Aziz, his accent broad Leeds. 'And I like the idea. How ambitious you are for this tournament. How you see it going London-wide within a couple of years. And TV rights after that. Tommy's been telling me all about it.'

Has he now? Other than Frankie clearing the idea of him running it here with Listerman last year, he'd not gone into any details at all. Meaning Tommy had been asking around and someone had been talking. Frankie felt a knot of dread inside him. Tommy sniffing a profit would certainly explain why he was here. But having Tommy involved was the last thing Frankie wanted. This was his baby. His chance to make it big. To get away from people like Tommy for good.

'Here's my card,' Aziz said. 'You give me a call if you need any advice. I've organized a few things like this up in my neck of the woods.' He gave him a wink. 'I can tell you all the pitfalls to avoid.'

'Er, thanks,' said Frankie. 'I'll do that.'

Aziz turned to Tommy. 'Right, well, I'd best be going,' he said, rubbing his hands together. 'Pleasure calls.'

Tommy smiled. 'Have a nice dinner. Oh, and my associate here . . .' He nodded towards the tanned guy who'd been eyeballing Frankie and was at it again. '. . . he'll wait for you while you eat at Quo Vadis and then bring you round to St James's.'

His brothel, he meant, not that he'd have put it quite like that. A 'Gentlemen's Club' was the phrase he preferred. The tanned guy nodded and waded firmly out into the crowd, cutting a path for Aziz to follow, leaving Frankie alone with Riley at the centre of the space his minders had carved out for him at the bar.

'Yes, this is turning into a very interesting evening indeed,' Riley said, lighting himself a cigar. 'A glimpse of a bold and exciting new future, eh?'

He held up his empty whisky tumbler to Slim. Crystal. Monogrammed. Riley must have had one of his goons bring it here for him. Frankie wondered what else they might have about their person. Personalized hand grenades? Or samurai swords? Embossed with a family crest – a skull and crossbones, no doubt.

'I remember them days,' Riley said, nodding at the photo montage behind the bar as Slim poured him a quadruple Dalwhinnie. 'I know all them faces. Every single one. Fuck me, we were all so bloody close back then.' His expression seemed to darken. 'And look at all you kids. You've all changed so much over the years.' His eyes narrowed. 'I forgot you all knew each other too.'

Which kids? Which photo did he mean? One in particular? Frankie couldn't tell. The holiday-snaps montage had plenty of group shots. Half of them faces he couldn't even remember.

'You never came out there with us, did you?'

'No, kid. Always too busy. But enough of the past, eh? Here's to the future.' Knocking his drink back, he smiled. 'So, you're quite the speech maker, these days, I see.' Was he taking the piss? Frankie couldn't tell. 'Not like your dad. He was always far more of a back-room boy, eh? Much like myself.'

If Frankie was meant to say something, he didn't know what. The Old Man and Riley's friendship – if that was even the right word – was a weird one these days and something the Old Man never spoke about. All Frankie knew was that while Riley might have offered him the hand of protection inside, he didn't think he'd visited him once.

'You must be pleased with how tonight's going.'

'Yeah, thanks. It's been a good turnout,' Frankie said.

'And, more important, the right sort of people.'

He was looking at Pat O'Hanagan when he said it. The owner of a Northern Ireland bookie chain, who Andy had introduced Frankie to earlier. Managed a couple of top-flight players as well and, judging by the two lumps in suits who were walking him to the door now after Aziz, was involved in a lot heavier shit than that too. Hardly someone Frankie fancied ending up in business with and he'd already crumpled his card up in his fist.

'You should pop along after as well,' Tommy said. 'With them lot. Down to St James's. Or do you still just not? With them?'

Tommy had a good memory. *I just don't. With them.* That was the exact same phrase Frankie had used when he'd turned down Riley's offer of some free entertainment round there.

'I hear you're off the booze as well,' he said.

'Yeah, that's right.'

'A good thing in a manager too.' There he was again – letting Frankie know exactly whose place this really was. 'And something your brother could have done with less of last night. How is the little rascal, by the way?'

So Tommy had already heard what had happened. No surprise there. 'He'll be fine.'

'Good. Who do you think done it?'

'I don't know.'

Riley cocked his head to one side. 'Really? No ideas? A smart lad like you?'

'He didn't see. No one did.' And no way was Frankie stirring things up on his own hunches. Not without any proof.

'The way I hear it, that young Dougie Hamilton . . . he's becoming quite the chip off the old block, and stepping up a rung or two, and making a right nuisance of himself all over the place.'

Was he saying that Dougie Hamilton was behind last night's attack on Jack? That he knew this for sure?

'Hardly surprising,' he went on. 'What with everything that's happened to his poor old dad.'

Again, meaning what? That Terence Hamilton was losing control of his own firm to his son because of what had happened last year? Or that word had finally got out about the cancer Terence had told Frankie was slowly eating him up?

Frankie waited for Riley to say more. But he just stared passively into Frankie's eyes. No point in asking him either. Information was power to this man. He'd not give a syllable of it away for free.

Time to cut to the chase, then. And see if Riley could really help him out.

'There's something I need to ask you,' Frankie said.

'Let me guess. A favour?' Riley smiled thinly. 'If I had a quid for every time someone asked me for one of them . . . and, come to think of it, don't you owe me one already? And a pretty bloody big one at that?'

He meant for the lead he'd given Frankie last summer, the one that led to him tracking down Susan Tilley's real killer.

'Yeah,' said Frankie.

'And yet here you are asking for another. Well, I'll tell you what,' he said, chiming his gold signet ring against the rim of his glass, 'seeing as I'm in such a mellow mood, I'll even hear you out.'

'I want him off the street.'

'Who? Dougie Hamilton?' Riley looked surprised. He made a gun out of his fingers and thumb and pulled the trigger. 'Bang fucking bang?'

'No, Jack. Off the street and out of the firing line.'

'Ah, I see. And how do you think I should go about

achieving that? By firing *him*, perhaps?' Another pull of that imaginary trigger. Riley smiled, clearly enjoying this particular little verbal link. 'Only, you see, he's quite a useful asset, your brother. Maybe not so useful as someone like Tam here . . .' He hooked his thumb over his shoulder to where Tam was gawping at Dickie Bird's date's cleavage. 'But everyone's got to start somewhere. And if he listens hard and learns to do what's he's told, who knows where he might end up in a few years' time.'

In an early grave was the only bloody answer to that. The same as Danny Kale and Christ knew how many other kids Jack's age who'd provided cannon fodder for Riley over the years.

'Actually, I'm not here to ask you to fire him at all,' Frankie said. Another look of surprise from Riley. But careful now. For Frankie's plan to keep Jack safe to work, he needed to pitch it right. 'There's no point, he's way too loyal. To you.'

Riley smiled, approvingly. Loyalty, he valued it above all else.

'Then what do you want?' he said.

'For you to move him into something legit.'

That was the word Jack had used. *Legit.* A legit job. The kind his lack of qualifications and normal work experience stopped him getting. Something out of danger and off the street. Because as well as having his grubby fat fingers in plenty of well dodgy pies, Riley owned plenty of kosher businesses too – like the Ambassador Club itself.

'Something where what you're talking about, his potential, can shine through? Especially if he sees it as something,

105

I don't know . . . positive? You know, like a promotion, I suppose.' Nothing to do with his big brother interfering, in other words.

Riley said nothing, just stared at Frankie for a second, two. 'And what if it doesn't . . . *shine through*? What if he screws up?'

'Then . . . you know where I live, don't you?'

'Meaning what? You're offering yourself up as some kind of collateral?'

'Just offering to sort him out if he strays. And keep an eye on him. Make sure he keeps his priorities right.' Until I can figure out a way of getting him out from under you altogether.

Another long, hard look from Riley. Letting him know this was for real, that he'd be held accountable. Then, finally, a nod.

'You've been hanging out with your dad's cousin too often,' he said.

'What do you mean?' Frankie glanced over at Kind Regards, still there at the end of the bar. Was Riley talking about the Old Man's case files? Had someone told him Frankie was looking back into them? But who? Maybe Snaresby? Or Lomax, or Dolf?

But no, he wasn't talking about the files at all.

'You make a good case,' he said. 'A tight one. Legal, like. And, yeah, I can see where you're coming from. And maybe our Jack would be better suited to a different kind of role.'

Our Jack. Frankie's skin prickled. But now wasn't the time to go picking issue with that.

'Your timing's not bad either,' Riley went on. 'In fact, I've just come into something that might tick the box perfectly. Quite literally, in fact.' He grinned, nudging Tam and the fat lump standing next to him. 'Here, you two, stop drooling over that bird's tits, and pay attention.'

The two of them quickly turned round.

'I was just telling Frankie here that we've just come into a business that might tick exactly the right *box*, regarding where his little brother might work. *Box*. Geddit?' He held up his fists and did a little shuffle with his feet.

'Er, no, Unc,' said the fat lad, who had a lazy left eye, and jeans and a fawn leather jacket two sizes too tight.

Tommy rolled his eyes at Frankie. 'My nephew, Darren,' he said, lowering his voice. 'Got dropped on his head when he was five.'

'Oh, yeah, right, boss. I get it,' said Tam, grinning. 'You mean Rope-a-Dope.'

'Exactly.'

'The boxing club?' said Frankie. 'Up Hanway Street?'

Riley nodded. 'The very same.'

'First place I ever donned a pair of gloves,' Frankie said. 'Dad took me and Jack down after I got done over as a kid. Said we needed to toughen up. Back when Sponge Eddy was running it.'

'Yeah, running it into the fucking ground, more like,' said Riley. 'The same as his dumb kid Eddy Junior's been doing ever since he took over. Instead of making a proper go of things like you've been doing here.' He nodded at the crowd. 'More like making a proper stop of it. And with me one of his fucking investors too.'

'And what?' Frankie said. 'You're saying Jack could go help this Eddy Junior out?'

'No, fuck that. EJ's history. Took early retirement, didn't he, Tam?'

'Very early. About five a.m.'

'Very funny,' Riley said. 'Almost as funny as mine. But, seriously, Frankie. He had to go. He was losing me money hand over fist.'

'Ended up falling out of the first-floor window,' Tam said, gazing evenly at Frankie. 'Very careless. Perhaps he was drunk or sleep walking. Poor git split his head open like a melon on the pavement, but luckily he'd signed the lease back over to the boss just before he did.'

The way he said it suggested he was thinking how easy it would be for something similar to happen to Frankie one day.

'Enough of the gory details, Tam,' said Tommy. 'The good news is that I've got real plans for it now. You know, to do it up. Expand its customer base and all that. And what I'm now thinking is that maybe there's a place for young Jack in all this.'

'Jack?' said Tam in disbelief.

'Yes, fucking Jack,' snapped Riley. 'For all we know he's got a brain every bit as useful as Frankie's here, hidden under that ridiculous barnet. Maybe it just needs channelling. You know, training up?'

'Yeah,' Frankie said, 'maybe that's it.' A foot in the door? A fresh start? He couldn't help thinking this might even work.

'Good. Then that's settled,' said Riley. 'Fix up a meeting,

Tam. Get Frankie and Jack round to take a dekko, and let's see if we can work something out.'

'Thanks,' Frankie said.

'Oh, don't thank me,' Riley said, fixing him with that look again. 'This is a favour. And we all know how those work, don't we? How one day they get called in?'

'Yeah,' Frankie said.

'Good.' Tommy Riley raised his glass to the montage on the wall. 'Happy days, eh?' he said, before turning back to Tam. 'Now bring us that bird with the big tits over here so I can chat her up. I've got a good mind to take her out for a ride in the limo, so I can fuck her hard up the arse.'

14

The weekend passed by in a blur, but not the kind Frankie was more used to last year – not the tequila kind. More the seriously hard bloody work and totally knackering kind.

Friday night's launch party went on until three, when he finally managed to pour the last of his guests – a couple of battered .bookies, who'd insisted on doing a bottle of JD and playing incoherently badly until neither of them could even hold a cue – into a cab. He managed to get himself about five hours' fitful shut-eye after that, before his alarm went off.

Of course, it would have been nice to take the weekend off completely. He'd earned it. Taffy was round to pick up the competition table at nine and a good thing too. Frankie wanted it well away by the time the punters started turning up for the England v Scotland footie match that afternoon.

While Frankie was hauling round the seating banks to face the screens across the otherwise empty club with Xandra and Spartak, they were stopped in their tracks by the radio. Half the city of Manchester had been evacuated after a telephoned IRA warning. Christ. When the bomb blast had gone off, hundreds of people had still got injured all the same. They looked at one another, shocked and saddened. But depressing as it was, life went on. A steady flow of customers started turning up around noon and were pissed by two and screaming at the screens by kick-off at three. Spartak watched the door like a hawk, wary of any interlopers from the Swiss game turning up. But the only excitement on show this afternoon was watching England beat Scotland two nil. Frankie's bet was still looking good then.

He fell asleep that night staring at the postcard from Mallorca on his bedside table and woke with the same questions rattling round his head. What if this card really was from her? What if his mum was alive and really was living in Mallorca? What if his dad was wrong and there really was a good reason why she'd not been in touch until now?

But what could he do about it? That was the even bigger question he just couldn't shake. There was no address or phone number. Just a picture of some street in a foreign city. It would be like looking for a needle in a haystack.

He drove round to Jack's Sunday afternoon and checked in on him. The lad was on the up, and he was healing fast. Jack even had a bit of a spring in his step, which Frankie reckoned had a lot to do with Tiffany having slept over the night before. Frankie told him about his chat with the Old Man, about how he couldn't see how that card was from her. Jack just nodded, changed the subject. Because that was it for him, wasn't it? Yet another reason not to believe. Frankie wanted to tell him about what Riley had said too, but didn't. For one thing, it still might not happen. For another, if Jack knew he was behind it, he'd not be half so keen.

Monday came and Frankie went over to meet Andy in his office in Haymarket House. Seemed like the launch had gone better than well, they'd knocked it out the park. Andy was well chuffed and already had a whole bunch of meetings chalked in. The Soho Open really looked like it was going to happen at last. Frankie's life, it seemed, was finally looking up.

Then on Tuesday, he got the call.

*

'So what's this all about then?' Jack asked as they wandered down Oxford Street to the Rope-a-Dope club. The stitches on his head were healing nicely. He'd lucked out, tell the truth, with the worst of the cut being on his scalp. All blending in nicely now with that topknot. Like Frankenstein modelling for Gap.

'I dunno,' Frankie lied. 'I just got this message from Tommy, saying he wanted to see us both.'

'Well I hope we're not in trouble.'

'Now why would you say that?'

'No reason. Just, you know, it feels like getting dragged up in front of the headmaster, that's all.'

Frankie had just been for a run, decked out in tracksuit and trainers. He held back a smile, cautiously not wanting to look too keen on whatever it was Riley had in mind regarding the gym – not until he'd at least heard the actual terms. 'You remember that time we broke into school over the weekend and released all them helium balloons up into the school gym on the night before prize-giving?'

Jack laughed, sending his cigarette bouncing, sparking off the side of a bus. 'Yeah, Cock-Eyed Keats went bat shit when he couldn't get them down.'

Cock-Eyed Keats. Their old headmaster. The balloons had been scrawled all over in black marker with words like 'TITS', 'ARSE' and 'TWAT'. Nothing too blue – nothing that might actually have got them expelled if they'd been caught. More certificate fifteen than eighteen. But enough to make every kid gathered there in assembly practically piss their pants.

'I thought he was going to have a bleeding heart attack,' Frankie said, as they turned onto Hanway Street and on past Bradley's Spanish Bar.

'A myo-cardial-in-*farc*tion,' they chimed in unison, impersonating their old headmaster, who'd taught them both biology.

'And what, may I ask, might you two be laughing at?' a deep voice boomed out.

Tam Jackson was leaning up against the wall, looking big enough and hard enough to be propping the whole bloody building up. Stood next to him was another bloke, an Adidas gym bag gripped in his tanned fist. Ten years younger than Tam. Wearing the same powder-blue suit Frankie had seen him in at the launch party in the club.

'Tam . . .' said Jack warily.

'Jack . . .' Tam nodded back.

'All right,' said Frankie. 'Who's your mate?'

'Jesús.'

113

'Hayzuz?'

'Yeah. As in Jesus.' Even Tam's normally impenetrable expression gave a little twitch.

Jesus? Frankie tried not to smile. Tried, but didn't succeed.

'Amusing something, is it? Me?' Jesús said, taking a solid step towards Frankie, all laced with intent. Something off about his accent. Spanish? Frankie couldn't be sure.

'No, mate. Nothing funny. Something you is not.'

Jesús watched him, unblinking, not sure if he was taking the piss. Probably a good thing too. Looked like he could handle himself and Frankie was hoping for a quiet start to the week. But then the moment passed. And Jesús took a packet of Gummi Bears, of all things, from his pocket and tipped a bunch into his mouth. Didn't even offer Frankie one at all.

He glanced up at the building. A regular redbrick like the rest of the street. A chipped wooden inn sign hung from a couple of rusty chains, with what looked like two lumps of mud painted on it, probably meant to be gloves. Cracked, blacked-out windows studded the building left and right, one of them smashed in altogether. The one through which EJ had taken his dive? Frankie checked the pavement below, half expecting to see a red splodge, but thankfully there was nothing but the usual London mosaic of dried gob and gum.

Tam Jackson flicked his cigarette into the gutter and nodded them both inside, a nasty flash of darkness in his eyes, like he knew something they didn't. Stepping through the open door into the gloomy interior, Frankie wondered

114

if Tam's face was the last thing EJ had seen before he'd smashed his brains out on the kerb.

'Christ, I remember it now,' Jack said, walking ahead.

Frankie screwed up his nose. Because, Christ, he remembered it too. The guff of Ralgex and stench of sweat and damp and mould and toilets too – the kind that hadn't been flushed. Tommy hadn't been kidding, this place really had seen better days.

A Capital Radio jingle blared out through the speakers way up in the high-ceilinged rafters. Some tune kicked in. Something about a firestarter. No kidding. This place could probably do with the purge.

'I'd forgotten what a shithole this was,' Jack hissed into Frankie's ear.

Frankie ignored him, looking round at the big, echoing space, full of grunts and orders and the clanking of weights. A double-height ceiling like the Ambassador, with a glass-fronted office up there on the mezzanine and a viewing balcony running round looking down onto the two rings below.

One of them was empty and two lads were busy sparring in the other. In spite of the stink in here, it still got the old blood pumping, and Frankie made a beeline for the ring, passing eight or nine other fellahs working out with jump ropes and barbells and drumming on speed bags.

The trainer egging the two fighters on had to be seventy if he was a day. GoGo JoJo. The same bloke who'd first shoved Frankie in a ring. Still tough as teak, by the looks of him, too. The muscles on his bare arms stood out like knotted ropes. As well as being a boxer himself, he'd been a top blood man back in the day and had worked for Muhammad Ali in '63. Frankie would bet his bottom dollar he still had the faded old snap of the two them together on him in his wallet now.

'All right, kiddo,' he said, clocking Frankie and grinning across. 'Jack,' he said, his smile a little less sincere.

Kiddo. He'd taught Frankie here between the age of thirteen and sixteen, before he'd moved on to kickboxing, and the Old Man twenty years before that.

'Good to see you, JoJo.' Frankie shook him warmly by the hand, trying not to wince, his knuckles nearly popping under the old man's grip. 'How's things?'

JoJo rolled his bloodshot eyes round the room. 'Been better. You heard about EJ?'

'Fell out the window.'

'Yeah. Fell. Right.' JoJo glared across at Tam Jackson and looked for a second like he was going to say something, then turned back to Frankie and said, 'So it's true then? What I've been hearing? About who's going to be running this place?' He stared pointedly at Jack, who was gazing absent-mindedly up at a noticeboard.

'Yeah.'

'A little late in the day, ain't it, for him to develop a love for the noble art?' He was referring to the fact that Jack had only managed three weeks here before quitting, complaining the training was too hard.

'Maybe. But you know what? Do us a favour, JoJo, and give him a chance at least to prove you wrong.'

'All right,' said JoJo, with a little click of his tongue. 'Seeing as it's you, I just might.'

116

'How about you two carry on with your little reunion later?' interrupted Tam. 'Let's not keep Mr Listerman waiting any longer than we have to, eh?'

JoJo ignored Tam, turning his attention back to the ring. 'Guard up, for fuck's sake, Jonny,' he snapped. 'How many times do I have to fucking well say . . .'

So Listerman the lawyer was here. Seemed like Riley really did mean business then. Frankie and Jack followed Tam further back into the building, past the multigyms and changing rooms. A couple of big lads in suits emerged from another door off to the left and marched past, both of them carrying black briefcases like they were guns. Slick-backed, suited and booted. Clearly not here to work out at all. Frankie thought he recognized one of them from round the club on Friday night. One of Riley's boys.

'What's in there then?' he asked Tam, nodding at the door.

'Nothing.'

'Well, there must be something, because two of your mates just came out.'

'Nothing you need to concern yourself with,' Tam said. 'Got a separate entrance. Meaning it's a separate business, OK?'

None of his business, then. Fine. Frankie got the message. Not sure he liked it, though. Not sure at all.

He followed Jack and Tam over to the right and up a steep flight of stairs. A heavy fireproof door at the top. An even heavier bloke standing sentry beside it. He knocked four times, then opened up the door and let them in.

The glass-fronted office Frankie had clocked from below,

the one with the bird's-eye view of the gym. Listerman was sat behind a wide, schoolteacher-type desk, punching numbers into a calculator, whilst scribbling down notes, his specs glinting in the harsh, fluorescent light. An air conditioner hummed. The old brass ship's clock on the wall ticked.

'I'll be with you in just a sec. Grab yourselves a pew, boys,' Listerman said, unsmiling, and without looking up.

15

Easier said than done. The only other chair in the room was a broken swivel seat with a torn orange cushion. Jack took it, flashing Frankie a cocky grin like he'd just beaten him in a game of musical chairs.

Frankie walked over to the giant pane of reinforced glass and gazed down into the recesses of the gym. If anything, it looked even worse from up here. The lighting flickered every now and then like it was about to short. Water pooled outside the changing room from some kind of leak, even the sprung floor of the ring on the left looked like it had a crack running down its right side.

'Nut, anyone?' Listerman said, putting down his pen and taking out a packet of dry-roasted peanuts from his jacket pocket.

'No, thanks,' said Frankie.

Jack lit a cigarette and Tam shook his head.

'Fine. Suit yourselves.' Listerman flipped a nut up into the air and caught it in his mouth. 'So,' he said, crunching down. 'What do we all think?'

Jack blew smoke out. 'About what?'

'This. The gym.'

'Well, it's a total shitho—' Jack started to say.

'What he means to say is it's got potential,' Frankie said, standing by his brother's side.

Jack laughed. 'You need to get down Boots opticians, bruv.'

'No, I mean it,' Frankie said. 'It just needs a bit of work.'

'A bit?'

'All right. A lot. But it's not much different to the Ambassador like that. It just needs some tarting up.'

'Exactly our thinking,' Listerman said with a thin smile. *Our* making it clear he meant Riley's firm. 'And a good manager, of course.'

'Of course,' said Frankie.

'Someone with a bit of vision who can see the future – fitness.'

Jack took another drag of his fag. 'Fitness?'

'Exactly, Jack,' said Listerman, reaching for another peanut. 'Well spotted. A booming market, just like you say. For lots of young people with plenty of money to splash. There's even this thing called boxercising. You heard of that? All the rage in Fulham, apparently.'

'I guess,' said Jack.

'And guess right. And just look around. You've got the boxing gym downstairs, but there's a whole floor up above here too that's not being used at all. You can run all kinds of classes in it.'

'Classes?'

'Yeah. Aerobics. Yoga. Need I go on?'

'No,' Jack said, swivelling round on his chair now and looking a little bored.

'Great. So you'll do it?' Listerman's eyes fixed on Jack, as he swung back round to face him.

'Me?' Jack looked aghast. Christ, he really hadn't seen this coming at all.

'Well, who else am I talking to? I don't mean Frankie here, do I? He's got his hands full already with the Ambassador and his tournament.'

'But I don't know shit about this,' Jack said, 'about running somewhere.'

'So you'll learn, like a duck to water. After all, you practically grew up in a club.'

'And I'll be on hand to advise you,' Frankie said. 'You know, help out any way I can until you find your feet.'

'But what about what I already do for Tommy?'

'Oh, don't you worry about him. This is *his* idea. And don't you go worrying about your money, either. This is a bump up the ladder, see? A promotion, if you like.' Listerman sat back in his chair, nice and easy, reminding Frankie of the Old Man, the way he'd used to love going sea fishing on holiday, getting himself strapped into one of them chairs on a charter boat, knowing it was only a matter of time before he'd get himself a bite. 'And this here,' he said, tapping the desk, 'would be *your* desk.'

Jack whistled.

He got up and looked round the room, like he was getting a proper feel of the place for the first time. Frankie smiled. There was a definite sparkle in Jack's eyes. One that had nothing to do with narcotics. Or bloody aerobics classes either. It was the spark of genuine excitement. Possibility. *Power*.

'Well, you know, now that you come to mention it,' Jack said, 'maybe I do have a few ideas about how to improve things. Like, for example, we could –'

'Yeah, yeah,' Listerman said, 'and we can go into all those details later. But, for now, can I just take it that your answer is yes?'

'Yeah.' Jack smiled again. Even puffed his little chest out a bit. 'Deffo. For sure.'

He walked over to the desk and stretched out his hand. Listerman rose and shook it. Deal done. Frankie's smile hardened a little. More like the easy bit done. Now he just had to keep Jack on the straight and narrow and make sure he didn't screw this opportunity up. Or get screwed.

'Well, I must say, Tommy will be delighted,' Listerman said, flicking another dry-roasted peanut into his mouth. 'I tell you what, Jack, why don't you head back downstairs with Tam here and get a feel for the place. I need a quick word with your brother here about some other business. Just some paperwork. Boring stuff. The kind of thing he's got to deal with over at the Ambassador, but you won't need to worry about here, because I'll be taking care of all of that.'

Frankie felt a tingle of alarm from the way Listerman said it, but Jack just smiled. Trusting, too trusting perhaps.

'I'll wait for you downstairs then, Frankie?'

'Su—' *Sure*, Frankie had been about to say, but didn't get the chance.

'No need for that. Tam and Jesús there will give you a lift home. I'm going to need to borrow your brother for a bit longer.' He looked at Frankie pointedly. 'Take him for a little ride.'

Frankie shifted uncomfortably, spotting the almost imperceptible crinkle at the corner of Listerman's mouth that was probably the nearest he ever got to an actual smile.

'And where would that be to?'

'All in good time, Frankie. All in good time.' He nodded curtly at Jack. A dismissal.

Tam walked Jack out and the door swung shut behind them with a heavy click.

Frankie stared down into the gym below. The Spaniard – Jesús – had got changed and was now in the ring, helmeted and gloved up and ready to fight. Then a big lad, twice his size, lumbered out from the opposite corner, fists the size of whole hams.

Listerman's half-reflection loomed up alongside Frankie's in the glass divide. 'I'm betting you're thinking it's *adiós muchachos* for our dirty dago friend down there?' he said.

'Quite the opposite, actually,' said Frankie. Something about that Jesús. The way he was just standing there watching. Like he could walk on water if he chose.

The big lad didn't even see the first punch coming. Or the second, or the third. The fourth one put him on his back.

'But back down to business, eh?' Listerman said, steering Frankie back over to the chair where Jack had been sitting.

'No, you're all right, thanks. I'll stand.'

Listerman walked back behind his desk. 'So how do you feel about it then? About' – he clicked his fingers – '*Alakazam* . . . us having turned your brother from blue collar to white?'

123

'Yeah, good,' Frankie said, 'so long as this is for real. A proper bump up, right? Because what you said just now about you taking care of the business side of things . . . you are still going to give him a chance to learn the ropes?'

'Of course. Of course. Because that's the arrangement, right?'

'Right . . .'

'The very essence of the favour.'

'Sure.'

'The one Tommy wants to call in right now.'

'Right now?' Frankie wasn't sure he'd just heard right.

'Here,' Listerman said, sliding a stapled A4 document across his desk. 'Allow me to explain.'

'What is it?'

'A contract,' Listerman said.

'For what?'

'The cost of all this – your brother's bump.'

Frankie had known it couldn't be as easy as just asking Tommy Riley and getting exactly what he wanted.

'How much?'

'Twenty.'

'*Grand?*' Frankie couldn't hide his surprise – and horror. Where the hell was he meant to find that kind of money? Everything he'd been working for . . . this was going to wipe him out.

But Listerman smiled, a proper one this time – all teeth. 'No, Frankie. You've got it all wrong. We're not talking money. We mean per cent.'

'Of what?'

'Well, what do you bloody think? Your tournament, of course. Or *our* tournament now. Because Tommy likes it, *really* likes what you've got planned. We both do. He wants in.'

16

The 'little ride' Listerman had planned for Frankie turned out to be not nearly as scary as he'd thought. Because words like that, 'little ride' . . . well, Frankie had seen enough gangster flicks over the years to know they sometimes ended in short, sharp swimming trips in concrete boots – and the weather still wasn't quite hot enough for that.

Perfect, on the other hand, for bazzing around London in a nearly new BMW 3 Series convertible – albeit one with some transit damage to the front bumper and a nasty little oil stain on the upholstery in the back.

Listerman had dropped Frankie round at the showroom off the Great West Road before the ink of his signature had even dried on the last page of that contract he'd drawn up. A 'sweetener', that's how he'd described the Beamer. Something to show how seriously Tommy Riley was going to be taking his responsibilities as a silent partner in the Soho Open from here on in.

Listerman told Frankie the car was another favour owed by someone else to Tommy. He'd be able to put it up as an additional players' prize for the tournament, to hopefully help tempt some seriously quality entrants. But for now Frankie had it to himself for a couple of hours.

But as what? That's what he wanted to know. A sop? Something to help him get over the fact he'd just signed 20 per cent of his future away? And maybe something much bigger than that too. What he'd wanted most of all. *Control.*

He caned it down the Westway and onto the M4. As his foot pressed down on the pedal, he tried not to think about Riley, the tournament. As he eased off the gas, his mind wandered to the postcard, and his mum. He didn't want to think about her, or the Old Man for that matter – for once in his miserable bloody life, he just wanted to *be*.

But as the exits flashed by and the petrol gauge dwindled, Snaresby kept on popping up in his mind. And those two cops too, including the one he'd said was dead. Frankie had to find out more about them. But how?

Something else about Snaresby was bothering him too. What he'd said about keeping in with the right people and protecting their interests . . . The way he'd phrased it was just too good a fit with what had just happened with Riley. Had Snaresby somehow already known that Riley had wanted a slice of the action, even then?

Frankie turned the car round at Reading services and headed back into London. Too many questions, not enough answers. For now all he could do was keep driving, keep his eyes on the road, and hope that whatever came next was better than what had come before – with a soundtrack of Pulp's 'Common People' blaring from the state-of-the-art CD player to guide him back home.

He dropped the car off at the dealer, then cabbed it back to the flat, so he could call the Old Man. Finally he could focus on the here and now, what with Jack getting offered his new position down the gym. Of course, the Old Man still had a blue fit, didn't he, when Frankie broke the news to him about Jack having been hospitalized. But the gym news tempered that a little. Even the Old Man had been impressed with that, so you could say one good thing had come out of today.

But at what a cost.

*

'*Déjà vu*, old bean?' Mackenzie Grew said, glancing across and flashing Frankie a clean white smile in the rear-view mirror.

Frankie was in the passenger seat of the classic shiny red Jag. Grew was Tommy Riley's driver, and God only knew what else besides, and the car belonged to his boss. Not that you'd think it from looking at the slickly dressed ex-Mod behind the wheel. He was sporting a flash suit, bespoke snakeskin shoes and a Toni & Guy-priced haircut, straight fringe à la Oasis mode.

Grew was talking about how he'd picked Frankie up last year to go see Tommy, at a meeting where Frankie had ended up asking for Riley's help in clearing Jack's name.

'I guess that all depends,' Frankie said.

'On what?'

'On what Tommy wants.'

Grew pulled the Jag up outside the four-storey, sand-blasted town house in St James's. Every bit as classy-looking as Frankie remembered it. The kind of place you'd expect to find barristers hard at work in their chambers. Not Eastern European hookers dressed up in chambermaid outfits servicing them and City boys who were playing away from their wives.

'Well, then, until the next time,' Frankie said, unbuckling his belt to get out.

'Oh no, pal,' Grew said, checking his watch – a Breitling, expensive as, the very same model that DI Snaresby wore – 'this time I'm coming too.'

The way he said it gave Frankie food for thought.

Riley was waiting for them upstairs, in the same dimly lit bar area Frankie had met him in last year. He wasn't alone. Two twenty-something women in translucent negligées were perched either side of him on a red and black velvet sofa in the centre of the room, both of them looking well stoned. Tam Jackson was here as well, leaning against the glinting chrome bar, a bottle of classic Coke in his hand. He looked up as Frankie and Grew came in and didn't offer a smile as they approached.

A Doberman glared at Frankie from where it was sitting on a giant purple velvet cushion over in the corner. It bared its teeth and started to snarl.

'Shut the fuck up, Whitney,' Riley shouted, sending the dog whimpering into silence. 'Sorry, son,' he told Frankie. 'She's not yet been fed and I think, between you and me, she might be on the blob.'

The *what*? Christ, Frankie couldn't even bring himself to ask. 'No worries,' Frankie said. But, God, he hated big dogs.

'Good game yesterday, wasn't it?' Riley said.

'Yeah,' Frankie agreed.

'England four, Netherlands one. My only regret is I wish I'd had myself a little bet.'

'Me too,' said Frankie. Even though, of course, he had. One that had bought that holiday of his one step closer to reality.

Grew fixed himself a tumbler of Smirnoff Red from the bar. Didn't offer Frankie one. Knew he didn't drink. Lit himself a smoke with his little silver lighter that was shaped exactly like a German Luger. Leant back next to Tam. A swishing at the back of the room. The bead curtain there parted as the big, chubby figure of Riley's nephew, Darren, sauntered through, grinning and buttoning up his flies.

'I heard the Ambassador was chocka for the match,' Riley said.

'Yeah. Rammed,' Frankie said. A record till day, in fact. Not that he was planning on telling Riley that. He'd dipped into Frankie's pockets enough already for one week – one life.

'Pirates,' Riley said.

'Eh?'

'The Dutch. Historically, they were just like us. Made a fortune bashing Catholics and nicking all their gold. We're natural allies, actually. I still like doing business with them today.' He smiled flatly and nodded at the sofa opposite, before giving it the Barbara Woodhouse: 'Sit.'

Frankie did as he was told, conscious of both girls looking him up and down . . . something Riley clocked too and clearly didn't like.

'Go on, you two, scoot off upstairs,' he said, giving them both a shove. 'And get yourselves warmed up, eh? I'll be up in a bit.'

He watched them sashaying side-by-side past the hanging drapes and tapestries on the wall to an arched doorway off to the left.

He turned to Frankie. 'So what did you think of it?'

'The match?'

'No, we're finished talking about that bollocks. I mean the gym.'

'Oh, I think it could be all right.'

'Not *could* be. *Will* be.'

'Yeah.'

'I'm sorry?' Riley cupped his hand round his ear, like he'd just missed something.

'And, yeah, I mean, thanks,' Frankie said.

Another flat smile. 'My pleasure, son. Always happy to help out a friend.'

A *friend*? Employee, more like. That's how Frankie felt more and more every time he and Riley spoke. Particularly now he'd got his name in ink.

'The name,' Riley said.

'The what?'

'Of the club. I mean, it's shit, isn't it?'

'Shit?' Frankie quite liked Rope-a-Dope. The whole Ali connection.

'Worse than shit. Old-fashioned. Old. No good any more, because now there's been a change of hands.'

'OK . . . so . . .' Frankie still couldn't see what this had to do with him. '. . . what were you thinking of –'

'The Bloodthirsty James Boys.' Riley grinned, watching Frankie's face. 'You know, after your grandfather and great uncle. More of a personal connection, see. Between the new management and the club. Because people like that, right? A story. A bit of history.'

It was certainly that. Both brothers had been professional boxers in their early twenties. They might not have made the big time, but they'd certainly made a big impression round here. Word was they'd ended up working as enforcers for the Richardson gang back in the fifties. Though this was something Frankie's dad had never confirmed or denied.

'You know, I met one of them once,' Riley said. 'George. Built like a brick rhino, he was. He was there at your dad's house one day when I called round.'

Yeah, Frankie knew this already. How Riley and the Old Man had been the best of mates.

'I know, Unc?' chipped in Darren. 'What about calling it Bloodthirsty's?'

'Hmm. Well, Darren, it does have a certain *ring* to it, excuse the pun.'

'What pun?' said Darren.

'As in boxing ring, Darren.'

'Ah, right. Good one, Unc.'

Unc. Riley visibly shivered at the word. 'But the kind of clients we're hoping to attract to the private gym upstairs are more likely to be interested in how their bodies look on the outside, than what's going on underneath.'

'Oh, yeah,' Darren said, and went back to picking his nose.

'Which is why,' Riley said, 'I've decided to call it "The James Boys Gym". A bit classier. And it's got a nice flow to it. Memorable, like.'

'That'll be the alliteration,' Frankie said.

'Exactly so. And, of course, it could also apply to the current generation of James brothers too.'

'Sure.'

'You approve then? Because I'm sure your dad would like it too.'

'Er, yeah. But shouldn't you be having this conversation with Jack? I mean, he is –'

'Yeah, yeah, and I will. But, you see, the thing is, there is one other matter I wanted to talk to you about,' Riley said.

'Yeah?' Here we go. What he'd been dreading since he'd got the call from Grew. Because no way had Riley just asked him here to shoot the breeze about the gym. Or even the tournament for that matter. Because on-going business . . . that's what Listerman was for.

'The favour,' Riley said.

And Frankie's heart fell proper hard then. *The* favour. Not *a* favour. The one Frankie still owed him for the information that had led to him proving Jack's innocence. A massive favour.

Whatever Riley was about to ask him to do in return, it was going to be no walk in the park.

17

'There's a girl,' Riley said. 'A beautiful girl. I've known her a long time and she's very fucking dear to my heart.'

Well, he clearly wasn't talking about Mrs Riley. Tommy was hardly the faithful sort. Word was, the only reason he'd been married for the last twenty years to the same woman was because she put up with his snoring, looked the other way where all his flings were concerned, and made a killer spotted dick.

'She's his goddaughter,' Tam said, 'before you go getting the wrong idea.'

Riley's dark eyes narrowed. 'Eighteen years old. A beautiful girl who I held in my own arms the very day she was born. The only child of one of my very best friends.' Riley ran his tongue across his very white teeth. 'Now little Tanya – that's my goddaughter's name – she's been a sweet little thing most of her life. Took after her mum, a model, the nice sort too – she kept her clothes on. Well, most of the time.' He glanced sidelong at Tam. 'Anyhow, little Tanya got packed off to a nice posh boarding school when she was eleven, to move the family up a rung. Cheltenham Ladies' College, it was. Y'know, I went there for a Sports Day once with her mum, in lieu of her dad, him unfortunately not being around. All jolly hockey sticks, tweedy green uniforms and actual cucumber sandwiches on the manicured lawn, would you fucking believe?'

Frankie thought the question was rhetorical and didn't answer. But then he realized Tommy was still staring at him, waiting for a reply.

'Er, yeah,' he said. 'I would.'

'But do you know what else?' Riley said. 'Even though little Tanya wasn't from that kind of background herself, she soon fitted in. Assimilated, I believe that's the word, Tam?'

'Indeed it is, boss.'

'Yeah, she learned herself some pretty manners. Picked up a lovely home counties accent. Made herself some hoity-toity mates. Minded her Ps and Qs. And even bagged a nice bunch of solid GCSEs to boot. Sounds like a dream, don't it? And this year, this month, to cap it all, she's only sitting her ruddy A levels before heading off to university, right?'

'Right,' said Frankie.

'Only she's fucking not,' Riley exploded. 'Because suddenly it doesn't look like that's going to happen. Leastways not unless we do something about it. And quick, eh?'

We. Frankie didn't like the sound of this at all.

'Because, you see, here's the kicker,' Riley said. 'Her mum, God rest her soul, died last year in a helicopter crash. She was on her way to Ladies' Day at Royal Ascot, bless her soul. I was meant to be flying there with her, but got detained. Talk about bloomin' lucky. Well, for me, yeah?'

But the way Riley had said it . . . the look in his eye . . .

did he mean he'd been seeing this woman? Had been having an affair with her? Was that the real reason for his interest in this girl?

'The only way they were able to identify her body was from her hat,' he snapped. 'A beautiful pink thing that I bought her from John Boyd – the geezer who does bloody Lady Di's hats. Now, Frankie, this is the problem, see? Tanya's mum's unfortunate demise caused a "trigger", that's what they call it, isn't it, Tam?'

'Yeah, boss. The thing what pushes people right over the fucking edge.'

'Exactly. And you see our concern is, Frankie, that this is what's happened to little Tanya. Because from that tragic moment onwards, she slowly but surely started going off the rails. There was word of her nipping up to London to see her older brother, who was living with their granny in their Knightsbridge home, and she'd be hanging out with his stoner friends. Turns out little Tanya liked going out clubbing an' all. She got herself a boyfriend, one of her big brother's mates. I see what you're thinking, Frankie, what's so wrong with that? She's an eighteen-year-old girl, old enough to vote, old enough to decide whose cock she sticks in her mouth. But the thing is –'

Frankie just kept his own mouth shut. Where the hell was all this going? And what the hell did any of it have to do with him?

'It didn't stop there, did it?' Riley said. 'The brother of my goddaughter moved out to their place in the south of France, to get himself straight, to detox, and she was left alone at weekends in London. You know what happens

136

when you leave a grieving, eighteen-year-old girl unsupervised? She ended up doing naughty things with increasingly naughty people. That was until last Monday, when she didn't even bother tipping back up to school at all.' Riley closed his eyes and breathed out slowly, then took a deep swig of his drink.

'Which is when the boss got the call,' Grew said. 'From the grandmother.'

'A dear old lady too,' said Tommy. 'And one I'd told after the funeral, any trouble and she was to come straight to me. Now she wasn't just missing a granddaughter, but jewellery too, paintings, furniture, even fucking *hats*.'

'They even smashed the glass case Tommy had paid for it to be displayed in,' Tam said.

'They'd been robbed?' Frankie said.

'Worse,' Riley said through gritted teeth. 'Little Tanya took her mum's hat herself. Or rather, her and her new fellah did. And what a horrible bleedin' fellah he is. Tell him, Tam.'

'His name's Jonny Dukati,' Tam said. 'But everyone calls him Duke. He's a fucking naughty boy. Not only is he a violent son of a bitch who's already done a two-year stretch for GBH up in Manchester, he loves the white stuff, too much bloody coke, thinks he can do anything he bloody well likes when he's on it. Anything at all . . .'

'And it's these ambitions,' Tommy said, 'these dangerous ambitions of his, that, unless he changes his ways and very bleedin' quick, are liable to get him killed . . . and if little Tanya's in the vicinity when this goes down, then I'm afraid we're going to be scraping her off the floor right alongside him too.'

There it was again – *we*. Did Riley mean that him and Tam were planning on doing the scraping? That this Duke's ambitions were ones that crossed with his?

'But do you know what the biggest problem with this fellah is?' Riley asked.

'No,' Frankie said. There was *more*?

'He works for me.' Riley drained his drink and held it out to Darren for a refill. 'Which is something little Tanya's father would not be very happy about were he to find out. And his is a friendship that I do not wish to risk. Particularly as he is a – how shall I put it?'

'Co-investor, boss,' said Tam.

'Yeah, that's it. A co-investor, or sleeping partner if you will, in many of my current schemes.'

Darren's bulk appeared wobbling between Frankie and Riley for a few seconds, as he topped his uncle's glass with Dalwhinnie.

'Now I know what you're probably thinking,' said Riley, as the big lad stepped aside. 'Why don't I just call old Jonny boy off? Tell him to stop dating her, or whatever it is these young folks call it these days? Tell him that if he doesn't I will cut off his cock and ram it up his arse?'

'Er, right . . .' Not exactly how Frankie would have put it, but yeah, that was certainly the gist of what he'd been thinking.

'Because – and now we really hit the nitty-gritty – he's no longer around to ruddy tell.'

'He was meant to have been doing some . . . *business* for the boss out in Amsterdam,' Tam said.

The pirates . . . No prizes for guessing what kind of

business that might have been in. Unless, of course, Tommy had sent him out there to discuss the price of tulips and cheese.

'Only instead, he went off radar,' Riley said. 'And not only did he pull a Houdini himself, but he absconded with my goddaughter. Now normally,' he continued, 'I am a patient man. But various reports I've received on young Duke's recent conduct have led me to believe that this situation needs shutting down and fast.'

Frankie still didn't get it. Why was he here? Riley slowly grinned then, leaning forward on his sofa and staring deep into Frankie's eyes, so knowing, Frankie knew, just knew, he'd just read him.

'Now *why me?*, you may well be asking. Why has Mr Riley got me in here today? And you may well have already come up with some answers. Such as you owing me a favour. And you having proved yourself so highly adept last year at sorting shit out, that even I haven't quite worked out just exactly what the hell it was you did to get your little brother set free.'

Frankie said nothing. No way was he ever going to talk about that. Not to anyone. It was the kind of information that could get himself put away for good.

'But there's another reason too,' Riley said. 'Why you're exactly the right person to help sort out a shit storm like this.'

Again Frankie said nothing. But this time because he didn't want to hear whatever it was Riley said next. Because whatever card Riley was about to play, Frankie already knew he was trumped.

'You know her,' Riley said.

'Who *me*?' Did he mean this Tanya girl? 'No, you're mistaken,' Frankie said, almost smiling now. Because maybe this meant Riley didn't need him after all.

'Mistaken?' Riley slowly raised his eyebrows. 'Tut tut, you disappoint me, Frankie. Surely by now you know I never make mistakes.'

'What I mean is,' Frankie said, 'there must be some mistake, because I don't know anyone called Tanya. No one at all. Honestly, I swear.'

'Ah . . .' Riley slowly nodded. '. . . well, that's because she wasn't called that when you last saw her. No, she was called "TT" back then.'

'TT?'

'That's right.' He screwed up his face, like he'd just smelt something bad. 'And, I mean, you can get why she ditched it, you know, a nickname like that, as she got older. What with it sounding like "titties", the way it does.'

'Yeah,' Darren grinned.

TT? Frankie frowned. Because there was something, wasn't there? Something about it. Something familiar. Not the way Riley was pronouncing it, but how it was spelt. Something he'd heard before. Only where?

'Ah, yes,' said Riley, watching him closely again, *reading* him. 'Now you're getting it.' He grinned across at Grew. 'Didn't I tell you he was smart?'

Grew nodded. But Frankie was still frowning. Whatever memory that name had just snagged, it still hadn't surfaced into view.

'TT Landy,' Riley said.

And – *boom* – there it was. The connection Frankie had been searching for. Now clear as day. Little T was how Frankie had known her back then in Marbella. Back when he'd gone away with his parents and their mates and she was a sweet little girl with blonde plaits always tagging along and trying to join in – that's how he remembered her. Back then, she couldn't have been more than seven years old, six years younger than him. Little T was the little sister of Freddie Landy. Christ, the same Freddie, if Riley was to be believed, who'd now turned into a junkie and was currently drying out in the south of France.

Gaz Landy was their old man and Sooze the wife. The same couple Riley had been describing earlier – Riley's silent partner, and her, the poor woman, now dead.

Frankie thought back to the photos Riley had been staring at behind the bar on the night of the launch. Was that who he'd been looking at? Gaz Landy? And Freddie? And Little T? Was that the connection with Frankie he'd made? Jesus Christ. Was that why Frankie was sitting here now?

Another knowing smile from Riley. 'Good, I see you know who I mean,' he said. 'Which means you probably also know that, much like your father, her pop's detained at Her Majesty's pleasure at the moment.'

For icing a security guard in a heist. At least, that's what Frankie had read in the papers a couple of years back when Gaz Landy had been put away.

Riley clicked his fingers at Darren. 'Show him the photo,' he said.

Darren fetched it from the bar and handed it to Frankie. A scrawny-looking, but pretty with it, girl with long blonde hair stared back at him. A heart-shaped stork mark there above her right eye, with dark-red lipstick and pale skin. So this was how Little T looked now, a mini-Kate Moss, even down to the heroin chic.

'So that's her, my goddaughter, who's at the mercy of this wolf of a man she's got herself hooked up with. Who you're going to help get her back off. Because of the favour you owe.'

'But how?' Frankie said.

'You'll work it out. You'll have to.'

'But what if she —'

'Doesn't want to leave him? Doesn't want to come home? Then you'll have to be persuasive.'

'But I don't even know where she is.'

'Ibiza,' Tam said.

'What?'

'You know, the Balearics,' Tommy said. 'Right next to Majorca.'

Frankie just stared at him, the image on that postcard flashing up in his head.

'See, boss,' Tam said, misreading him. 'He knows it. That's him halfway to finding her, I reckon.'

'Finding her? But how —'

'The same way you found Susan Tilley's killer last year, son,' Riley said. 'By using your bloody snout. And by not bloody giving up until the job's bloody done.'

Frankie's heart was thundering now like he was about to have a seizure. Little T, Ibiza, his mother and Mallorca, all blended into one. But this was crazy, right? And dangerous, if what they said about this bloke Duke was even half true. He wasn't the right person to be doing this at all.

Only Riley was grinning like it had already happened, like finding Duke and the girl and bringing her home were just a few little details that needed ironing out. He was already up on his feet and rubbing his hands together.

'Right,' he said. 'Well, if we're done here, I've got an appointment upstairs with a pair of double Ds and a Brazilian.'

'What's the Brazilian's name, boss?' Grew asked.

'Christ,' Riley said, rolling his eyes. 'Do us a favour, will you, Frankie? Try and teach this bent bastard some decent jokes while you're away.'

'What do you mean *away*?'

'Well, you didn't think I'd be sending you off on your own, did you? I mean, I know you can handle yourself and all that. But our friend Duke, in addition to being balls deep into my beautiful little goddaughter, ain't such a shrinking violet himself. So I thought having a little professional backup on hand probably ain't a bad idea. After all, let's not forget, you are still fairly new to this game.'

This game. His game. The one Riley wrote all the rules for and called all the shots in.

*

'Don't look so worried,' Grew said, 'I'm sure we'll get along famously.'

'Sure,' said Frankie. Because it wasn't exactly like he had a choice, so he might as well be social, eh? And it could be worse. Christ, what about all them other bellends that made up Riley's crew. At least Grew had a brain and a half-decent dress sense. At least he wasn't called Tam.

Grew walked him back down the spiral marble stairs and into reception. Frankie remembered the fit bird – Chloe, wasn't it? – who'd been on the desk last year, the one who'd slipped him her phone number and had told him she wasn't a pro. He never had called her, had he? Not because he hadn't wanted to, more because of Sharon. Because he'd still hoped back then he was in with a chance. But feet clicking across the black and white chequered floor today, he felt different. Like instead of getting closer to Sharon, with each day passing, now he was getting further and further away. And the girl sitting behind the desk in that Chloe's place today, he'd never seen her before. But her bored look said it all – he was just another one of Riley's hoods.

'You want her to call you a cab back to Soho?' Grew said.

'Nah, but . . .'

'What?'

No harm in asking, was there? While he was on Riley's books, he might as well try and get something out of it for himself. 'There is something.'

'So shoot.'

'What you told me last year . . .'

'When?'

Frankie slipped a business card out of his jacket pocket and held it up. It was waxy white and embossed with

Grew's name and phone number printed on it in a neat black font.

'About giving you a call if I needed any help,' Frankie said.

Grew said nothing. Meaning what? His offer had had a time limit on it?

'Well, I do,' said Frankie.

Grew checked his watch. 'Right now?'

'No, afterwards. When we're back from the Balearics.' Not just *Ibiza*. Nah, because he was already seeing this little trip as far more than that.

'And who's this favour to do with?' Grew asked. 'Tommy?'

'No,' Frankie said. 'My dad.'

The tiny vein beneath Grew's left eye pulsed so slightly Frankie wasn't sure he'd even seen it at all. Grew had known Frankie's dad before he'd gone away. Frankie remembered them sometimes playing snooker together after hours in the club. Grew sparked up a cigarette and gazed out through the bright, sunlit window across the garden square outside. He took a long drag and blew out.

'Well, I don't suppose there's any harm in asking,' he said.

'I got two names,' Frankie said. 'And I need addresses to go with them.'

'So go look them up in the phone directory.'

'It's not that simple.'

'Yeah? And why's that?'

'Because both of them are cops.'

18

'What the hell is he doing here?' Frankie said.

Mackenzie Grew grinned. 'Oh, whoops. *Mea culpa.* Didn't I mention it wasn't just me coming along for the ride?'

'No.'

Jesús shot Frankie a cold glance, before flipping open the overhead locker on the opposite side of the plane aisle to stow his bag. He grunted, annoyed that it was already full.

'This bag, it is yours?' he asked the bloke in deck shoes, chinos and a Fat Face shirt sitting below it, who was jabbering into his mobile phone.

The bloke ignored him and carried on talking. Something about share prices.

'I said, is it, this bag, yours?' the Spaniard repeated, taking the briefcase down this time to illustrate his question more clearly.

'Oi. Hang on, Alan,' the suit said into his phone. 'Look, mate,' he told the Spaniard. 'You can't just move that. I –'

The Spaniard slammed his case hard into his chest, knocking his phone from his hand.

'Australia,' he said, glancing down at the man's lap and grinning.

'Whuh-what?' the yuppie said, confused. He was clutching his case like a shield.

'Is there a problem?' a stewardess asked, her accent Spanish.

'*Este hombre acaba de decir que se estaba moviendo,*' said the Spaniard, slipping flawlessly into his home tongue, all bright-white smiles now for the stewardess. They rattled off a couple more sentences in Spanish Frankie didn't get a word of. He'd bought himself a phrase book down Foyles on Charing Cross Road the day before yesterday after his meeting with Riley, but had only got as far as mastering the necessities for ordering himself a fry-up and asking directions to the bog, neither of which struck him as particularly likely to be of very much help now.

But the Spaniard seemed to be doing pretty well without his help anyway. Because as she walked away, the stewardess glanced back over her shoulder at the Spaniard and flashed him a coy smile, eyeing every inch of his bespoke powder-blue suit. He waited for her to turn, before fixing his glare back on the yuppie.

'I make an explanation to her that we are the very best of friends and you are agreeable to swap seating with me and sit at the back of the plane. Next to the toilet. Because you feel sick.'

'But I'm n—'

The yuppie was obviously a slow learner. The Spaniard flat-palmed his case hard against his chest again.

147

'Did you hear what he just –' the yuppie asked Grew.

'No, pal. But if you know what's good for you, you'll do what you're told.' Grew turned back to his Jackie Collins paperback.

'You go now,' the Spaniard hissed at the yuppie, leaning down and eyeballing him right up close. 'Or . . .' He held up his forefinger. '. . . I take this digit and make insertion in your anus. Very hard. So you understand it comes out of your ear.'

He was actually pointing at the yuppie's nose when he said this, which threw into some doubt whether his heavily accented English had indeed conveyed the message that he wanted. But the yuppie's resistance was gone, and he promptly scrabbled up quickly from his seat and scarpered to the back of the plane with his case clutched in his hands.

'Why don't you persons just listen?' said the Spaniard, after he'd stowed his bag and sat down. He pulled a pack of Gummi Bears out of his pocket and tipped some out on the fold-down table in front of him.

'You persons?' Frankie said.

'I think he means us Brits.'

Jesús was ignoring them. He was separating the little bears out into different colours.

'Oh,' said Frankie.

'And I reckon it was South Africa, actually,' Grew said, grinning across at the Spaniard.

'*Qué?*'

'You might be OK at languages,' Grew explained, 'but

your geography's all over the shop. That piss stain on his chinos didn't look like Australia at all.'

*

Frankie nodded off some time after Grew's fourth double G&T, in the middle of a story he'd been telling him about some legendary eighties weekend of his that had started off with the David Bowie Glass Spider tour and ended up with him and an old boyfriend of his who'd since died of AIDS nicking a speedboat from Brighton Marina and caning it over to Calais. Or was it Le Havre? Waking up, Frankie couldn't be sure, and no point asking Grew as he'd passed out and was slumped snoring on Frankie's shoulder with his straw trilby pulled down over his eyes.

The Spaniard, on the other hand, hadn't moved. Literally. He was still staring at the back of the headrest in front like there was a TV playing there that only he could see, the nut. Frankie wasn't happy, not happy at all, about having this bastard along for the ride. Sure, he might be good muscle – Frankie had seen enough of his moves down the boxing gym to know that – but he was a liability too. Hardly exactly professional, was it, throwing his weight around like he'd just done with that posh bloke before take-off.

Not that Frankie had been given any much more of a clue as to what he was meant to be doing over on Ibiza anyhow. All he was sure of was he had to find this Duke character, and the girl, then get the girl back home. Yeah, sure, Riley had spelt out the basics of the mission pretty clear. But there'd still been no word on how exactly all that was meant to be achieved.

Frankie had tried quizzing Grew on it back at Gatwick Airport. But no dice. He'd just said all would be revealed in good time. It was easy for him to relax, mind. Enforcing his boss's demands, this was his bread and butter. But Frankie wasn't a crim and didn't want to get sucked in on that. Even though he knew he had no choice.

He'd thought about just saying no, as *Grange Hill* used to put it. Of trying to wriggle out of going. Of even telling Riley he was sick. But even though he wasn't a part of this world, he still knew it well enough from the Old Man. You paid your dues, your favours, because if you didn't, you were an outlaw – disconnected. Fair game. And not just you, but yours – Jack, the Old Man, the club. It was all fair game. If Frankie reneged on a deal, Riley would bring his whole world crashing down just like that.

Frankie had called in on the Old Man yesterday. He'd told him he was flying here today – a last-minute bargain getaway, he'd said, the same as he'd told Slim and Xandra. Just to help him unwind after the last few days. No point telling him the real reason. He'd have just spat his teeth. He hated the thought of Jack being involved in his world, and Frankie the same. Frankie didn't tell him anything about his other plan either, about hot-footing it over to Mallorca and trying to find that street shown on the postcard. Because the Old Man would have just thought he was crazy for that too. They'd not even mentioned his mum, not after how near they'd come to falling out over her big time last week.

And he'd given the same last-minute-getaway bullshit to Jack when he'd popped round to say goodbye too.

Frankie's ears popped as they started their descent. Looking out of the window as the plane banked round, he saw they were passing a higgledy-piggledy town, all ochre and white in the blazing hot sunshine below, stretching along a coastline of white, sandy bays.

Ibiza Old Town, if he wasn't much mistaken, from this map here in the in-flight brochure – a place chocka with bars, restaurants, boutiques and clubs. Not to mention *muchos*, *muchos* pills and thrills and bellyaches and spannered Brits on tour. There were plenty of them on the plane who'd already had more than their fair share of in-flight beers. Bar the lack of music, it felt like a pub.

He felt a little tingle in his gut then, just at the thought of it all. But not of anticipation, not like every other Herbert on board . . . well, apart from Jesús here. It was a tingle of dread, because he'd have to be bloody careful and keep his shit together. Frankie was here for one reason only – not for fun, but to pay off a debt.

The more he kept his shit together, the sooner this spoiled little rich kid – aka the sweet little girl he'd known as a child – was found, the sooner he could go looking for the other woman missing in his life. Just eighty miles northeast across that glittering blue sea on Mallorca.

Half an hour by plane, but potentially a whole world away.

19

Scorchio.

Was there any other word to describe it? Frankie couldn't think of one. And not just the temperature. The fashions. The people. The music. Everything about this place was hot, hot, hot.

They'd ditched their bags in the Mandalay. A boutique hotel up in the top half of Ibiza Old Town, or *Vila d'Eivissa*, as the locals called it. Not that many of them he'd met had spoken much Spanish to him at all.

The whole island was geared up way too fast for things like stumbled conversations – Frankie looked pale as milk, marking him out as a tourist on sight.

Everyone had instead addressed him in flawless English. Even the cabby who'd driven them from the airport and the waiter who served him an iced water, along with two glistening, perspiring pints of San Miguel for Jesús and Grew.

They'd wandered into town about half an hour ago now from the hotel. Both Grew and Jesús already seemed to know their way round pretty well. Had clearly been here plenty before.

They were sitting outside a bar called the Twisted Lemon on the packed *Paseo*, as the sun slowly started to sink over the twinkling blue sea. A steady flow of holiday-makers and clubbers trickled past, young, beautiful, hip and rich. This was the posh bit of the island and the bistros, bars and boutiques stretching off either side of them were already packed. The smell of sizzling *gambas* and steaks hung in the air, offset by the familiar tinge of weed. On this pleasure island, not even the local cops, sauntering past in their neatly ironed little uniforms, seemed to give a shit.

'Ah, yes,' said Grew, sparking up a smoke and taking a long, cool sip of his beer. 'Now this is the life, is it not?'

Hard to disagree. It wasn't like Frankie had had a choice in coming here, but Christ he'd had worse views in his life.

'And far from the madding crowd of vomiting Brits who'll shortly be clogging up the clubs and bars of Sant Antoni, eh, Jesús?'

'True.' Jesús still hadn't spoken a word to Frankie since he'd sat down beside him on the plane.

'So what time's he get here, then? This Balearic Bob?' Frankie asked. Bob. Their man on the ground. Soon to be their guide.

'Dunno. Jesús?'

'Soon.'

A man of few words. Frankie reckoned he'd been watch-ing too many spaghetti westerns. Fancied himself as a bit of a Clint Eastwood, strong, silent type. Fat chance. He looked more like he was auditioning for the Eurovision Song Contest. All brand-spanking-new stripy white shorts and billowing white shirt, with box-fresh pastel-blue espadrilles.

Frankie was almost tempted to ask him for a tune. But there wouldn't have been much point. For one thing, Jesús didn't have a sense of humour. And for another, all the bars along the strip here already had the music side of things well covered. Competing bass lines. Bongo bongo. Exactly the kind of shit Jack and his mates had been playing in that club. Total rubbish, in other words.

'*Aw*-wight, geezers,' a rich Essex accent boomed out. Belonged to a big, fat, bearded fellah who'd give Jabba the Hut a run for his money in the lardarse stakes. He was all billowing cotton, chest hair, gold chains and waistcoat. Like a hideous Cockney version of Demis Roussos. 'Yo, Migsy,' he shouted out at the waiter who was lurking in the shadows beyond the door. 'The usual, mate. Five of your namesakes. An' a bottle of tequila.' He nodded at Grew and Jesús in turn. 'He's called Miguel and that's what they've got on tap here. It's like he was destined to serve us what we want. Gentlemen, nice to see you both again. And to meet you too,' he told Frankie.

'Balearic Bob, I presume?'

'Frankie James.' He had bloodshot, sixty-something eyes, but not a wrinkle on his fat sunburnt face. 'Tommy wasn't wrong. Quite the young detective, aren't you, I see.'

He was looking at Frankie, all teeth, but was he actually smiling? It was hard to tell, his skin was stretched so tight from all the work he'd had done. He shot out a pudgy little hand for Frankie to shake. A strong grip, mind. Took Frankie a little by surprise. Even made him wince. Something Balearic Bob clocked and looked pleased about too. Just letting Frankie know he still had a bit of muscle left under all that flab. Not quite the pussy Frankie had taken him for at all.

'So that new hotel to your liking, lads?' he asked, pulling up a chair and scratching at a couple of scars just under his chin.

'Yeah,' said Grew. 'Very nice.'

'You're booked in for a week, but I can't see it taking us that long, to be honest, to track this little girl and that prick down.'

That *prick*. The way he said it was full of venom. The nod that followed from Grew had Frankie feeling that it was him, every bit as much as her, that Riley wanted to get his hands on. Good news, mind. That Bob here was feeling optimistic about how long this would all take. Grew lit a fag off the one he was already smoking.

'Don't that kind of depend on how hard she's hiding?' he said. 'And how much she don't want to come home.'

'I understood that's where he came in,' said Bob, looking from Grew to Frankie. 'You're friends with her and her brother, isn't that right?'

'*Was*. A long time ago. The last time I remember speaking to her properly, I was helping her build a sandcastle on her seventh birthday,' Frankie said. 'And as for him . . .'

'What?'

'It don't matter.' The last time Frankie had seen Freddie Landy, Jack had reminded him only yesterday when they'd said goodbye, had been round at Jack's old flat just before Christmas. Frankie remembered the two of them drinking vodka and chatting about the old days. But Jack said Tanya had been there too. Later on. *And* this bloke of hers, this

Duke, whose nuts Riley wanted to cut off, was off his head on coke. They were only calling round to pick up Freddie, who was carrying their ketamine stash which they'd needed to bring them down. The only problem was that Frankie had been passed out in Jack's bedroom by then and didn't even remember them being there at all.

'Yeah, well, let's find the naughty little cow first and worry about how we get her home later. On which preliminary investigations are already under way. Oh, and before I forget, here's your goody bags,' Bob said. He dug into his leather shoulder bag and pulled out three padded envelopes, one for each of them.

Grew opened his up and took out a phone, along with a photo. Of Tanya, Frankie saw. The same one he'd been shown in St James's. Grew peered inside the envelope and nodded, the trace of a smile round his lips.

'Very decent of you, Bob. Very decent indeed.'

He slipped the envelope into his jacket pocket. Frankie followed suit. He dreaded to think what was in there and would check it out when he got back to his room.

'Cheers,' he told Bob.

The waiter brought over the beers and the bottle and some shot glasses and started filling them up.

'Not for me, thanks,' said Frankie, covering his with one hand and nudging the lager away with his other. No mean feat, either – it looked like a bloody advert for good times.

'Different rules over here, mate,' Bob cackled, knocking his back. 'It's never too early in the day.'

Frankie kept his hand right where it was. 'Every day's too early for me.'

'Oh, I see. One of the fallen – an abstainer.' His piggy little eyes narrowed even more, so much so you could hardly even see they were there. 'Well, fine, suit yourself, and good luck with that. It'll be interesting to see how long you last on this island.'

For the first time, Frankie saw Jesús smile. 'Maybe you and I, Bob, we'll have ourselves a little bet?' He raised his glass first to Bob, and then Frankie – staring him well hard in the eyes as he did – then knocked his shot back.

Frankie thought about saying something. Less to Bob, more Jesús. Letting him know he was no pushover. Shoving the bastard right back. But then he remembered Rope-a-Dope. That poor bastard flat on his back. If him and Jesús ever did come to blows, he reckoned it would end up every bit as messy as that. And might mess up everything they were doing here. So maybe, just for now, he should show a little restraint.

'All right, all right, we can do without any handbags at dawn,' Grew said, picking up on the spark, 'or dusk, for that matter. Suffice to say, you two aren't exactly going to be best mates, but can we at least just leave the argy-bargy out of it. Some of us' – he raised his glass to Bob – 'are attempting to have a civilized night out.'

'Amen to that,' said Bob, and both of them necked theirs down. 'Welcome to Ibiza, heaven on earth. Now, anything you lads want while you're here. *Apart* from bloody alcohol,' he said to Frankie. 'Pills, powders, pussy . . . whatever, just let me know and I'll switch the tap on.'

'You got anything for mozzies?' Frankie said, smudging one across the back of his hand.

'What?' Bob grinned. 'Like a gun?'

There was something about his little eyes when he said it. Like maybe he was packing. Frankie bloody hoped not. It was one thing coming out here at the behest of a gangster to find a missing girl. But that was as dark as he wanted it to get.

'So where exactly are we up to regarding preliminary investigations?' Grew said.

'I put the word out Wednesday as soon as you said you were coming. I've put out some copies of that photo of her you faxed over.'

'Who with?'

'A few of them who owe me . . .' He waved at a couple of cops walking past, different uniforms to the last time. '. . . and, of course, our very good friend, who's keeping an eye on the clubs . . .' He was looking at Jesús when he said this, but didn't go into any more detail than that. '. . . or the posh clubs anyway, the kinds of establishment where a posh piece of arse like her will probably be hanging out.'

'I'd be careful what you're calling her,' Grew said, suddenly no longer smiling. 'Don't forget this is Gaz Landy's little girl we're talking about, which is why it's so fucking important we get her back.'

'And get her back we will.' Bob gave him a reassuring squeeze on the arm, before sloshing more tequila into their glasses. 'But for now let's all just loosen up our sphincters and have a nice evening of it. Oh, and before I forget, I've booked us a table at Rikitik's Beach Bar to watch the footie tomorrow.'

Even Frankie smiled at the idea of England versus Spain

out here – he couldn't think of a better place to watch the match, even back at the club. But he'd better call Slim and Xandra to check that everything was going well back home. Shouldn't be any trouble, mind, with Spartak booked in for the door again.

'I don't know why you smile,' Jesús said. 'Tomorrow you will only lose.'

'More like our lads are going to wipe the floor with yours,' Frankie said, switching up his smile to a grin.

Right on cue, a fanfare of trumpets started up from somewhere further down the strip. Punters in the bars all around started getting to their feet. Cheering and whooping and whistling broke out as the trumpets rolled through a progression of jazz riffs that would have done New Orleans Mardi Gras proud.

Frankie got up and craned his neck to see. The head of the procession making its way down the strip came into view. A tall woman, wearing a Venetian mask and a Red Indian headdress, led a group of burlesque performers, bedecked in heels and nipple tassels, each handing out flyers to the public gawping at either side.

'Oh yes, lads. Get in,' yelled Bob, grinning. 'Here they come. Just look at the totty tottering. Enough to give the Pope wood. By God, I love this place.'

As the procession drew level with them, Frankie caught the lead girl's eyes and she blew him a kiss from the end of her white-gloved fingertips. One of her minions, a dwarf painted head to foot in gold, rushed up to Frankie and handed him a book of matches.

'Mistress likes you,' he shouted. 'Don't be late, don't be late.'

Frankie read the logo on the matches. It was promoting some club called Indigo Blue.

'You know this place?' he asked Bob.

'Intimately,' he grinned. 'As the kids might put it, it is where it's at.'

Frankie turned to look at the woman again. But already she'd gone, moving on, her entourage with her.

Jesús, he noticed, was glowering at him and the book of matches in his hand.

'Right, let's get back to the bloody drinking,' Bob said.

20

The call came at just gone 1 a.m. It might have been bed-time for Frankie, but for most people round here the night seemed to be just getting going.

Him, Grew and Bob had long since moved on from the Twisted Lemon – to Roca, via Bacchus, Mona Lisa and Ibo. Grew and Bob were pretty hammered, but still drinking and, even more surprising, still standing up. No doubt a result of whatever it was they'd been sticking up their noses, which was plenty, if the amount of trips they'd made to the bogs was anything to go by.

'We've had a sighting,' Bob said, lurching back from the bar with his phone in his hand.

Grew looked at him unsteadily. 'Blimey. That was quick.'

'Told you, didn't I? That my network was good? I'm like the fucking CIA.'

'Him or her, or both?' Frankie said.

'Her.'

Frankie clocked the look of disappointment on Grew's face.

'At least maybe,' Bob added.

'Only maybe?' Grew frowned.

'They're keeping an eye on her. Seeing if Duke turns up. He's harder to mistake, the tattooed freak.'

'Who called it in?' Grew asked.

'Our friend.'

The same one he'd mentioned before? The one who was Jesús's friend too? No way to tell from reading his expression. He'd headed off half an hour ago, to go 'set up that thing' was all he'd said.

'Where was she spotted?' Frankie said. 'If it's her.'

'Kooks,' said Bob. 'A right little hedonists' haunt. No pikeys. Cognoscenti only, all locals and trustbusters, on the other side of the island. The middle of nowhere.' He sighed. 'And here we were just getting started. It's gonna take us at least an hour to get there, I'm afraid.'

'I'll go,' Frankie said. He'd been about to make his excuses anyway. These two had reached that repeating themselves stage of drunkenness a good hour ago. He wasn't exactly ready for bed, though, either. It was still too hot. Frankie questioned his choice of outfit, maybe shouldn't have worn this suit, even if it was linen. A little jaunt across the island in an AC cab to a posh club might be just the ticket. Plus, no way was he letting a possible sighting of this girl slip by just because these two were too pissed to check it out. He wanted this dealt with, and fast.

'And if it *is* her?' Grew said.

'Then I'll do my best to persuade her to –'

'Wrong,' said Grew. 'You call me on that phone. She might not be on her own and whatever we hit, I'd rather we hit it together.'

Hit. Not exactly the kind of word you'd use if you thought this was going to be as easy as Riley had made out.

'All right, I will,' Frankie said.

'All the numbers you're going to need are already pro-grammed into that phone I gave you before,' said Bob, meaning the one in the envelope Frankie had here in his jacket pocket. 'Jesús is one, Grew's two, I'm three. And you're four.'

Frankie remembered that phrase from those reruns of *The Prisoner* he'd used to watch as a kid: *I'm not a number, I'm a free man!* Yeah, right. It was horribly clear the reverse was the case.

*

Frankie checked out the contents of the padded envelope as he travelled across the island in the cab he picked up just off the main drag. As well as the phone and a nice, tidy wedge of pesetas, there were five wraps of doo-dah, for God's sake. Enough to get him banged up. He ditched the lot out the window. Some favours he could do without.

There were a couple of pix too. That one of Tanya and one of a shaven-headed, heavily tattooed bloke, who looked half thug, half male model. Frankie was guessing it had to be Duke.

Frankie had asked Jack about him yesterday, when he'd called round to see him to say goodbye. Had done it just casually, via talking about Tanya and those holidays they'd gone on. Just to try and get the lie of the land without Jack twigging that's why Frankie was coming out here, in case

163

he'd done something like ring her or this Duke up. Jack said he was a real headcase, scary, like – which was rich, considering the nutters he usually hung out with himself.

Two business cards tucked into the envelope as well. One for a club called Secrets. All roses and lipstick marks. Had to be a brothel. And another with the legend 'Hotel Visits' written on it in embossed white print. Charming. And how convenient. He sent them both the same way as the wraps.

The image of the lipstick, though, it stuck with him. For the whole forty-five minutes it took them to get out of Ibiza town. Forty-five minutes. Jesus, what was wrong with this effing island? The traffic was worse than south London. What if it was Tanya there in that club? What if he missed her because of this?

As he sat back, telling himself to cool it, telling himself he might still be in with a chance of finding her tonight, he reprogrammed the phone with Jesús, Bob and Grew's names instead of their numbers. What was this, *The Man from* fucking *Uncle*? The last thing he wanted was to end up ringing that bastard Jesús by mistake.

He took out the card with lipstick on he had on him in his other jacket pocket. *Palma, Mallorca* . . . he traced the letters with his finger. He'd already asked back at hotel reception about how easy it was to get over to Mallorca. He could either fly or get a ferry. A piece of piss either way. Only question was when.

When Balearic Bob had said the club was tucked away, he hadn't been kidding. After Frankie's cab finally broke free from the second glut of congestion they got snagged up in round Sant Antoni, they hit the countryside proper. It was like a different island. No music. No neon. No queues. Hardly a house or a car in sight. A maze of single-track roads. With a star-studded sky and a crescent moon above. Frankie was just about to tell the driver to turn back, assuming they'd got lost, when there it was. A glow in the distance. Red car tail lights. A trail of them, a hundred long, slowly edging on. Then noise. A steady, rising wall of drum and bass.

They finally reached the car park on the cliff edge and were greeted by a sea of motors – the place was rammed. He'd never seen so much wealth. Porsches and Mercs littered the car park, some of them even with drivers standing by. Frankie paid the driver double what the fare showed and asked him to stay put. He didn't fancy getting stuck out here without a ride back.

There was a queue to get in, a snake of beautiful people. They were all dressed up like time travellers, some like they'd just stepped out of the sixties, others the seventies. Some straight out of Buck bleedin' Rogers central casting. He joined the back of the queue. He couldn't remember the last time he'd done that in London.

But while half these punters might have been dressed up like hippies and what have you, their jewellery and their accents gave them all away. This lot were minted, no different to what you'd find down some posh den like Annabel's at home. He got talking to some bird in a white leather bikini and not much else. She told him she loved his suit. He reckoned she was probably taking the piss, because her mate she was with rolled her eyes. Not quite the vibe these others were aiming at, was he? But sod them. What was it Jack had said? The whole point about clubbing these days was that it was broad church. Yeah, even including him in his suit.

When he finally reached the gate, he gasped at how much the entrance was. Cash entry. He shook his head slowly at the black-leather-jacketed bouncers either side. But sod it. It wasn't his money. Tommy Riley was funding this whole shebang after all.

As he weaved his way in, there were yet more beautiful people beyond the fence, getting pissed and high. Flaming torches lit up the perimeter of an outdoor courtyard, with a lit swimming pool, of all things, at its centre and a grand, sandstone building beyond – the club proper, he guessed. With yet more bouncers on the door. Frankie headed for one of the three bars by the pool.

'Mineral water,' he said.

'For inside?' asked the Courtney Love lookalike behind the bar.

'Does it matter?'

She pointed to a sign. 'No glasses inside.'

Hilarious that no glasses were allowed, just gak and pills. Of course. 'Yeah,' he said. 'For inside.' Because he was going to have to check everywhere, wasn't he, to see if she was here.

He paid for the miniscule bottle of water with a fifty and she gave him his change. He guzzled down his drink. Christ, it was still so hot, he was parched.

'You seen this girl?' he then asked, taking Tanya's photo out and showing it to the bar girl.

She looked first it, then him, up and down, suspiciously. 'What are you? Cop?'

'No.' He leafed a bunch of pesetas down onto the bar, but kept his hand on them. 'Just an old friend.' Well, it was true. 'I'm meant to be meeting her here tonight.'

The barmaid checked out the photo again. 'The hair,' she said. 'It's different. Shorter. I think it's possible I saw her with a group of friends over there.' She pointed to another bar at the end of the pool.

'What was she wearing?

'What?'

'Wearing. Her clothes,' he explained, tugging at his own.

'Oh.' She smiled. 'White. She was wearing white.'

Great. Just like every other prick in here. Why couldn't someone he was after just be dressed up like *Where's Wally?* for a change? 'Thanks for you help,' he said, taking the photo back off her and leaving the cash behind.

The second bar was a little rum shack kind of a thing, all bamboo and woven palm leaves. Frankie put another bunch of pesetas down less than a minute later. The bar girl there hadn't seen her, bollocks. He went through the same routine three more times with three more of the models masquerading as staff here before he got lucky. One of the lads clearing away glasses said he'd seen her and that she was dressed in white too. She'd gone inside, he reckoned, with a bunch of mates about half an hour ago when some DJ called Altro had started his set.

Frankie headed in through the main doors into . . . another bloody world. He was blasted by sirens, bass, lasers and strobes. If outside had been ethereal, this here was more of the kind of sweat pit Frankie was used to avoiding in London. Because, seriously, he just didn't get the point of it.

A bunch of whacked-out muppets worshipping at the altar of some bellend whose only apparent talent was being able to spin someone else's discs.

Mind you, it wasn't all bad. You had to admit that. Some of the birds were off the clock. Off their heads too, though. Jesus, the second he set foot on the main dance floor in an attempt to cross it, some blonde lurched into him, sloshing his water all over his suit.

'Sorry,' she mouthed at him, the green and yellow silk butterfly hairclip on the top of her head looking like it was about to fly away. Then, laughing, she pushed up on her tiptoes and kissed him hard on the lips. 'Cheer up, it might never happen,' she yelled in his ear over the noise.

Yeah, right, it already had. But he didn't get a chance to tell her that. She was already off, swallowed back up by the surging crowd, as the DJ screamed out above the track, 'Are you having fucking fun?' Frankie chugged his way slowly towards the back of the dance floor, feeling like an uncle, because no, he bloody wasn't.

Through the fug of sweat, smoke, perfume and booze, he tried checking out the faces he was forcing his way past. Almost impossible. All of them twisting, turning, grinning, gurning. How the hell was he ever going to find her in here?

Then he spotted the kind of vantage point he was after. A roped-off VIP area at the back. A bunch of raised booths, overlooking the dance floor and stage. Packed with über-rich party punters, sucking on joints and hookahs, and guzzling vodka and champagne. Hah, what a joke. The amount of money it cost just to get in here and that still didn't mean you were *in*.

Two ways in. Both of them guarded. Two geezers on one entrance. One on the other. He plumped for the one. Dressed in regulation bouncer black leather jacket. A short bloke. But tidy with it. Looked like he could handle himself. Frankie grinned at him like he'd seen him just two minutes back and tried walking right by him. But the little bastard wasn't falling for it. He jutted out a metal-hard arm to hold Frankie back.

'You need a wristband.'

Jesus Christ. Would you believe it? Another Scouser.

'Yeah, I lost it.'

'So go find it.'

'How about I just buy another one?' Frankie held up another fifty, but the bouncer's eyes just smiled *piss off*.

'That won't even buy you a gin and tonic in here, pal. So why don't you sod off back to the plebs' bar over there where you belong.'

Frankie gritted his teeth. Charming. But not a lot he could do about it now. One of the other bouncers was already worming his way over through the VIPs towards them, sensing trouble. OK. Shit. Fine. He'd have to find somewhere else to get a good look round from.

Thanks for nothing, you prick, Frankie was about to say. But then he saw her. The bar girl said she was dressed in white – unless it was someone who looked a lot bloody like her? Her hair was shorter than in the pic, but she still had that heart-shaped stork mark just above her right eye and she was walking right towards him from the dance floor.

It was bloody fate.

21

The bouncer started to push him backwards, to move him out of her way. She was with two other girls, all of them dripping with jewellery and sweat. Or rather, she was with two women – more like Frankie's age. But they looked even older behind their eyes. They had that same look as those birds Tommy had working for him over in St James's.

'Hey, Tanya,' he yelled, nice and loud, just as she reached him.

'Huh?' Her eyes narrowed. No mean feat, either, seeing as they were the size of saucers. Her face was even paler than in the photo he'd just been showing around. Her once-beautiful eyes nestled inside black circles.

'Tanya Landy.'

'Do I know you?' she shouted back.

'Is this guy bothering you?' the bouncer bellowed, his hand still firmly on Frankie's back, spring-loaded and ready to shove him right back down these steps.

'TT,' said Frankie.

Her whole expression changed from confusion to curiosity. 'No one calls me that any more.'

'Or Little T, I'll bet.' He searched her face for signs of

that little girl he'd once known, but there was nothing left. She looked gaunt, messed up, like the junkies he sometimes found asleep by the bins round the back of the club.

'A friend of yours?' asked one of the other girls, giving Frankie a once over. Eastern European accent.

'Um . . . I mean, yes, but . . .'

But could she remember him? Because of course the last time their paths had crossed, when she'd tipped up high on coke at Jack's flat, Frankie had already been passed out.

He had to move fast, before he lost her attention. 'Yeah, yeah, you remember me. We saw each other just before Christmas and we used to go on holiday,' he said. 'When we were kids. I'm Frankie . . . Frankie . . .'

'Frankie James!' she shouted, and beamed over at him – she looked so pleased with herself, she might as well have been yelling *Eureka!* Like she'd just solved the biggest god-damn problem in the world. She threw her arms right round his neck. Christ, she was thin, he could feel the bones of her arms digging into his flesh. 'Cool Frankie James!' she laughed.

Cool? Even the bouncer smiled at that. He finally took his hand off Frankie, his frown smoothing out from red alert.

'And, yeah, yeah, I *do* remember it now. We saw you and Jack round at his?'

'That's right.'

'Only you . . . Oh, my God, I remember it now. You were really drunk, weren't you? You were sleeping it off in his bedroom.'

'So much for being cool, eh?'

A big, wide smile crossed her face. 'Oh no, you're still that. The cool big brother I never had.' She rolled her eyes. 'Instead of the one I did get. Come on, come meet everyone. Sergei,' she shouted ahead, pulling Frankie past the bouncer, who just slowly shook his head.

Sergei had clearly been to the same school of fashion as the bouncer, and the same went for the four other guys he was sitting with. All of them were dressed in black, like a troupe of mime artists. There wasn't a primary colour in sight. The two women Tanya had been dancing with draped themselves over two of the men, who didn't look like they much cared for the attention either way. None of them were dancing, or speaking, and it was pretty bloody hard to guess what any of them were thinking. They were all wearing shades.

'Drink?' Tanya asked, patting the red leather banquette beside her for Frankie to sit down.

'Er, no. I'm OK.'

'So how long are you over for?'

'Well, that kind of depends.'

'On what?'

On you. On how fast I can get you out of here. Which couldn't be fast enough either. Because, Christ, just look at her. Here in the candlelight, away from the disco lights, she looked even sicker than before.

'This and that,' he said. 'How about you?' The million-dollar question.

'Oh, I don't know. I suppose when this stops being fun . . . *If . . .*' Her grin made it clear she didn't reckon this would be until at least the end of the summer.

'You've got a place here, have you?'

She shrugged. 'We're staying with these guys.'

Sergei was standing closer now and turned to face them as she said it. Was he listening? Hard to tell with all this music. The two of them were having to shout just to be heard.

'Who's *we*?' Her and Duke? He was guessing so, but he wasn't meant to know it, was he? Not as far as she was concerned. Not unless he wanted to admit right from the get-go that Riley had sent him here. Which was something he'd bet would just frighten her off – he needed to win her trust first.

'Me and my boy. Man,' she grinned. 'You never did actually meet him that night, did you? He's a little bit older than me. More your age. I always did like an older man.'

What? Was she actually flirting? Or maybe she was just on ecstasy, she did look off her box.

'Is he one of these guys?' Frankie said. None of them looked anything like the snap of Duke he had in his pocket.

'What, the Russians?' She rolled her eyes. 'God, no. They're . . . I don't know . . . business associates, or something like that.'

Which made sense, because none of them looked that friendly. Half of them weren't even drinking or, if they were, they were keeping their shit together. At least that's how it appeared.

'His name's Duke,' she said.

Frankie shrugged like it meant nothing.

'Your brother knows him. They both work for Tommy Riley. Or, at least, Duke did.'

173

Did. Meaning what? That he'd quit? That him and Riley had jointly agreed to go their separate ways? Fat chance. Absconded, that was the word Riley had used. Meaning Duke had done one. A flit. But from what? And why?

'So this place you're staying at. It nearby, is it?' Frankie fished. Because he was already thinking that might be the best place to talk to her. When she was sober. To tell her why he was really here. Because her old man and her god-father wanted her home. Because they weren't going to take no for an answer. And because it increasingly sounded to Frankie like her boyfriend was in trouble if he didn't head straight back home to see Riley as well. But not with this lot watching their every move.

Her turn to shrug. 'It's out on the north coast some-where. I'm not actually sure where.' She shrugged again. 'These guys drive us everywhere.' She meant the Russians. 'I wouldn't have a clue how to get there on my own.'

No way was he just going to be able to pop over for a visit then.

'You got a number I can call you on?' he said. Next best thing. 'It might be fun to hang out with you and your fellah while I'm here. I mean, if you want.'

'Yeah. Good idea. You two would get on like a house on fire.' She pulled a pen out of her little black bag and scribbled down her name and number on a little book of matches that fell right out alongside it. Restaurante Ca'n Costa, he read, picking it up. 'Oh God, you've got to check that out too,' she said, folding it into his hand for him to keep. 'One of Duke's old mates runs it. It's a *chiringuito*.'

'A what?'

'A sort of old-school beach restaurant. They have the best seafood on the island, but you can only get there by boat. Only open on Fridays and Saturdays. Hardly anyone knows it's even there. It's the perfect place to get away from it all.'

'Great,' he said. 'Thanks, I'll make sure to check it out.' He tucked the matchbook into his pocket alongside the one he'd been given earlier for the club.

'You want a line?' she asked, pulling out a wrap from her bag.

'Er, no. Thanks.'

She started to rack one up, right here on the glass table in the booth. But Sergei tapped his finger on the back of her hand and shook his head.

'No point inviting trouble,' he said, nodding across at the bouncers.

A fair point and one she took, though to be honest the way the bouncers were guarding these guys, Frankie doubted they'd give much of a toss. Winking at Frankie, Tanya hooked arms with one of the other girls and made off for the bogs.

Frankie smiled at Sergei, but got nothing in return. He didn't like the look of these twats, not one little bit. The sooner he could get her away from them the better. But when? Because no way was he going to be able to do it tonight. At least, not on his own. But what if this was it? What if he didn't manage to get hold of her tomorrow on the phone? He heard it again, what Riley had said, about her ending up being scraped off the floor. He got up and went towards the fire door at the back of the club. Another bouncer was guarding it, but, now he'd been allowed into the VIP area, this guy just waved him through.

Outside was a wide balcony area, looking down over the car park and beyond that the sea. A few people were smoking joints, sitting at tables chatting. Frankie walked over to the railings on the far side, taking out the phone. It was time to call the cavalry and get them out here too. Bob might know who these Russians were and where they were staying. With any luck, he might even end up clearing the whole thing up, nice and quick.

But no such luck. He dialled both Bob's and Grew's numbers, but got nothing but rings. Bloody pissheads. He couldn't bring himself to call Jesús, better to deal with whatever this was himself than end up with just that unpredictable jerk as backup. He left a message on Grew's phone. Told them where he was and what was going down.

He spotted some movement below him then, in a dimly lit bit of car park round at the back of the club, away from the queues. And, blimey, if it wasn't some of Little T's Russian pals having a little conflab at the back of a shiny as mercury four-by-four silver Range Rover. And, as if that particular model hadn't been clue enough, the Russkis were busy filling in the rest of the dots for any casual observer like Frankie to work out. Five or six little scrotes hanging round them, seventeen or eighteen years old. Girls and boys. Baggies full of God knows what being doled out to each of them to get selling to the clubbers inside.

Aye, aye, lemon pie. So that's who Little T was hanging out with. Wheeler-dealers. And shifting plenty of product too, if this little scene was anything to go by. Then, turning, he saw Sergei, smoking a fag a few yards away, watching him. Had he just followed him out?

Tanya was already sitting back in the booth when Frankie got back inside. Right, so what to do now? Stick with her and wait for the cavalry to show? That made the most sense. This Sergei bloke clearly had suspicions about him, but so what? He hadn't got enough to act on. And even if Grew didn't get Frankie's message, if he hung around here long enough, who knew what information he might pick up to help them track down Tanya again?

But before he even reached her, Tanya leapt to her feet. Frankie turned to see who she was grinning at. Two more Russians, walking her way in the same regulation uniform as the rest. Then a third bloke with them, stocky and good-looking, dressed down in a T-shirt and jeans, with tattoos on just about every part of him but his head. He had to be the boyfriend.

Duke.

22

Frankie watched Tanya hug Duke and start chattering into his ear, as the club continued to throb all around. Then he saw Sergei talking to one of his boys – one of the lads who'd been out in the car park – and getting all animated now, and nodding Frankie's way. *Moodak*. Frankie caught the word, even over the music. Knew what it meant too. Bastard. One of Spartak's favourites. The only bloke Frankie knew who swore more than him.

'Here he is. Jack's brother, Frankie,' Tanya said, pulling Duke over.

But Duke didn't look pleased to see Frankie at all.

'You sort of met him once,' she went on, 'round at Jack's flat last year. But he was a little the worse for wear, weren't you?' She grinned.

'Er, yeah,' Frankie said.

'And you just happened to be here tonight, did you?' muttered Duke in his Mancunian drawl.

'Yeah, that's right.'

'He spotted me coming off the dance floor,' Tanya said.

Duke eyeballed Frankie, his lip curling. 'What, and you just happened to recognize her, yeah? Just like that?'

'That's right.'

'From the last time you saw her, right? From when you were unconscious and we called round at your brother's flat?'

Duke was openly mocking him now and the logic of his message was even getting through to Tanya's drug-addled brain. She slowly turned to Frankie, saying, 'What does he mean? What's going on?'

'Who fucking sent you?' Duke said, shoving his face right up in Frankie's grill.

'Whoah.' Frankie took a step back. 'I don't know what you're –'

'A problem?' said Sergei. Another one not slow on the uptake.

'Yeah, there fucking is,' said Duke.

'You,' Sergei told Frankie. 'Outside.'

They steered him back then, five of them. Gave him no choice. Out through the same fire escape as before. No bouncer there this time to even clock what was going on. Like bloody buses, they were.

Outside was just as bad. The smokers and jokers who'd been out here before had vamoosed. One of Sergei's goons slammed the fire escape door shut behind them. Frankie's adrenalin was thundering now. This really wasn't looking very good at all, even less so as Sergei opened his jacket. Shit. He was carrying a holster. He flipped the guard off, giving Frankie a good look at the weapon's grip, and nodded at two of his goons, who grabbed hold of Frankie, while a third one patted him down.

Of course, they found the padded envelope straightaway.

Though, thankfully, missed the thinner one in his other inside jacket pocket, the one with the lipstick postcard and the photos of his mum. Sergei took the phone out and held it up and muttered something in Russian. No prizes for guessing what – he was most likely grassing him up for having been out here earlier making a call. He handed it over to Duke.

'You look,' he said. 'See who he called.'

Duke's tattooed finger started punching the buttons. 'Bob, Jesús . . .' He started reading the short, *very* short, directory out loud. 'Grew . . . *Grew?* Mackenzie Grew? You prick,' he shouted at Frankie.

Great. So much for being too much *The Man from* bloody *Uncle*. Clearly Bob hadn't been quite as paranoid as he'd seemed. Duke tossed his phone away and Frankie watched it skitter across the floor and up against the wall.

'Sergei, he's working for Tommy Riley,' Duke said.

Tanya timed her entrance perfectly, squeezing in past the bouncer at the fire door, coming in right on those words.

'What the fuck?' she said, staring at Frankie. 'What the hell is going on? What do you mean, he's working for Riley? Are you?' She turned on Frankie. 'Is it true?'

'Yeah,' he said, watching Sergei now opening the padded envelope. No point in denying it. He could see exactly what was coming next.

The photo of her was proof enough that he'd been sent here to track her down. Sergei gleefully held it up.

'But . . . but why?' she said.

A good question, one that Frankie suddenly realized he

didn't have the answer to. Because whatever was going on here with these Russians, it was about a hell of a lot more than just someone wanting their goddaughter and her naughty boyfriend home. Whatever this Duke had got himself mixed up in here, it was big time and deadly. Frankie wanted no part of it.

'Because your father wants you home,' was all he could say. 'And Riley does too.'

'Because of *him*?' she spat, nodding at Duke. 'What? You think I don't know that Uncle Tommy told him to stop seeing me? Well, Uncle Tommy can fuck off. I love him. Don't I, babes?' she said, kissing Duke hard on the cheek. 'And I'm not a kid,' she snapped at Frankie. 'You can't tell me what to do.' She clawed a pack of Winston cigarettes from her little black bag, spilling a wrap of coke onto the floor by her feet as she did.

'But you are still a schoolkid,' he said. Why not? He wasn't exactly going to get another chance to talk to her, was he? And no matter what the bigger picture was with Duke, Riley and these Russians, little Tanya was still way out of her depth. 'You've got exams to take, your whole future. And all this, everything you're doing out here . . . it's not going to get you anywhere. And the only reason your dad and Tommy want you back is because they care about you.'

At least, he hoped that was true. He hoped for all their sakes that Riley wanting her back wasn't just to do with *this*, with whatever else was going down here.

'What? Those two jackals?' Her pretty lips curled into a sneer. 'Fuck them both and you.' Her own dad, a jackal. He watched Duke's dark eyes sparkle at this. Had he put that into her head?

She spat at Frankie then. *Spat*. Right in his face. He felt her saliva trickling down his cheek and, suddenly, he did remember her then. Tanya was the little girl he'd helped teach how to swim that last summer they'd been together as kids, the little girl who he'd bollocked Jack over for taking the piss out of her stork mark and making her cry. But only because he now saw that kid was long dead.

Sergei said something to the two Russians holding Frankie. They pinned his arms even tighter behind him. Good and professional, like. Sergei rolled up his sleeves.

'Now we find out why else you really here,' he said.

Bollocks. Frankie readied himself, closing his eyes and tensing his stomach. But at the same time he knew there was no point. This was going to hurt. It was going to hurt like hell.

'Right, what's going on here?'

What the hell? Frankie looked right. The Scouser. The bouncer from the front of the VIP area. Him and four of his mates had just stepped out through another fire door. Just over there to the left. But was this just more bad news? Because wasn't he working for them?

Only Frankie then realized he might be wrong. Because the two Russians holding him let go. The others stepped back too, meaning the bouncers weren't in their pocket after all. They were working for the club.

'Nothing.' Sergei stood between Frankie and the bouncers, all smiles, but not budging an inch.

'Doesn't look it, pal,' said the Scouser. He stared at

Tanya. 'She doesn't look like nothing either. Looks like she's been crying. These boys been bothering you, love?'

'She's with me,' said Duke, taking her hand in his.

The bouncer cocked his head. 'I don't believe I was talking to you.'

'She is fine,' said Sergei.

'Ditto, pal,' said the Scouser. His eyes flicked back to Tanya. 'I asked you a question.'

'Yeah,' she said, 'I'm fine.' But her shoulders had started to shake.

'You don't look it. Actually you don't look old enough to be in here at all.' He took a step towards her. 'And 'ello, 'ello, 'ello, what's all this then?' He was looking at the wrap right next to her feet. 'Underage and doing drugs and with a bunch of n'er-do-wells.'

'You what?' said Duke.

The Scouser ignored him. One of his lads behind him was already muttering into his radio. Clearly more troops would soon be on the way. 'In fact, you know what I'm thinking?' he said. 'I'm thinking the least we can do for this young lady is keep her here with us until she sobers up.'

'You can't do that,' Duke said.

'No? Or maybe you'd rather I just called the police?'

'No, you will not do that either,' Sergei said, opening his jacket, letting the Scouser see the holster, just like he had done with Frankie.

'Easy, mate,' said the Scouser. He slowly raised his arm, pointing up at the CCTV camera staring down from the rooftop.

Sergei barked something in Russian at his boys and they

moved fast to form a ring round Duke and Tanya, who were swiftly marched down the metal fire escape leading into the car park below.

'You're fucking dead,' Duke shouted, glaring back at Frankie.

Then with a clattering of boots, they were gone. The Scouser ran over to the edge of the balcony and stared down. An engine roared. Tyres squealed. Frankie watched the silver Range Rover race out through the car park entrance and into the night – right past where Frankie's cab should have been waiting, but no longer was. Frankie picked up his phone from where Duke had tossed it. Looked like he'd lucked out, it wasn't broken.

The Scouser was walking towards him already talking into his radio. 'Yeah, sorry, boss,' Frankie heard him saying. 'Their headman had a pistol. We had to let them go. But, yeah, I got the plates.' He switched off his radio and looked Frankie up and down. 'Looks like that was a close call for you then, mate.'

'I don't know how to thank you enough.'

'How about just getting the hell out of my club and not coming back?' the Scouser suggested, with what might even have been a half-smile.

Frankie stared off in the direction the silver Range Rover had gone. He suddenly felt dog-tired. 'I don't suppose I could ask you a favour,' he said.

'What? Another one? As if saving you from a beating weren't enough?'

'You never know, I might have won.'

This time the Scouser did smile. 'Jimmy,' he said, sticking out his hand.

'Frankie. Frankie James.' They shook.

'So what's this favour then?' Jimmy said.

'I need a cab, the one I paid to wait for me's buggered off.'

'Fine, stay put here and we'll call you one. I'll send one of the lads up to fetch you when it gets here.'

23

The black convertible Porsche shunted forwards then back-wards across the car park, then forwards again.

From where Frankie was standing on the club's back balcony, waiting for his cab to show, it reminded him of this little remote control car he'd had as a kid. *Whizz. Bang. Whizz. Bang. Whizz.*

He remembered the day it had died. Its battery had been low and he hadn't been able to navigate it out quite in time from behind the bar in the Ambassador Club where his dad had been working. The Old Man had been drunk and for some reason it had got right on his nerves. Frankie still remembered the sound it had made when he'd stamped it practically flat with his size ten boot.

'Now I must say she does look a tad tiddly to be trying that,' said a man, appearing at Frankie's side. A tall geezer. The kind who got rained on first in a storm. And wearing nothing but a pair of gold-rimmed mirror Aviator shades and a pair of matching, stretchy gold lamé pants. 'Oi!' he shouted down. 'Stop crunching the gears, or you'll kill the bloody box.'

'You know her?'

'Sure. Jeremy.'

'Funny name for a bird.'

'No, not her. Me.' Frankie saw he was smiling and holding out his hand. 'Jeremy Algernon Entwhistle,' he said.

'Frank Antonio James.'

They shook hands. 'Frank James? Like the bank robber?'

He meant the Wild West bandit, brother of Jesse. An old joke Frankie had heard plenty of times before.

'Yeah, which is why most people call me Frankie,' he said.

'And are you having fun here tonight, Frankie?'

'Sure. A real blast.'

'Good. I'm delighted to hear that.' He pulled a half-smoked spliff out from where it had been tucked into the waistband of his pants. 'You don't happen to have a light, do you?'

'As a matter of fact, I do.' Frankie dug into his pocket and pulled out the two books of matches and handed them over. 'Take your pick,' he said.

'Indigo Blue, get you,' Jeremy said, noticing the logo on the first book as he sparked up from it. 'You've been there?'

'No. A dwarf gave them me.'

'Ah, one of the proppers.'

'The what?'

'That's what they call them, all the cool young things working back in the West End in Sant An and outside all the bars, handing out matchbooks and flyers and trying to get tourists like you into their clubs.'

'And it's a good one, is it? This Indigo Blue?'

'The best.' He took another long drag of his spliff and

smiled. 'You should check it out, a player like you. It's the biggest party of the year there tomorrow night.'

'A player?'

'Well, yeah. Look what it says here.' He nodded down at Tanya's name and number scrawled on the other match-book, the one for the beach restaurant.

'Oh, yeah. That. It's complicated,' Frankie said, taking it back.

'*And* I saw you partying with all of those dudes in black back there,' Jeremy said.

What? Had this bloke been watching him too? Surely not, because when Frankie looked up at him, he didn't seem remotely interested. Instead, he was staring back down into the car park, where the Porsche had ceased its shunting at last. He must have been hanging out in the VIP area, that's all.

'They looked pretty hardcore,' he said.

'Yeah,' Frankie said. 'They were. Russians. Or most of them, anyway.'

'Bloody foreigners. No offence,' he quickly added to Frankie.

'Er, none taken,' Frankie said. Because surely this guy was more English than him? His voice couldn't have been more plummy if he'd tried.

'But, God, I hate them, the way they just come here and think they can take what they want . . . I mean, it's just not *cool*, you know? And it's just not how it works on an island like this. You've got to be much more . . . well, respectful. And pay your dues, and attention to traditions, because that's how it's always worked . . .'

'Well, I wouldn't worry about it too much,' Frankie said, not really getting what he was on about, and figuring he was probably just stoned. 'I don't reckon they're going to be back here in a hurry. The bouncers saw them off fairly firmly. They were pretty hardcore too.'

Jeremy grinned at this. 'Hmmm. Scousers, eh, and ex-Paras, that's a pretty lethal combination.'

Paras? Frankie had made the right call there, then, not taking that fellah on when he'd stopped him getting past that rope.

Down below, the Porsche's sunroof had now started sliding back and forth. Frankie caught a flash of blonde hair at the steering wheel, a glimpse of a green and yellow butterfly on top. Shit. Really? That girl from the dance floor? So that's where she'd gone.

'Maybe someone should tell her,' Jeremy said.

'Tell her what?'

'That she's too drunk to drive.'

'Oh, I'm sure someone or something eventually will. Maybe a sheep, or a tree, or a car.' Frankie sighed. 'Or maybe me. My guess is I'm the only one sober enough round here to help.'

'Good man,' said Jeremy, smiling. 'A knight in shining armour. Or linen, anyway.' He pinched the collar of Frankie's jacket between his forefinger and thumb. 'And good linen too.'

'Right, well I'd best be going then. Nice talking,' Frankie said.

'You too.'

'And can you let them know for me, the bouncers, the Paras, that I won't be needing a cab any more?'

'Consider it done.'

Frankie headed down the metal fire escape, the same way Duke had gone.

'Take good care of her,' Jeremy called after him. 'I mean the car as well as the girl.'

'I will.'

'And next time you feel like paying a visit to the VIP area up here, make sure to just tell them my name.'

'Yeah, sure,' Frankie called back. But he wasn't even sure Jeremy could hear him any more, with the bass rising up from the club.

'How about you let me do you a favour?' Frankie said, reaching the car. He leant against the passenger door and stared into the girl's eyes.

'Do I know you?' she asked, gazing up, more curious than alarmed.

'No. Well, apart from on the dance floor just now – you accidentally spilled my drink.'

She looked him slowly up and down. 'Oh, yeah, the boy in the suit. *And* I kissed you afterwards, I remember you now.'

'Boy?' Frankie smiled. It had been a while since anyone had called him that.

She took a cigarette out of a half-crumpled Marlboro Lights pack on the dash and fumbled with a box of matches to light it. He reached in quickly and grabbed the burning match from where it had just landed on her bare thigh.

'Thanks,' she said, shuffling in her seat and pulling her

short skirt down as near as it would get to her knee, 'that would have hurt.' She passed him the matchbox and asked him, 'Do you mind?'

He lit her cigarette for her.

'So where exactly is it you're trying to go?'

'Trying?' She looked annoyed for a second, but then laughed. 'Huh. Yes, I suppose that is right, isn't it? I can't seem to get this bastard into the right gear.'

'A hire car?'

'No, just not my car, I'm used to automatics – a friend lent it to me.'

'Nice friend,' Frankie said. Jesus. What kind of friend lent out a motor like this? Someone with way too much money, of course. But that was this place all over, wasn't it? Unreal.

'Why don't you budge over a minute?' he said. 'And let me have a go.'

'You're not going to nick it, are you?' She pouted, clambering over into the passenger seat. 'Only the friend of mine who lent it to me wouldn't be very pleased.'

'Likewise if you wrote it off.'

'Fair point.' She looked him up and down again. 'But what about you? Are you sober?'

'As a judge.'

'And the drink I spilt?'

'Water.'

Jeremy was still up there on the balcony, waving down at them. A red-haired girl had joined him and he already had his arm round her waist.

'You a friend of his?' the blonde asked.

191

'Who, Jeremy? Nah, we've only just met.'

She was looking up at the balcony. Jeremy waved again and gave them a big thumbs-up.

'Well, he obviously seems to approve of you. So I suppose I'd better give you the benefit of the doubt.'

They introduced themselves; her name was Sky.

'In that case, why don't I drive you home?' Apart from doing her a favour, this was going to be a lot more fun than a cab.

'OK, but I'm warning you, don't get any silly ideas in your head. Either about me or the car.' She tapped her little black handbag knowingly. 'I've got a gun in here and know how to use it,' she joked.

Not funny, he'd seen enough guns for one night. Strike that, one life. 'Don't worry,' he told her. 'I won't.'

He got in and turned the ignition. The engine gave a satisfying purr.

'For a knight in shining armour, you've got a very wicked glint in your eye,' she said, gazing across at him.

'I just like speed.' Shifting the car into gear, he headed for the exit. He glanced up at the balcony to wave goodbye, but Jeremy had already gone.

'It was him, Jeremy, who suggested it, actually, that I drive you home,' he said.

'Ah, well, you should have said earlier, any suggestion of Jeremy's . . .'

'He's that smart a fellah, is he?'

'Well, you'd have thought so, owning a club like this.'

'This is *his*?' So that's why he knew all about the

Russians, because those Scouse Para bouncers were working for him.

'Well, I say his. It's actually more his mother's.' They pulled out onto the road. A steady stream of cars was still heading into the car park, but ahead of them the road was clear. Frankie let it rip, gunning the Porsche along the straight, before cutting tight into the next turn.

'His mother?' he said, slowing back down. 'Christ, I hope she doesn't know what her little boy's going out dressed up in these days.'

'Oh, she knows and doesn't give a monkey's so long as he makes her a decent profit and he definitely does that. She's one of the ten, you know.'

'The ten what?'

'The families who run the island, stupid. Loads of the clubs are run by women who've been here since long before the tourists came.'

'Why women?'

'Because the men, the old men, way, way back in the old days, used to leave the best land, the farmland, to their sons, and give the useless land, the impossible-to-farm coastland, to their little girls. Only now . . .'

'Ha ha. Yes. Guess who lucked out. Sounds like some kind of rough justice to me.'

'Well said.'

'But if it's all girl power out here, then what's he doing in charge of the club?'

'Well, that's the funny thing, his mother's only had boys. Three of them. One from an English daddy.'

'Which is Jeremy.'

'And two more from Spanish stock.'

Well, at least that explained Jeremy's apparent irritation at foreigners like those Russians. This was his island and he didn't like seeing it messed with.

'As well as Kooks, his mother owns Indigo Blue.'

'Yeah, he told me to go there tomorrow night. Said it was the best.'

'Oh, it's the best.' Sky looked at him knowingly. 'And I'll be there too so you should definitely come. What happens there, well, as they always say round here, you've got to see it with your own eyes.'

The way she looked at him when she said it . . . that little half-smile . . . well, there was obviously something that was amusing about it, maybe something he really did need to see.

'Maybe I will.'

'Jeremy owns a few hotels too,' she said.

'Including, let me guess, the Mandalay?'

She looked surprised. 'Yeah, but I thought you said you didn't know him.'

'And I don't, but I'm suddenly thinking he might know me.'

Because, yeah, suddenly it was all falling nicely into place. Bob getting that call. Frankie haring it over here. Frankie leaving a message on Bob's phone confirming Tanya was here. And then bouncer Jimmy and his boys turning up in the nick of time to help save Frankie's arse, *and* doing his damnedest to split Tanya off from those wankers as well.

Yeah, no wonder old Jeremy had just been checking in on him and had even arranged for him to get a ride home.

It was almost certainly him who'd put the call in to Bob to begin with, to let him know Tanya might be there.

'But even though the boys have got it good now, one day they'll settle down, and whoever they marry, well, you can bet their mummy's going to want that female line to take over again . . .'

'And what about you?' he said. 'How do you know him?'

'Oh, it's a funny story, I used to be one of his proppers.'

'Oh, right,' Frankie said. 'Like the girls you see back in the West End?'

She elbowed him hard in the ribs. 'A lot bloody classier than that, I'll have you know. I used to work for Privilege, or Amnesia, and get rich kids up from their parents' yachts in Botafoch Marina into the clubs. I was bloody good at it too, so that's why he wanted me working for him. That and because we were tribe, still are.'

Tribe. Yeah, that made sense. You only had to look at the two of them. And what they were both wearing. Or, rather, what they weren't.

'And your destination, please, madam?' They'd reached the main road junction at last.

'The Marina. Straight on.'

'Where you used to sign up rich kids?'

'Exactly.'

'Any hotel, club or bar in particular?'

'No, I just want to go back to my boat.'

The roads around Sant Antoni and the Old Town were still logjammed. Luckily, though, Sky knew plenty of short-cuts. As he drove, she explained she'd been brought up on the islands – here and Mallorca – which was where her father still lived.

'I'm heading across in the boat to Palma tomorrow,' she told him, as they finally pulled into the Marina car park.

Despite being knackered, Frankie's heart still thudded in his chest at the word. He thought of the envelope in his pocket, the one Duke hadn't taken, the one with the postcard with the lipstick on it and the photos of his mum. Sky took his hand in hers as he switched off the engine and gently turned his wrist round to face her so she could see his watch.

'Or rather, today,' she said. 'Do you fancy coming along for the ride?'

He didn't need to answer, it was clearly written all over his face.

'But first I need a couple of hours' sleep,' she said. 'Come on, let's go crash. You look pretty knackered as well . . .'

24

'Well, I hope you're wearing some swimming trunks under those trousers.'

'Whuh? Huh?'

'Because, if not, I guess you're just going to have to come skinny-dipping, like me . . .'

Well, that certainly made Frankie open his eyes all right. A shadowy flash of movement in a circle of bright light and a tinkle of laughter and she was gone. Where? In fact, whoah? Where the hell was he anyway?

He rolled over onto his back and tried sitting up. Big mistake, shit, that hurt. He gripped his forehead tight with both hands where he'd just hit it. And rubbed it, gritting his teeth – it was all he could do not to yell out. But what had he hit it on? He peered into the gloom. A padded ceiling. He reached out and ran his finger over its soft white leather, less than two feet above him.

Then came a *splash* from outside, followed by a whoop. Phew. He twisted round to look, that circle of bright light making him wince all over again. Ugh, he was knackered, even worse than hungover. Christ, he couldn't remember being this tired in his whole life.

'Come on, what are you waiting for?' The same woman's voice as before.

And, oh yeah, now he remembered. The beautiful, drunk girl from last night. The one he'd driven back from that club to the harbour to her boat. The one she'd said she was planning on taking to Mallorca today. He half rolled, half crawled off the double bed. Shit, did that mean she'd . . . ? Had they . . . ? No. No, surely he'd have remembered if they had? And no way would he have either, right? Not with her being as pissed as she was.

But, even so, it was weird he couldn't even remember coming to bed at all. The boat, he remembered that for sure. It was a fast-looking speedboat, called something crazy-sounding. Yeah, the *Savage Monkey*. He could remember parking that Porsche in the posh private car park she'd had a gate pass for. Then climbing on board and making them both a coffee. Christ, they'd stayed up talking for ages, up on deck with a billion stars shining down from above, and her sobering up. He remembered her making him laugh.

There'd been a moment too. A 'maybe we could' moment but he'd been too far gone by then and had a headache of all things. That was it, the last thought he remembered, but certainly not getting to bed.

Then more splashing sounded outside, so he crawled across the tiny cabin to the steps leading up into the light and ducked to make sure he didn't make the same mistake again with his head. Slowly he climbed up out of the cabin, into the cockpit. Instantly, something felt wrong.

Fuck a duck, the harbour was gone. And not just the goddamned harbour, the whole bleedin' island. He grabbed hold of the steering wheel to steady himself, suddenly becoming aware of the boat rocking gently beneath him, and looked around. All he could see was clear blue sky and deep blue sea, with a couple of white sails on the horizon. But apart from that they were in the middle of nowhere. Alone.

'Off! Off! Off!' the girl – Sky, that was her name, right? – started shouting. She was swimming five yards from the boat, grinning across at him, her wet face and hair glistening in the sun.

Well, in for a penny . . . He turned his back to her and stripped off, then walked over to the side railing and took a deep breath. Hardly his natural environment down there . . . and bloody hell it looked bottomless. Were there sharks in the Med? Jellyfish? Giant squid? Only one way to find out.

The water hit him like a sledgehammer. He surfaced, gasping, to see Sky already swimming across to join him.

'Isn't it glorious?' she said.

'Er, yeah . . .' He was trying to be a gentleman and not look down, or too obviously, anyway. Well, hell, he was trying, at least.

'You certainly look refreshed. I told you that pill would work.'

'I took a pill?' No wonder he couldn't remember.

'We both did but don't worry, it was just Valium. I didn't actually tell you it was a Valium, I just said it would sort out your headache, which of course it did.'

He shook his head, a little annoyed. Pretty hard to do, actually, whilst treading water and trying not to get a stiffy. Talk about multitasking.

'Because you're like Adam Ant, right?' she said, grinning and wrapping her arms around him. 'Don't drink, don't smoke, what do you do?'

There wasn't exactly much talking after that, not much swimming either. Apart from the four or five strokes it took them both to get back to the boat. It was the first time Frankie had done it at sea, then the second time too. Funny, because he'd never been a great one for bunk-ups in cars and had never much fancied the mile-high club either, both too bloody cramped. But this on-board malarkey, well, it suited him just fine. In fact, he'd go as far as to say he was a natural at it. Probably got it from his granddad on his dad's side, the younger of the Bloodthirsty James Boys, who'd been a plumber in the merchant navy in the war.

'It's nice that, isn't it?' he said. 'The rocking motion.'

They were lying naked on the foredeck. She'd just got back from fetching them both a much needed bottle of icy water from down in the galley.

'You weren't doing too badly on your own.'

'Nor you.' He rolled over onto his side to look at her. Christ, she had beautiful green eyes. 'So, do you mind telling me where the pissing hell we are?' he said.

'The middle of nowhere.'

'Clearly.' What would happen if it was just the two of them? No Grew, no Bob, no Jesús, no Duke or Little T. No reason for him to do anything other than just hang here with her and see where it all might lead.

'What?' she said.

'What?'

'You?'

'Me?'

'You're grinning.'

'I am?' He was. 'I was just thinking, that's all.'

'About what?'

'About how nice you are.'

'Nice?' She pulled a face.

'All right. Not nice. Sexy.'

She pulled a pout.

'Funny, smart,' he tried.

'You should see me with my glasses on.'

'Nah,' he said, 'I prefer it like this. With you wearing nothing at all.'

He kissed her. Slowly, sensuously. It felt so good, he found himself wishing it could last for ever, but eventually she pulled away.

'Halfway between Ibiza and Mallorca, to be precise,' she said.

'What?'

'Where we are, you asked.'

'Blimey.'

'What? You did say you wanted a lift.'

'Yeah, I know.' He did kind of remember saying yeah to her offer. Probably around the same time he'd done that bloody Valium. Because it had kind of made sense at the time. But what was Grew going to say when he found out? Another half-memory surfaced. 'And you did say you were heading back to Ibiza later tonight?'

'That's right, after I've picked up the food for the party I'm running.'

That was it. She'd been kind of vague about her job last

night, but basically it sounded like she was a party planner. Tonight she had some rich dude's bash that she needed to get some stuff for from the big foodie markets over in Palma.

'And are you still up for meeting up? At that club you were telling me about? Indigo whatnot? Later tonight.'

'Blue . . . yes. Only my boyfriend's going to be there too . . .'

'Ah, I see.' He nodded. Idiot. Because that's what this was, right? Something casual. Something that happened in places like this a thousand times a night. But somehow it hurt more than it should.

'What about you?' she asked, watching him. 'Someone special waiting for you at home?'

'There is someone special, all right. It's just she's not waiting for me.' He tried picturing Sharon how he'd last seen her, but he couldn't. She was all London skies and concrete, it seemed like a different planet.

'Her loss, my gain.'

Rolling on top of him, she kissed him hungrily again. He pulled her in close, but then a harsh ringing sound started up below.

'Sorry, this might be work, but hold that thought,' she said, squeezing him hard between the legs, 'and I'll be back in a mo.'

She climbed off him and hurried back into the cockpit, and then out of sight down below. He couldn't understand much of her conversation in Spanish: his phrase book only took him as far as his first beer in Ibiza town. He shut his eyes and must have dozed off, because next time he opened them, he could hear the engine running and she was sitting there beside him dressed in some hippy tie-dye poncho with a mug of steaming coffee for him.

'Bloody hell, you really are an angel, aren't you?' he said, sitting up. He took a swig. 'Nicely sugared too. How did you know?'

'I didn't. Just figured you could probably use the energy after all your exertions this morning.'

He grinned. 'Ha ha, you're not wrong.'

'There's some food down below too. It's not much. Just some bread and Manchego.'

'Man what?'

'Cheese.

'I don't suppose you've got a toasted-sandwich maker, have you?' he asked. 'Because you'd be surprised at what I can rustle up.' She looked confused. 'Never mind,' he said. 'Bread and cheese will do just fine.'

'Come on, then, let's get back to the cockpit. Believe me, you're not going to want to be up here when I open this baby up. Oh, and maybe put some clothes on?' she joked. 'That's a coastguard ship over there heading our way and the last thing we want is you getting done for indecent exposure. You can shower off down below.'

This baby, as she explained twenty minutes later, over the roar of the boat's engine, was capable of doing forty-five knots on the flat and a happy thirty-eight over choppy waves like this. He felt seasick, but kept it to himself.

A good thing too, because Sky was clearly in her element, loving this shit, and he didn't want to make a tit of himself by revealing what a total landlubber he was. She obviously had him pinned down for someone far more cosmopolitan and he was enjoying playing that role just fine.

'So it's full-time, is it?' he shouted. 'This party-planning business of yours?'

'Pretty much. High season, anyway, like now. Then things quiet down in the winter when Ibiza turns into a ghost town.'

Giving the horizon a three-sixty scan with a pair of binoculars, she pushed up the throttle another notch. They were now going so fast that he nearly asked her if they needed to wear crash helmets. But she looked totally chilled, like they were out for a walk in the park.

Turning round, he saw the coastguard ship was just a dot in the distance now. A double-decker bus compared to a nice sporty little number like this. He grinned across at her. Blimey, she was some girl. He wondered who her boyfriend was – one lucky bastard, that was for sure.

'How about you, you're over here on business?' she asked, putting the binoculars down again and seeming to relax.

'No, not really.' He didn't know how to explain.

'The suit,' she said.

'Oh, right. Nah, that's just force of habit. I hardly ever dress down at home, because I run a club,' he said. 'No, not that kind of club,' he laughed. 'Not like your mate Jeremy last night, a snooker club.'

'Really?'

'Yeah, you know, a bit like pool.'

She smiled. 'I do know what snooker is. Not too much call for it out here.'

He shrugged. 'Might be that the tables don't travel so well in this heat,' he said. 'They can be pretty temperamental at times.'

She stood up and pointed. 'Look,' she said. 'Mallorca. Another half-hour and we'll be there.'

He still couldn't believe that he'd done one like this. But what if instead of worrying about what Grew was going to say, he just made sure he never found out? Yeah, sod it. Just give him a call and tell him he was still on Ibiza and make up some shit about having got lucky last night and being back at some bird's.

He ducked down into the cabin and grabbed his jacket and took out his phone. No reception. He went back up and grabbed hold of the railing to head up front where he could be out of earshot.

'Forget it,' she said. 'That's not going to work till you get to Palma. You can use the radio, though, if you like?'

'Nah, you're all right. It's nothing urgent anyway.' Grew could wait. The state he'd been in last night, he was probably still in bed. He put his phone away. Pulled out the postcard. And held it out to Sky. You never knew your luck.

'What?' she said.

'Do you know it?'

He held the card steady with the image facing her. Didn't want to risk losing it either, or he was screwed.

'Old town, it looks like. Maybe Santa Catalina,' she said.

'Where's that?'

She handed him the binoculars. 'North of the cathedral,' she said.

He focused in on the island that was growing bigger by the second now. The cathedral was impossible to miss. A massive bastard of a thing. Pretty bloody impressive for an island like this. The city of Palma stretched out in a wide arc to the right and left of it. *Never Eat Shredded Wheat*, he recited in his head, checking the compass on the boat's dash. To the left of the cathedral, there was a sandstone-coloured quarter, a jungle of mismatched stone walls and balconies.

'It's the old red-light district,' she said. 'It used to be really run down. But now it's full of up-and-coming bars and restaurants.'

'Sounds like my kind of place.' Just like Soho, in fact. But what about her? His mother? Could he really picture her living somewhere like that too? And again *why*? Why the hell would she be there? Making a new home for herself right the other side of Europe, knowing him and Jack were still there back home?

Sky flipped over the postcard and looked at the back. 'So who's the mystery girl?' She handed it to him, lipstick side up.

'That's what I'm here to find out.'

'What do you mean?'

'It's just someone who's been missing a long time. Someone who I'm hoping to find.'

'And that's all you've got to go on? A postcard? Not even an address?'

'Yeah.'

'Well, you're certainly a romantic. I'll give you that.'

'It's not like that,' he said, putting the card back in his

jacket. 'Not a girlfriend. Not an ex. Just someone I need to know's OK.' He didn't want to get into it now, about how he hoped it was his mum who'd written this, but he didn't want her thinking he was some crazed stalker either.

She gunned the engine again, bringing them swooping round into the bay, heading for shore. Showing off, she was. It was a right buzz, so much so that it nearly killed off Frankie's nerves about coming here and what he might find. Almost, but not quite.

'Maybe my dad will be able to help,' she then said, cutting their speed suddenly right down as they approached a wide grid of jetties, lined with gin palaces and yachts.

'Your dad?'

'Yeah, that's him over there. The big bugger who's waiting for us with the boathook in his hands.'

25

Sky wasn't kidding when she said her father was big. All eighteen stone and six feet of him. Alejandro was bald as a hazelnut, olive-skinned, mustachioed and wearing an oil-stained white singlet and palm-tree-patterned Bermuda shorts that showed off his weightlifter physique.

'This is Frankie,' Sky said, as Frankie stepped off the boat to join them, 'my *friend . . .*'

Alejandro nearly crushed Frankie's hand as he shook it. So much so that it left Frankie wondering if maybe he'd somehow guessed what him and his daughter had been up to out at sea.

But as they headed for the Club del Mar members' bar for a coffee, he also got to wondering who exactly was really in charge here. Because, sure, Sky might be his little girl and they clearly cared for each other, but Frankie couldn't help remembering what Sky had told him last night about the women on these islands being the real bosses, not the men.

The three of them found themselves a nice little table with a view of the ocean, and got stuck into some of the best coffee Frankie had ever tasted in his life.

There was plenty of footie banter already going down on the tables around them, where an assortment of wealthy-looking Spaniards, Germans and Brits – probably yacht owners or their skippers – were tucking into brunch. Hardly surprising. England were up against Spain this afternoon in the quarter-finals and it was bound to be a belter.

With all the strife that had gone down this last twenty-four hours, Frankie had almost entirely forgotten until he'd overheard a couple of old boys talking about it just now. And already he was thinking that, bugger me, he was going to be in even more shit than he already was. Because Balearic Bob had booked that booth down at that beach bar for them, hadn't he? And no way now was Frankie going to show.

'Hey, Frankie,' Sky said, as their waiter started clearing their coffees. 'Let me show my father that postcard.'

Frankie handed it over.

'I cannot . . . how you say?' Alejandro said, a few moments later. 'Be certain? Because these bars . . . I do not recognize them exactly. And this is strange, because I know so much of this town.' He smiled at his daughter, placing his hand on hers. 'But yes, this street looks familiar, I think Sky is right. This is somewhere nearby here in the Santa Catalina district. Or it is maybe possible somewhere around La Seu too?' He looked to his daughter for confirmation.

'*La So?*' Frankie said.

'The cathedral,' Sky explained, pointing to where its buttressed roof dominated the city skyline further along the bay.

Alejandro handed back the postcard. 'OK, yes, I think it

is that you must start over here . . .' He pointed at part of the city just above up Club del Mar.

Sky had a quick word with the waiter, who then returned a few minutes later with a guidebook. They studied the map in the back. He should be able to cover the area they were suggesting he search and still have plenty of time to get back here to meet up with Sky and cadge himself a ride back to the White Island, as she liked to call it.

'Er, *la cuenta, por favor*,' he said, snagging their waiter once more on his way past.

'Certainly, sir. Right away, sir,' the waiter answered in flawless English with a smile.

Sky and Alejandro were both trying not to smile.

'That bad, eh?' he said.

'You'll get better with practice,' she said.

Frankie banged down some cash and thanked them and said his goodbyes. Time to leave them to it. Alejandro needed to get back to the millionaire's yacht engine he'd been fixing before Sky had radioed in and Sky was picking up a shed load of *pata negra* – some kind of local ham, he'd just learned – and other delicacies to take back for her exclusive party.

Frankie set out for the main road. When he glanced back, he saw both Sky and Alejandro watching him. She'd told him he was a friend of a friend from London, but he wasn't sure how much he'd been taken in by that. Any more than Frankie had by him. A boat engineer he might be, but that endless-hours-of-mindless-dedication physique combined with those doodly little tats on his fingers, neck and arms, they spelt out just one thing: hard time. But for what? Now there was a question Frankie would love to know the answer to, but doubted he'd ever dare to ask.

He found Santa Catalina by following the signs to the burgeoning touristy district, just like she'd said. He walked through the beautiful indoor market just off the first street he hit – you could get anything here, fish, meat, fruit and veg, you name it. The outside edges were littered with little cafés and bars, a bit like Smithfield meets Borough Market. Surely he could take five minutes to enjoy another of those banging coffees – *cortado*, just like Alejandro had ordered him back at the club. With *muchos muchos azúcar*. Yeah, lovely. Now he was feeling wide awake. He picked up a few slices of that *pata negra* from one of the deli counters on the way out. Black foot pig. Even better than Pepperami. Christ, he could get used to this life, just a shame he wasn't really here on holiday at all.

He put in his call to Grew. Still no answer. Shit, he must have been battered last night. He left him a message, telling him to call him back. Then he got down to it and began working the area in a grid system from a map he picked up. As he concentrated, sweat built up on his brow. He was the only mug out here in a suit and he was one knife away from turning his trousers into shorts.

Every street he entered, he kept getting the card out and checking it against what he saw but none of them came close. He must have hit twenty or thirty businesses as well, showing the people working there her photos from the envelope in his pocket, but each time lucking out.

Restaurants, bars, clothes boutiques, tourist tat stores, he tried them all. Even the porn shops – oh yeah, this town was feeling more and more like home the longer he was here. All those questions kept popping up inside his head again about his mum. Could she really have made a home here? Was sending him this card her way to tell him well done for looking after his brother, or because she'd wanted him to come here too?

For the first time he started thinking about it. What the hell he might say to her if he did actually track her down. *Hi, Mum. So how've you been keeping?* Or, *Thanks for the card. I thought I'd just pop by and say hello.* And what would she say? Would he even bloody recognize her anyway?

He started to feel sick at the prospect. Frightened, like. Because whatever way he tried playing out meeting her in his head, somehow he just couldn't make it feel real.

As he kept on pounding the pavements, he tried keeping her face in his head, but that didn't work either. All he kept getting of her was stills, the same frozen poses from the photos he had of her at home on the mantelpiece and walls. And the same laughs and asides of the half-hour or so of video he had of her from the VHS camcorder that the Old Man had got her the year before she'd disappeared.

Finally he made it over to near that cathedral, La Seu, off the main drag, overlooking the bay. The pavements were crawling with Brits wearing England T-shirts and flags. Sweating, swearing, swigging cans and pushing prams. All blisters and bra straps and *Eng-ger-land!, Eng-ger-land!* Crikey, it didn't look quite so pretty abroad. There were Spanish flags out everywhere too, mind, hanging off the courtyard balconies, pinned up above the tapas bar doors.

He looked down at his watch, it was noon – no wonder he was feeling the heat now. Was thirsty like a camel and hungry as hell so he headed off the beaten track, sticking to his grid, still scratching every street he walked off on his map with a pen. But already, he'd pretty much covered the whole area he'd been told to search. What would he do next, give up, get himself into a bar and watch the game? Suddenly a bar seemed mighty appealing indeed. A bar and beer. Yes, a beer. He could almost feel it in his hand, taste it in his throat.

Then suddenly he stopped. What the hell? Had he just been daydreaming? He looked around, trying to get his bearings, and searched for a street sign to match up to where he reckoned he was on the map. It was easier said than done, this whole street was all scaffolding and netting. A grand exercise in sandblasting, it looked like. But still something about it gripped him, wouldn't let him move.

Feeling his heart starting to race now, he took out the postcard yet again and held it up. And, hang on, hang on. Wait one bloody minute. Because, yeah, take away all this bloody work being done and there was definitely something familiar about it all.

Yes. Bloody hell. Get in, my son. Because, right there, in between the last two bars on the strip, he saw it – and not just because he was still thirsty as hell. Right ahead was a stone water fountain with a little imp or fairy on top. Again the buildings above, stretching three more storeys up, with their neat little shutters, were exactly the same as the postcard. Yes, this was bloody it, no doubt about it, he'd hit the bloody bull.

He ran across the road and into the nearest bar where a TV was blaring in the corner. The usual pre-match guff was being chewed over, only it was in Spanish, not English. A bunch of locals glued to it, drinking coffees, smoking fags.

'Oi, mate,' he said, hurrying over to the grizzled bartender. '*Señor*,' he corrected himself, suddenly wishing they'd taught Spanish back at home instead of just bloody French.

'*Qué?*'

What? Yeah, he knew that much. 'This, mate. This,' he said, putting the postcard down on the bar top and stabbing his finger at it. 'This bar, here. Is this here?'

'Here?' the man repeated, staring down. 'Here. *Aquí? Sí. Sí es aquí.*'

Sí. Yes. Grinning, Frankie held out his hand, and when the man took it, he pumped it up and down. Un-be-bloody-liev-able. He'd done it, he'd found it. But did that really mean it? That she was somewhere near?

He pulled out the envelope with the photos of her in it. Showed them to him. But this time he got nothing. Not a flicker of recognition. But that didn't mean anything. Not necessarily. Because the photos were all of them eight years old or more, from before when she'd gone away.

He tried saying her name, even wrote it down. He tried explaining who she was, slowly, in English, but the guy didn't understand. All right, fine. Then he'd need to find someone who did, or who could translate. What about Sky? No, he checked his watch again, he wasn't meeting up with her for at least another three hours. There must be someone

214

else. Right, how many shops and bars were there showing on this card? At least a dozen. Thanking the man profusely, he headed back outside.

Time to check out every single one.

26

But, heart still pounding, ten bars later Frankie had got no further. Yeah, he'd found three or four people who spoke good enough English for him to be able to explain that he was looking for this woman in these old photos who might be living somewhere around here – none of them recognized either her or her name. But that was another thing, who said she was even using her own name any more?

He needed to get his thoughts together and headed across the road. At the end of the street was a little restaurant with red-and-white tablecloths on tables out on the pavement in the sun. This was a perfect spot for something to eat and drink, decked out with Italian football scarves in the window – and another flag he didn't recognize, a golden eagle on a pink and black shield.

It looked busy, always a good sign, but even as he was watching, a couple finished paying their bill and left. The closer he got, the more he could smell the oregano and basil. It was exactly what he needed right now, pasta, pizza, something filling. The sign up above the door said Al Duomo, half hidden by the scaffolding netting hanging down.

'This one's free?' he asked the waitress who was just starting to clear the empty table. She was a tall twenty-something with long, dark plaited hair and big brown Sophia Loren eyes.

'*Sí*, just one moment,' she said as she cleared the plates onto a tray.

Her voice was soft and friendly, but her accent was different to the rest of the people he'd been chatting to. And way more familiar too.

'You're Italian?'

'Yes.' She smiled at him curiously. '*E tu?*'

'Er, yeah.' He blushed a little. 'Well, sort of. My mum was. *Is*,' he quickly corrected himself. 'I don't really speak it myself.'

'Then maybe you should learn.'

'Yeah. Maybe.'

She smiled. 'Or maybe I should teach you a little?'

'Sure,' he said, sitting down. 'Why not?'

'*Vuoi venire a bere dopo il lavoro?*'

'*Vuoi venire a bere dopo il lavoro?*' he did his best to repeat what she'd just said.

'Not bad.'

'What does it mean?'

'You've just offered to take me out for a drink after work.'

'Right.' He laughed, embarrassed. 'And what's your answer?'

'*Ci penserò . . .*'

'Meaning?'

'I said I'll think about it.'

'Right.' Was she joking? He couldn't tell, but she looked dead serious as she continued to clear his table, before disappearing inside.

A waiter with the same thick dark hair and big brown eyes as the girl came to serve him. Her brother maybe? He spoke OK English and recommended the specials. Tuna *carpaccio*, followed by *tagliatelle pomodoro*, with truffle oil and rocket salad. Frankie smiled, thinking of Riley footing the bill – who was he to disagree? Frankie decided to ask him about the photo too, but in a bit, once he'd eaten and got his shit together.

The food was bang on, beautiful. The only problem was Frankie's craving for something a bit stronger than Diet Coke to wash it all down with. He got the starter in as fast as he could to line his stomach and, by God, was it decent. Something about it, especially the pasta sauce, proper soul food – took him right back to his childhood, it did.

'What do you mean, you don't know where you are?' It was half an hour later and he had Grew on the other end of the phone. He'd finally called Frankie back.

'Just that I met some bird and she gave me a ride back to hers.' Well, it was sort of true, wasn't it?

'More like just gave you a ride.'

Frankie ignored it. Better off just moving the conversation on, less chance of slipping up.

'So what about you? Where the hell were you last night when I rang?'

'Hammered.'

'Clearly.'

Grew laughed. 'Anyhow, you managed all right on your own, didn't you, love? At least, that's what I heard.'

'And who told you that then?'

'Never you mind. Just a little bird.'

A big posh fellah called Jeremy, more like, son of one of the ten. Who, more and more, sounded like exactly the kind of family Tommy Riley might make an alliance with if he fancied getting somehow involved in the action out here. Yeah, Frankie reckoned his theory had been right.

'Yeah? And this bird of yours, did it tell you about the bunch of dodgy Russian gangsters this Duke and little Tanya have got themselves mixed up with?'

'Something along those lines was mentioned. I did warn you not to get involved in anything without us being there.'

'The way it went down, I didn't exactly have a choice. But I'll tell you this – they're not amateurs. And whatever Duke's up to, I reckon Little T's in more danger than she thinks.'

'Which is all the more reason why we need to get her out of there and quick. And, talking of which, enough idle chitchat. Have you any idea how much these phones are costing the boss? Now what time are you getting back here, so we can have ourselves a proper powwow? You're cutting it a bit fine already if you want to watch the match.'

'Realistically?'

'Yeah.'

'It's going to be a few more hours.'

'That fit, is she?' Grew laughed. 'All right, well, make sure you come find me when you're back. But I warn you now, Bob's not going to be happy with you for standing us up at Rikitik's.'

The waitress still hadn't reappeared by the time it came for Frankie to pay the bill, but the waiter was just as keen to practise his English as she'd been. He was a big football fan too. Explained that the flags here in the window were for Unione Sportiva Città di Palermo, the Italian club the Sicilian restaurant owner supported. The waiter was from Sicily too, his father being an old family friend of the owner. He wasn't too happy about Italy having been eliminated from Euro 96 by Germany, mind, and was going to be cheering for Spain this afternoon against England. On account of how he was now living out here.

'And me also,' said the waitress, appearing by his side, and waggling her Spanish scarf at Frankie with a grin. It wasn't the only change she'd made either. The traditional black skirt and white shirt had been replaced with a red halter-neck top, three-quarter-length jeans and high heels.

'So I have decided that the answer is yes,' she said. 'About you taking me out for that drink.'

'Right. I mean, good. I thought you might have forgotten about me altogether.' Frankie stood up. 'Oh, and you look great, by the way.' He meant it. She looked knockout, in fact.

'Well, thank you.'

She looked a little taken aback, or was it amused? He really couldn't read her at all, which left him wondering if that had been the right thing to say. Because was that what this was? A date? He was none too sure about that either.

Maybe his consternation was showing on his face,

because suddenly the waiter was half smiling, half laughing at him too.

'You be careful with this one,' he warned. 'She's a real man eater.'

'Stupid brother,' she hissed, punching him hard on the arm – something that just made him grin even more.

'OK, so now we go?' she said, turning to Frankie. 'The match begins in one hour and I know the perfect place to watch.' She smiled. 'But I think perhaps first we go for a walk. To show you some sights. Oh yes, and so . . . my name is Isabella.' She shook his hand formally and even did a little curtsey. 'It is very nice to make your acquaintance.'

What the hell? Frankie could play this game too. He bowed theatrically and kissed the back of her hand. 'My name's Frankie James and it's very nice to make your acquaintance too.'

She laughed and linked her arm though his and steered him down the street. They talked about London, how she'd never been but had always wanted to visit. And a bit about her too. She was working here to improve her Spanish before going back to finish her modern languages degree in Italy. Apparently her brother was hoping to stay here and perhaps own his own restaurant one day. She pointed out various sights on the way, until finally they reached the cathedral.

'Come on,' she said. 'Even if you're not religious, it's cool as air conditioning inside.'

She wasn't kidding. It was like lying in a cool pool in a shady forest. Frankie sat on one of the pews under the vast, vaulted stone ceiling, as she went in to confession – something Frankie would never be able to do. Not just because the Old Man had blocked him and Jack getting confirmed as kids, but because of what had happened last summer.

He knew some of the things he'd done hadn't been right, but he'd had no choice, he had to help Jack. But people had got hurt and he could never forgive himself for that.

'Anyone you're missing?' Isabella said, coming back to find him after she was done. She looked too kind, too decent to have anything proper to confess. Or maybe her brother wasn't kidding. Maybe she wasn't quite the angel she appeared.

'You what?'

'Come with me and we can light a candle for them,' she said.

'Oh, right. Yeah, I suppose. Good idea.'

He walked over with her to the little collection box with the pyramid of flickering, glowing candles beside it and stuffed one of Tommy Riley's fifties in. Christ, he wondered when Tommy last set foot in a church, as Irish Catholic as he was. He'd probably have burst into flames.

'So who was it you lit it for?' she asked him, as they stepped back out into the blinding sunshine outside.

'My mum.'

'Oh, I'm sorry,' she said. 'I didn't realize.'

'No, it's OK. I mean . . .' He sighed, taking out the envelope from his pocket. He slid one of the photos out and handed it over.

'You've got her eyes *and* her cheekbones,' she teased,

gently nudging him in the ribs. 'She's very beautiful,' she said. 'How did she die?'

'She didn't, I mean, she isn't. At least, I don't think so. It's complicated,' he said. 'I meant to show this to you and your brother in the restaurant, to see if, well, to see if you knew her, but . . . well, the food was so good, I forgot.'

He took out the rest of the photos and handed them across, as he started to explain what he'd told the others. They sat down on a stone bench in the shade of a fountain and he pulled out the postcard too, the one showing the opposite side of the street to Al Duomo.

'And you really think this could be from her?' she finally asked, looking up.

He shrugged, feeling his stomach tightening. The more people he'd shown today, and the more headshakes he'd got in return, the stupider it had somehow all seemed.

'You don't recognize her then? Or her name?'

'No, but I can ask at the restaurant if you like, one of the Vaccaros might know?'

'The *Vaccaros*.' He rolled the word round his tongue. 'And who are they?'

'The owners.'

She meant the Sicilian family her brother had been telling him all about. 'Relatives of yours?'

'Our families were close back home in Sicily and they are now a very big local family here. Second-generation immigrants. Very – how do you say it? – *influente*?'

'Influential?' Frankie guessed.

'Yes, just so, which is why my brother and I came here this summer, because we knew they could find us work and we would be safe. Because in addition to being *influente*, they are exceedingly *potente* also. Powerful,' she explained.

Influential. Powerful. The way she said the words and the look on her face when she did reminded him of home. It was the same kind of wary and respectful way people spoke about families like the Rileys and the Hamiltons. Was that what these people were, gangsters? He guessed, but any help he could get with this, he'd take.

'Between them they know everyone,' Isabella said. 'In addition to the restaurant, they own a number of bars and clubs, as well as Les Roques? You've heard of it?'

'The *rushes*?'

'*Les Roques*. The Rocks. It's probably the most famous hotel on the island. In Deià. Their family home is part of it, on the hillside behind. It's where the British writer Robert Graves used to throw his parties, or so they say.' She smiled at him. 'You have heard of him, yes?'

'Actually, yeah,' Frankie said. '*I, Claudius*, wasn't it?' Blimey, she looked suitably impressed.

'Not only a pretty face,' she smiled, blushing almost as soon as she had. 'If you like, I can photocopy this and maybe ask around?' she said.

'Sure. Why not?' he said. 'That would be great.'

'And, of course, it is a good reason for you to come back and visit me.' She waggled the photo at him. 'I promise I'll keep it safe.'

'Deal.'

*

They watched the quarter-final in a place called the Corner Bar in a little square near the cathedral. The place was packed with expats – a right old adrenalin rush it was too. Most of them were yacht crews, all blonde hair and deep tans. True to form, all of them getting hammered on anything they could get their gnarly hands on. The crowd roared at all the near misses through the first ninety minutes and then extra time, chewing their nails down to the knuckles during the penalty shootout, where for once England didn't falter at all.

Frankie could almost smell it, his Ladbrokes winnings. England were going to be up against either Germany or Croatia, depending on who won that quarter-final tomorrow. He knew who he'd rather win, that was for sure.

He gave the Ambassador a quick bell while Isabella stepped out for a fag and an unfamiliar female voice picked up. Maxine, it turned out. Xandra's girlfriend. The place was so rammed, she was helping her and Slim out behind the bar. He had a quick natter with Slim and asked him to thank the others. Told them he owed them big time for running the show while he was away. He'd pay them too. A decent-sized bonus. They'd have earned it this month, that was for sure.

Slim put Jack on the line. He was absolutely wasted and wanted to know how Frankie was enjoying his cheap last-minute Ibiza break. It was on the tip of Frankie's tongue to tell him about where he actually was and what he'd been doing today. He wanted to tell him how he'd tried, but how he'd come up empty-handed, but what would have been the point? Jack would have just told him he was crazy for thinking it could have been any other way.

He asked Jack how he was healing and who he was hanging out with. He'd already asked Spartak to keep a seriously bloody close eye on him until he got back and Jack said he'd been chilling with him a lot, so Frankie felt he could rest easy over that much, at least. But even so, saying goodbye, he couldn't help thinking about that note that had been left on his car windscreen. *Had* it been about Jack last year? From that bastard Dougie Hamilton, or something further back? Could Frankie being here now be putting them all in more danger again?

He walked Isabella back to Al Duomo, where she was starting her evening shift at six, they swapped numbers and he told her he'd be in touch soon and asked her to call him straight away if she had any news for him about the photo that he'd left. She kissed him softly on the cheek when he went. Glancing back just before he rounded the corner of her street, he saw she was still standing there and could have sworn he saw her smile.

27

Sky got him back to Ibiza for just gone eight. This time there were no interludes, not even a swim, just a hardcore burn back to the Old Town that would have given Damon Hill a run for his money, the bloody speed that they'd gone.

The sun was melting on the horizon by the time they hit the port, with the whole sky burning pink, and another Ibiza night about to begin. Frankie stepped off the back of the boat onto the quay, with the two ropes Sky had just given him. Dib dib dib . . . He hooked them round the two big lumps of metal she'd just pointed at.

'How's that?' he shouted over the idling engine.

But Sky was already disappearing from sight, down below. Still in a right old rush to get all that food she'd got stashed down there in ice boxes back to the *finca* where this party of hers would be kicking off in a bit.

She'd been pretty short with him the whole way over, so much so that he wondered if she might have somehow clocked him with Isabella some time during the afternoon. Not that anything had happened. Not really, right? But, Christ, he couldn't stop picturing her eyes.

'Do you want me to call you a taxi to get you back into

town?' Sky said, climbing back up into the cockpit, having changed into a loose-fitting silk gown thingy, tied off at the waist with a belt.

No offer of a second ride in that Porsche, then. But, still, Frankie had plenty to thank her for, even if his little trip to Mallorca guttingly hadn't really turned anything up.

'No,' he said, 'don't sweat it. I'll walk.'

She grinned at him. A good grin. He reckoned he was just being paranoid then. She'd not seen him with Isabella. There were no hard feelings. She probably really was just mega bloody busy. And maybe even feeling a little guilty about this boyfriend of hers. For all Frankie knew she worked with him and was heading off to meet him in a bit. Yeah, time to make himself scarce.

'I hope your mates aren't too pissed off,' she said.

He'd told her a bit about them. Or a story about them anyway. Enough to let her know he wasn't just some weirdo hanging out here on his own. He'd said he was just over with a few lads from back home to watch a bit of footie in the sun.

'They'll be fine, they'll have to be nice to me anyway,' he said. 'The last I spoke to them' – which had been just before they'd set out from Mallorca – 'they'd sounded like they were going to need someone to carry them home.'

Grew had been well slurry. Hopefully he'd be in bed by now and Frankie could get an early night.

'But, listen, I just want to say thanks,' he said. 'For everything. What can I tell you? It's been a wicked day.' Wicked? In both senses of the word, in fact. Good times, but with big disappointments too.

'Well, stay in touch,' she said.

They'd already swapped numbers. 'I will.'

'Who knows? We might even see each other sooner than we think?'

On an island like this, anything was possible, he supposed.

*

Grew was waiting for him in reception at the Mandalay when he got back. Jesús was there too, with his shades on and an unimpressed look on his face. Clearly he'd not much enjoyed the match.

'Ah, and finally, the wanderer returns?' Grew said, looking Frankie slowly up and down. 'We are meant to be working here, you know.'

Frankie didn't even answer that. Grew was already nursing the tail end of a pint, while Jesús had a spliff poking out of his jacket pocket, and eyes like a knackered bloodhound.

'So what was the name of this lucky lady?' he said.

'Cielo,' Frankie said.

'Cielo?'

'Yeah, it's Spanish for sky.' Something he'd learned from his book. And something else he'd learned, from bullshitting the Old Man back when he'd still been at school, was to always stick as close as you could to the truth, as there was less chance of getting caught out on a lie that way.

'A local was she, name like that?'

'Yeah.'

'Nice place?'

'Yeah.'

Grew pointed at the seat opposite him at the little table. 'So break it down a little bit more for me about what the fuck happened last night.'

Frankie took him through what had happened from the moment he'd blagged himself into the VIP area at Kooks.

He then concluded: 'The long and short of it, at least insofar as what Tommy sent me out here for, is that Little T is not interested in coming home.'

'You got a chance to ask her, then, before . . . ?'

'Before they decided to kick the living shit out of me.'

'And before the security boys there turned up to ensure that this did not occur . . .'

'Your security boys – your mate Jeremy's, at least.'

'Ah, so you've worked that little connection out.' Grew looked impressed. 'Yes, he is indeed *our friend.*'

'Duke also made it perfectly sodding clear to me that it was his hide you were after as much as hers,' Frankie said.

Grew's face hardened. 'That's no concern of yours.'

'Apart from last night it nearly resulted in me getting a free Russian facelift.' Frankie smiled thinly. 'A danger I'd have liked to have been warned about, seeing as I was thinking I was only there to warn some kid off her boyfriend and persuade her to go home.'

'All right, I hear you,' Grew said. 'And, yeah, it's true. As you no doubt picked up at your meeting with him in St James's, the boss isn't exactly best pleased with young Duke.'

'What's he done?'

'That don't matter, not to you. The truth is we're not

even sure what the exact details are of what this twat's up to – especially not how these here Russians fit in. You seeing them there last night was the first any of us knew they were on the scene.'

Fine, so Frankie hadn't just been thrown out there to the wolves. He felt a bit better about that, at least.

'*Fortuna* . . .'

'What?'

'*Fortuna*,' Jesús said again. It was the first thing he'd said since Frankie had got here. Or rather, slurred. Fuck a duck. Was he drunk too? Frankie could hardly believe these two. Laying down the bloody law to him, with both of them getting merrily off their tits.

'You what?' said Frankie, still having no clue what he was on about.

'Lucky . . .' Jesús said, slowly waving his finger back and forth. 'Very . . . very . . . lucky. The best side most assuredly did not win.'

'Oh, God. You're talking about the football,' Frankie said. 'Which you bloody well lost.'

Grew lit himself a smoke, trying and failing to hide his own smile.

'You think this is funny, Grew?' Jesús said.

'No, mate. Not at all.'

'Good, because it's a tragedy.'

'I didn't know you were a Bee Gees fan,' Frankie said.

But the joke went right over Jesús's neatly coiffed head.

'All right, enough of this bollocks,' said Grew. 'Both of you please pay attention. Because as well as the bad news

231

of losing both Duke and the girl last night, we've possibly got ourselves some good news too.'

'How so?' said Frankie.

'Because 'tis the season to be jolly,' Grew said.

'You what?'

'Or to get totally off one's knockers, at least. It's the season opening of Indigo Blue,' he explained. 'Anyone who's anyone, or is planning on being anyone, is going to be there. Including, hopefully, Little T and our man Duke.'

And not just them. Sky as well. What was it she'd told Frankie last night about Indigo Blue? That had amused her so much? *What happens there, well, as they always say round here, you've got to see it with your own eyes.* Well, it now looked like he would.

'And lookee here, we got lucky,' said Grew, digging into his pocket and producing three wristbands. 'VIP tickets, no less. Which gives you twenty minutes to get shitted, showered and shaved, Frankie. Because we're leaving here in half an hour.'

So much for an early night, then. Looked like his day had just begun.

28

Indigo Blue was already rammed by the time they got there. The queues of whacked-out, half-naked clubbers stretched around the block, all of them itching to get in. Whatever hippy charm had been on display at Kooks last night, this was the opposite. Here was a way more urban crowd – the type Frankie was used to seeing round Soho on a Friday night. Nothing old school about it at all.

Balearic Bob waded right to the front of the queue, dressed in a black pork pie hat and a Hawaiian shirt so loud you could have used it to order a kebab from Romford. It wasn't to the front of the plebs' queue either, but the one roped off for VIPs. After a smattering of muttering and snarky complaints behind them, the bouncers waved Frankie and their posse through. Bob was no bullshitter, he really did know every player on this island.

They split up to search the place once they got inside, which was no easy task. First up, Indigo Blue had an 8,000 punter capacity. Second, it wasn't even just one club at all. More like a massive one with several other satellite clubs inside, each with its own separate entrance and vibes. But, lucky for them, these wristbands Bob had scored were getting them into every one.

Also it wasn't just them looking: all the bouncers and half the proppers too had been given snaps of who to look out for. After an hour or so looking, Grew decided the four of them might as well camp out in one of the better VIP areas and just wait. If Duke showed up, it was hopefully only a matter of time before they heard.

Frankie kept himself hydrated on water. These tunes were doing his head in. Yet more repetitive bollocks, and his ears were still ringing from last night. Frankie knew one thing, he was fed up with these loonies dancing all around and he wanted his bed.

The heavy beats didn't seem to be bothering the others, mind, they just kept on drinking. They all seemed to be having a great old time – plenty more trips to the bogs for all three of them. Frankie wasn't sure how smart being hammered would prove if it turned out Duke had them Russians in tow. He did try pointing this out to Grew and Bob, but they both just told him to chill.

Only then, about ten minutes after he'd got back from going to the bogs for a piss himself, Frankie found his feet starting to tap along to the music. Because – you know what? – it suddenly didn't seem half so bad. The same went for the people too, he couldn't understand why they'd been annoying him before. They were just having a good time and, frankly, what was so wrong with that?

But then *WHOOOOOOOOSH!* Frankie felt it right here in his gut like he'd just hit a speed bump at sixty miles an hour. He grinned at Jesús, who was grinning right back. Laughing, in fact.

And only then did Frankie realize what was going on.

'What the fuck have you done, you bastard?'

Jesús screwed up his perfect, tanned face in a frown. 'I don't know what you mean.'

'Don't lie to me.' Frankie felt another wave of whatever the hell was now inside him. Something way, way stronger than coke. 'What have you given me? You've slipped me something, haven't you, you twat? I can tell.'

Jesús's eyes narrowed. He looked down at the table. 'Oh no.'

'What?' said Frankie.

'I think this is a real problem. I think you're going to be off your head.'

'Wanker,' Frankie said, throwing himself halfway across the table and grabbing him by the throat.

'I would not do that, my friend,' Jesús said through gritted teeth.

'*Friend?* You wouldn't know the meaning of the word.'

Bizarrely, Jesús looked genuinely offended at this.

But Frankie wasn't falling for it. 'What have you given me? You tell me now, you prick.'

'What's going on here?' It was Bob, grabbing hold of the both of them, trying and failing to pull them apart.

Some bald bastard of a bouncer started wading in too.

'No, back off, mate, I've got this,' Bob snapped.

Frankie tightened his grip on Jesús's collar. 'This arsehole's just spiked me,' he said.

'Done what?'

'Spiked me.'

Jesús moved fast, twisting free from Frankie's grip. He was suddenly up on his feet and caught Frankie off balance and pinned his face flat to the table.

'Right, that's it. Pack it in,' Bob snarled.

'You're dead,' Frankie growled, trying and failing to tear himself free.

'It was an accident,' said Jesús.

'You bloody liar.'

'No, look!'

Jesús flung him then, actually flung him, some kind of judo throw. Frankie had no idea this bastard was as strong as that. He landed in a ball on the sofa and spun round to get up. But then he saw Jesús wasn't even trying to defend himself. He was just pointing, aghast, at his drink.

'It's true,' Jesús said. 'You took my drink, it was meant for me.'

Frankie stared across the table to where he'd been sitting. Shit, he was right. His glass of water was still sitting there, untouched. But the one next to it was empty. Jesús's. Not his.

Grew then got back and Frankie watched Bob whispering something into his ear.

'Oops,' Grew giggled, and he sat down to watch.

'What the fuck? You think this is funny?' Frankie said.

When WHOOOOSH! Here it came again. That whole wave of – what? Well, no other way to put it – pure *pleasure*, washing up and down his spine, making his whole body shiver with delight.

'What was in that?' he snarled at Jesús. 'Ecstasy?'

Because, yeah, he'd done a few pills in his time, but only when he'd already been pissed. And what he was feeling now was something way more powerful that that.

'MDMA.'

'You what?'

'The best bit of the pill. Pure. Without any crap.'

Pure. Yeah, Frankie could see that working for Jesús, just look at the bastard. Everything about him was squeaky clean. 'But how? Why?' Frankie asked, not even feeling pissed off any more, more curious.

'Most people eat it. I prefer to dissolve.' Jesús checked to see the bouncer who'd intervened earlier wasn't looking, then produced an origami sodding frog of all things and opened up its legs to reveal a little pile of well muddy-looking crystals inside. He licked his fingertip and dabbed it in before wiping it on his tongue.

'See? Tastes like death,' he said with a wince. 'Try it, if you don't believe.'

'Er, no,' Frankie said. 'But that's quite a sales pitch. You never know, it might even catch on.' He laughed again. Because, hell, it was hard to stay angry when you were feeling as bleedin' brilliant as this.

'Sorry,' Jesús said. 'Mate,' he added.

Frankie and him just looked at each other, then Frankie felt his mouth stretch into a smile.

'What's so funny?' Grew asked, lighting up a fag, and watching them shake hands.

'Nothing.' Frankie reached out for the packet. 'All right if I bum one of them off you?'

'I didn't think you did.'

237

'Yeah, but you know . . .' He sparked one up himself and sucked the smoke deep down into his lungs – and, bloody hell, it tasted good. '. . . when in Rome.'

'Ibiza,' Jesús corrected him.

And this time it was both Jesús and Frankie who started to laugh – they couldn't stop.

Frankie couldn't remember exactly when it was he decided it was a good idea to hit the dance floor, or exactly when he decided to take off his shirt. Both decisions felt spot on at the time, though, because it was melting hot in here and the tunes were ace. Banging, wasn't that how Jack had described them? Frankie had thought he was being a right knob back then, but suddenly it all made sense.

Not the only thing either; hugging suddenly made a whole lot of sense too. With this girl here now and this geezer too. He couldn't exactly hear what either of them was saying. It felt like his whole body was one big echo chamber for the bass being pumped out of the massive banks of speakers underneath and either side of the DJ's decks. But who cared, right? Words, what did they matter anyway? Everyone was happy and moving together. That was all that was really important, right?

The bloke kissed him on the cheek. Whoah, steady, mate. But that didn't really matter either, did it? The girl grabbed his hands, hauling him deeper into the crowd. Faces swirling. The bass pumping. After a while, he had no bloody idea how long he'd been here.

Water, that's what he needed now, so he headed for the bar. He'd lost the girl somewhere back there on the dance floor. But, sod it, she didn't matter. He was talking to someone else now and this bird had a bottle of iced water in her hand and poured it into his mouth then right down his chest. Bloody lovely, it felt. Then this barman was asking him what he wanted to drink. Next thing he was handing the girl a gin and tonic and was necking one himself. If the water had been good, this was nectar.

'Another,' he told the barman.

And another after that. He checked back in on Grew and the others, who were quite comfy in the VIP booth, necking their second bottle of Grey Goose vodka. In for a penny, in for a pound. So he got himself stuck into that too, neat, on ice. Bloody beautiful, it was. Then he tucked into a little bit more of that mandy too, but dabbed it this time – and, bloody hell, Jesús was right, it did taste like shite.

Jesús was faring just fine. Frankie wondered if maybe he'd misjudged him – they were having a right laugh now he'd loosened up. Frankie spotted that girl from the dance floor and waved her over past the bouncers. Next thing there must have been twenty or thirty other nutters in here round their table, off their heads, dancing. Grew chatting up some Spanish lad in a black leather codpiece, Bob up on the table swigging from a champagne bottle. Then Frankie and Jesús being pulled back onto the dance floor.

The whole crowd moved as one, Frankie with it. Hell, yeah, he never wanted to go back home.

He was turning, twisting, pumping his fist in the air, watching his arms fast forwarding then slowing up again. Faces and bodies twitched and shattered in the strobe. Then her. Was it her? Was it really her over there? Shit.

Thunk.

He was plummeting. Like he'd just dropped off a cliff. Like the bass had been pulled right out of him. Like suddenly none of this was important, none of this was real. He pushed away whoever it was who was pressed up next to him and shook their arm off. Jesus, it was Jesús.

'It's her,' Frankie screamed.

But Jesús just grinned and shrugged and pointed at his ears, carrying on dancing, turning away. Frankie twisted him back round to face him and stabbed two fingers at his own eyes, then pointed where he'd just looked. To make Jesús look that way too. Then . . . *oh, yeah* . . . He watched the Spaniard's expression switch. *Fuck, yeah.* Totally.

Because Jesús had just seen Little T too.

29

Or *them*. Because it wasn't just Little T any more. Duke, bare-chested and tattooed up like bloody Braveheart, was there too. But none of them Russians, thank God.

So what now that they'd found them? Frankie had already tried talking to her last night and had failed. Had got nowhere. Nothing had changed. Why the hell would she listen to them now?

But it didn't matter what Frankie thought because Jesús clearly did have a plan and was already making his move. *Oomph.* He grabbed hold of Duke by the back of his neck, swinging his right arm up tight into a lock. *Ouch.* A look of pure agony crumpled Dukey-boy's face, then Jesús began steering him like he was on bloody wheels – *whoosh* – deeper into the crowd.

But where? Glancing back to check that Frankie was following, Jesús headed right and now Frankie saw it – the backstage door. Just past a block of speakers to where Balearic Bob was standing hobnobbing with a bunch of miked-up thugs. Safety in numbers was always a good plan.

Frankie clocked the Russian moving in from the left just a second too late. He stepped in sharply behind Jesús, wrapping one arm around his neck and pressing the other up tight against it. He'd caught him deep in the shadows, half hidden from the rest of the club, and still out of Bob's line of sight. Just from the way Jesús froze then, it was obvious what was going down. The bastard had a blade.

Frankie grabbed a beer bottle from the shelf of one of the mirrored pillars as bass boomed up loud inside his chest. His ears hissed, then popped. Shit-a-brick. Here we go again. That last dab of MDMA he'd done was kicking in again. He was starting to soar.

Shit, he needed to focus, because it was all unravelling. Another one of them Russian bastards from last night had appeared out of nowhere and Frankie recognized this sod too. It was Sergei. The prick with the shooter who'd planned on giving him a beating. Well, up yours, mate. My turn.

Frankie moved in fast. Right in front of the wanker. Surprise, surprise, motherfucker. He swung a punch at him. Missed. Too pissed. Instead he spun himself right round and almost fell, but didn't. He saw Sergei's fist in the nick of time, ducked, smashed him hard on the bonce with the bottle. Connected. The bastard fell writhing, gripping his head as he hit the deck.

Frankie looked round for Jesús. Shit. The other guy still had hold of him and hadn't noticed Frankie yet. Frankie lurched forward, then stopped. Because, shit . . . what now? What the hell was he going to do about that knife? He couldn't go charging in there. Because the twat might just cut Jesús. Simple as that.

He turned and shouted to Bob. Then *crack*, white light, he felt the ground twisting out from under him as his head hit the sticky black floor. He felt boots piling into the back of his head and his ribs. Bastards. Bastards. He managed to grab hold of a leg and twisted it as hard as he could. Thankfully something gave and someone screamed.

Stumbling, Frankie forced himself up, cursing himself – what had he been thinking of, getting this pissed? Bodies were flying all around now. Bouncers. Russians. Duke and Jesús nowhere to be seen. Someone lamped Frankie and he smacked them right back, enough to slow them, but not stop them. He kicked out hard, but totally missed and landed on his arse.

Balearic Bob bundled past then, belly first, fast as. Who knew? All eighteen stone of him swept into the bastard who'd just been stepping in to stamp on Frankie's head and sent him flailing backwards.

Two white-shirted bouncers followed like angels sent from heaven. The Russians were driven back and he could see Duke too along with Tanya, and their mate who'd stuck that knife to Jesús's throat, nearly already at the exit now, with no one daring to slow them down.

Frankie forced himself up, his head throbbing. Jesus. Where was Jesús? He came staggering past, his face livid from where he'd just been punched. Not cut, though. No. The Russian hadn't done him, at least.

He started shouting all kinds of shit in Spanish. Then marched right forward like he was going to wade single-handedly into the Russkis. Only to suddenly stand stock-still and throw up all over the floor.

*

'Well, that was a bloody shambles, wasn't it, lads?'

Grew was furious. All four of them were back in the booth. Frankie's eye was already swelling up, he'd have a right old shiner tomorrow. Sitting next to him was Jesús, looking even worse. There was blood and water all over his shirt from where he'd tried cleaning himself up and a bit of bog roll stuffed up each nostril. It was a million miles from the Eurotrash glamour boy Frankie had first seen with Tam Jackson back on the night of the launch.

'We had one job tonight,' said Grew. 'And the backup to do what we needed. Only you two had to go getting off your heads on this shit.' He held up Jesús's little origami frog.

'It wasn't just us,' Frankie said. 'You've been in and out of that bog all night.'

'That may be,' said Grew, 'but my indulgence in the old Colombian marching powder does not put me off my game, it enhances it,' he shouted, throwing a punch at Frankie that stopped half a millimetre from his chin – one that Frankie didn't even see coming, fair cop. 'Unlike you muppets on this bollocks,' Grew went on, 'which don't seem to have enhanced anything about you apart from your ability to throw shapes.'

Jesús nudged Frankie hard in the ribs. He'd spotted a phalanx of bouncers heading their way and none of them Bob's lads from the ruck. Meaning, shit, here we go, thought Frankie. They'd probably been sent over to sling them all out.

But then he watched as they split into two groups and guess who emerged from the middle? None other than

Jeremy Algernon Entwhistle. Dressed exactly the same as last night, only this time with the addition of a matching bronze cape.

'I hear there's been some trouble,' he said.

Er, yeah, Frankie nearly said. *But luckily Superman's just flown in to sort that shit out.* He kept his trap shut, having already caused enough trouble for one night, and Jeremy didn't exactly look in a joking mood.

'The Russians,' Bob said, coming over from where he'd been calling someone on the phone.

Jeremy smiled grimly. 'I still can't believe they had the nerve to show up here.'

'Well, you did say they might.'

'*Might*, not would. It's like I told Frankie here last night, these people think they can come over here and take what they want . . . Not like you gentlemen, who are prepared to put in the work, and make the right alliances, and respect how things are done . . .'

Meaning his way. Oh yeah, Frankie could see that now all right. Him and Riley were like two peas from the same pod. They weren't the only lookee-likees here either, because Jesús was now up on his feet, and Jeremy and him gave each other a right old once over, before giving each other an even bigger hug.

It was only then that Frankie noticed it properly, when they were side by side. They had the same hooked nose and blonde hair combo, bloody hell they looked similar. Of course they had their differences too, height, for one. The tasteful lounge suit versus the superhero cape for another.

They must be brothers. What was it Sky had told him

when he'd driven her back from Kooks? That Jeremy's mum had got two other sons, both of them by local dads? Well, Frankie was guessing that Jesús here, from the way big brother Jeremy was now playfully head-locking him, was number two out of three.

'So I hear you and my brother have been misbehaving?' Jeremy said, coming over to Frankie, still steering his brother by the head.

'We had a bit of a mix-up.'

Jeremy let Jesús go. 'With your water glasses. Yes, I heard. Well, don't worry too much, it's good, pure stuff, should be wearing off soon. With any luck it won't drop you down with a crash.'

'I'll remember to feel grateful,' Frankie said.

'But, meanwhile, I hope you're not trying to get this exciting venture of mine the wrong sort of reputation? Of *ours*,' he added, nodding at Grew.

And *boom*, there was yet more confirmation – if any were needed – of what Frankie had already guessed: Riley was sticking money into this club, and whatever else Jeremy's family might need a partner, and some muscle, for. Like the drug trade, for example. Which clearly these Russians had an eye on an' all. But where did that leave Duke? Because if he was now in with the Russians, did that mean he'd screwed over Riley and Jeremy both?

'I need you to tell me what the hell is going on,' Frankie said.

'No, son,' said Grew. 'What you need right now is to get yourself back to the hotel and get a good night's sleep. I mean it,' Grew told him. No longer a mate. His boss.

'Because this shit that's gone down here tonight has only just begun.'

'We've already traced their names from their car registrations,' Jeremy said. 'It's only a matter of time before we find out where they're staying.'

Meaning he had the cops round here in his pocket too? Fuck me, this whole island was bent. No wonder the Russians fancied a piece of it.

'I tried tracing her number as well,' Jeremy told Frankie.

'Whose?' What the hell was he on about now?

'Tanya's. The one she wrote down for you on that little matchbook.'

The one for that restaurant she'd recommended, the Ca'n Costa? Hell's tits. Old Jeremy here didn't miss much, did he? He must have only gone and bloody memorized it when he'd lit himself that smoke.

For the first time Frankie started to think that maybe they would track down Duke and these Russians after all, but he started to worry about Little T too. This Jeremy wasn't someone you wanted to get on the wrong side of and he very much doubted he'd give a shit about her.

'But unfortunately we didn't get anywhere,' he said. 'Which makes me think she probably destroyed her phone. It also makes me think that her Russian friends aren't nearly as stupid as they look.'

Jeremy started talking to Jesús, and Grew shot Frankie another look. The kind that said *oi-didn't-you-hear-what-I-told-you-the-first-time-so-why-are-you-still-here-just-fuck-off*.

Frankie made to get up, but then he saw her. At least he

thought it was her – Sky. But, Christ, did she look different. All dressed up in a red corset and a black leather skirt as short as a belt, looking even more amazing than last night. To cap it all off, she was wearing a feather headdress and it was only then that he realized – was it her he'd seen in that first bar he'd sat in with Jesús, Bob and Grew? Had she been the one leading that procession? The girl in the mask? He remembered how he thought they'd even caught each other's eye.

Jeremy spotted her too and walked over and gave her a hug. Frankie watched her huddling up with him, kissing his glittery cheek, whispering something in his ear. Then she was sitting down by Frankie, kissing him on the cheek as well. He caught a whiff of her perfume and it cut right through to his brain.

'You look bloody wasted,' she said.

'I am.'

'Here, drink some water.' She giggled. 'Nice-y, icy, cool, cool water. You look like you need it,' she said.

He felt sweat pouring off his brow and he suddenly wished he could click his fingers and sober up. Whatever fun he'd just been having, it was over. All of this now, it was doing his head in. The music, these people, the noise.

'So how did your exclusive private party go?' he said. 'Whose was it?'

'My boyfriend's. His.' She tilted her head slightly towards Jeremy.

Yeah, that figured. Frankie didn't want to feel jealous, but he did. 'So what was the big occasion?'

'Well, I thought it was for his birthday, but it turned out to be this.' She waggled her engagement finger at him.

'Well, you certainly weren't wearing that on the boat . . .' He knew he sounded like an arsehole, the second he said it.

'That's because he only asked me today.' He remembered what she'd said about Jeremy settling down and marrying, and how one day that female line would pass down from his mother once again . . .

'And what are you two so busy chitter-chattering about?' asked Jeremy, sitting down next to her and draping his arms confidently across her shoulders.

'Your fiancée here was just showing me her ring.'

'And that's not all I hear you've seen of hers today, you naughty boy.'

Jeremy stared hard into his eyes and Frankie felt his skin burn. Shit, this didn't look good, did it? But then Jeremy smiled.

'And if you play your cards right tonight,' he said, 'you might even be able to do it all again.'

What the hell did that mean? Frankie watched him kissing her lingeringly on the lips, but his eyes never left Frankie's, not even for a beat.

'Because where better to continue our celebrations?' Jeremy went on, plucking a fresh bottle of champagne from the ice bucket on the table and starting to pour. 'One for you, Frankie Antonio James?'

'Er no,' said Frankie. 'Thanks, but I'm all right. I'm going to take Grew's advice, actually, and get some shut-eye.

Make sure I'm fresh for whenever you find out that address.'

One of the bouncers called Jeremy away then, leaving Frankie alone with Sky.

'He doesn't mind, then? About us?' he asked.

'*Us*. Oh, you are sweet, aren't you?' Sky said.

'What do you mean?'

'Thinking that that's what happened. That I was . . . I don't know . . . being unfaithful . . .'

'Well, weren't you?' It had certainly looked that way. The second time too.

'It's just that . . . Jeremy and I . . . we're not exclusive . . .'

'Exclusive?'

'With each other. I mean, we're kind of renowned for being the opposite, actually.'

'Renowned?'

'Yes, I thought you knew. I thought everyone did.' She put her hand on his thigh and began to gently, slowly massage it. She grinned up at Jeremy, who Frankie now saw was again watching, smiling back. 'But don't worry,' she said. 'You can see for yourself in a minute – I do hope you come play.'

Two girls appeared then, almost as if what she'd just said had been a prompt, and pulled her to her feet. Between them they were holding what Frankie at first thought was a white-feathered coat, but then realized, as they hooked it over her shoulders, was a pair of giant angel's wings. She winked at Frankie, blew him a kiss, then walked back to

250

Jeremy, who took her hand, and led her away from the booth and out into the crowd.

'Come on, lad, you're going to love this,' said Bob, pulling Frankie up onto his feet.

Frankie felt it then. The whole atmosphere of the place changing. And not just the music – though that had changed as well. The house beats were replaced by fanfares and something much more tribal underneath. The dancing began to slow and died off. Then hundreds, thousands of people's eyes were turning with the crowd parting, as Jeremy and Sky crossed the dance floor. They walked out to a raised platform in the centre, where Frankie saw semi-naked, painted performers had begun dancing and juggling and were spinning down from the ceiling on ribbons.

Frankie stayed where he was. So much for this shit being pure and him not crashing, he hardly had the energy to move. Certainly not to fight through that lot, to come play *what*? What had she meant? Enough had happened already tonight. He wasn't sure his heart could take any more.

And, besides, he could see perfectly well from up here, right? Whatever it was they were about to do. It wasn't good enough for Balearic Bob and Grew, though. The two of them were wading right in, Grew being led by the hand by the same Spanish lad in the black leather codpiece he'd been chatting to before. Bob, following, cackling in their wake.

Frankie swore he saw Sky looking back over at him then as Jeremy climbed up onto the stage and began parading himself before the baying crowd. In an instant, she was up there beside him, and as she took her clothes off, the crowd erupted in applause.

He couldn't handle any more, his skin was burning up and he knew there were only two ways out of this. Either carry on getting wasted or do like Grew said. Get himself the hell out of here and into bed.

*

The rest of his night was a blur, as his cab wound through the thronging streets before dropping him at the hotel. What he needed now was a cold hotel shower – but first he drank the water from the tap like a kid in the school gym after sports. All the while he was slapping the wall repeatedly, asking himself the same questions over and over. *Why? Why* had he done it? Screwed himself over? Not just the MDMA, but the smokes, the booze. Why hadn't he just left?

Finally he was lying down soaking on the bed. Sweating . . . spinning . . . repeating . . . half awake . . . half dreaming . . . Her in his head . . . Sky . . . the procession . . . that mask and headdress. Then up there on that stage . . . surrounded by them . . . baying . . . pointing . . . drumbeats thumping. Mixed in with the boat . . . swimming naked . . . gently rocking . . . And Isabella . . . her smiling . . . cathedral candles flickering . . . Mallorca . . . his mother . . . and then what Isabella had said –

His eyes flashed open and he sat bolt upright on the bed as the first light of dawn was creeping in through the gap in the curtains. He half fell onto the floor and stumbled for the desk and grabbed the notepad and pen and quickly scribbled the word down.

No question, he was sure of it now.

He'd heard that name before.

30

Frankie woke to the sound of ringing. Was it just in his head? He couldn't tell. He groaned, as he opened his eyes, and was met by a pristine white wall and translucent curtains shifting in the breeze. Where the hell was he? Oh shit, yeah, the hotel in Ibiza. A block of bright sunlight blazed on the ochre-tiled floor.

He started to turn his head, but grunted in pain, his neck aching. Rolling carefully onto his back, he opened his eyes again and saw that the room had started spinning. No, not the room. Just the fan. Bloody hell. It was like the beginning of *Apocalypse Now*. But who did that make him? The drugged-up poor sod who'd been given the mission of bringing Colonel Kurtz back from the jungle? Yeah, that felt about right. The poor schmuck who'd just been thrown into the thick of it without being given the full picture at all.

The ringing. It was his phone. He snatched it off the bedside table, moving away from the half-chewed pizza slice next to it, with a bite taken out of it – his? He didn't remember getting back here at all.

'Yeah, what?' he said, hitting answer.

'And a very good morning to you too.'

Mackenzie Grew. 'Bloody hell. What time is it?' Frankie said. His heartbeat spiked. Where the hell was his watch? But then he saw it on the floor, along with his pants, trousers, shirt, jacket and – bollocks – his snapped credit card. How the hell had *that* happened? All of it strewn across the suite like the fallout from a plane crash.

'Luckily for you, not wakey, wakey, rise 'n' shine time. That's going to be tomorrow morning. At five a.m., to be precise.'

'What? Why?' There was no point in even trying to kid him. Frankie didn't have a clue what he was talking about. Was it something they'd discussed last night?

'Duke, Little T and them Russians. That's when we're picking them up. We just got the call from Jeremy. We've got their address.'

Jeremy . . . oh God, yes, now he really felt sick. The room started spinning doubly. For real. Because, bloody hell, all that, it had really happened up on that stage, with all those people watching. Christ alive. With the whole crowd ogling, for God's sake.

'Some old country pad over the other side of the island,' Grew said. 'Built like a fortress. Used to be bloody owned by Denholm Elliott, I heard. A man after my own heart in more than one way. Anyway, the plan is to hit the bastards early and hit them hard.'

'Hit them?' Frankie sat up.

'Yeah, but don't you worry, we're going to have lots of backup. Everything'll be fine, so long as we play it right.'

The Russians. Little T. Duke. Jesús. Jeremy. Yet another of Riley's bloody turf wars that Frankie had somehow got himself embroiled in. He noticed the pad on the floor with just the one word written on it. He snatched it up but even the letters looked drunk – that didn't stop his heart thumping hard, there was a name.

'And how are you feeling this morning, young d'Artagnan?'

'D'ar what?'

'Tagnan. That's what Bob reckons we were last night, the Three bloody Musketeers . . .'

'Making him bloody Porthos,' Frankie said.

Grew said something he didn't catch.

'You what?'

'Nothing, I wasn't talking to you.'

Another muffled voice at the end of the phone. Sounded like Grew had company. The Spanish lad in the black leather codpiece.

'And what about today?' Frankie felt his stomach twist and he gritted his teeth, trying not to spew.

'I thought we'd take in a few sights,' Grew said. 'Maybe run a marathon or two.'

'I was thinking we wouldn't.'

Grew laughed. 'Now why doesn't that surprise me? I always did wonder what a lad your age was doing giving up so many of the good things in life. But it's obvious now, you've got no bloody brakes.'

'As I think I remember pointing out last night, I was spiked.'

'Accidentally.'

'Allegedly.'

'Oh, come on, you two boys had yourselves a right royal time.'

Got themselves a right royal kicking, more like. Oh yeah – Frankie got up and studied his black eye in the mirror – he remembered that an' all. But, Jesús, he remembered him too.

'I thought he hated me,' he said.

'Nah, he's like that with everyone when he first meets them. Aloof, I think's the right word. I reckon it's cos he's so rich.'

Rich? Oh, yeah. Minted. Him and Jeremy, both.

'So what's the story with him? What's he been doing in London?'

'Just learning the ropes, really. Kind of like a foreign exchange student, I suppose. Forging closer European ties, only with knuckledusters and guns.'

'Yeah, well, I'm going to be taking it easy today, all right?' Frankie said, pulling out his passport from his case and already gathering up his clothes. 'Probably just sleep this off then maybe hit the beach.'

More muffled voices Grew's end. Frankie smiled,

'I'll catch you later,' Grew said. 'There's something I need to do.'

Some*one*, more like.

The second he hung up, Frankie put in a call to the Ambassador. Luckily Xandra answered. He got her to go upstairs *toot sweet*.

'Yeah, yeah, that's it, through in the living room,' he said, covering the phone as he threw up in the toilet again.

'Are you all right there?' Xandra's voice came back.

'No, not exactly.'

'Food poisoning?'

'Yeah, a dodgy burger.' He couldn't bring himself to tell her the truth – that he'd just fallen off the wagon with a resounding thud. She'd been so brilliant about him getting on it in the first place. He felt shit about letting her down.

'Gross. OK, I'm here,' she said. 'And in the desk drawer, you say?'

'Right. The er . . .' He tried to visualize it. Which drawer *had* it been? 'I think it might be bottom right, or bottom left. The folder you're looking for, it's blue with elastic bands round it.' He could hear her opening and shutting the drawers.

'Top right, actually,' she said.

Frankie pushed himself up off the porcelain and flushed it, walking back out of the bathroom and doing his best to avoid his minging reflection.

'Good, that's the postcards, yeah? Have a flip through them. It's one from my mum to my dad. There's about twenty of them in all, mostly from Italy and Sicily. But the one I need you to find has a picture of a church on it and a donkey standing outside it.'

'A donkey?'

'Don't ask.' His mum had told him some hokey story about there being a religious tradition out there to push a live donkey off the top of a church.

He slid open the French doors and stepped out onto the balcony. Christ on a bike, it was shaping up already into another suffocatingly hot day.

'Ah, yeah. Here we go. I think I got it. Ha ha, very funny. Seems like your mammy had a bit of a naughty sense of humour, hey?'

Oh, yeah, there'd been a reference to the donkey's undercarriage, hadn't there? 'Right, but it's not her views on male anatomy I'm interested in. It's the name. The name of the family in Sicily she was staying with.'

'Va . . . vak something . . .'

'Just spell it out.' Frankie was already staring at the pad.

'V-A-C-C-A-R-O,' Xandra said.

'Vaccaro,' Frankie said quietly to himself, aping the way Isabella had said it when she'd told him about the family she worked for who owned the Al Duomo restaurant, and a bunch of other establishments on Mallorca besides.

'Why?' Xandra asked. 'Why's it so important?'

'Just some old family business that needs sorting.'

No way on earth could that name be a coincidence, could it? That the name of the family of Sicilian relatives his mum had used to go stay with was the same as the people who owned the only Sicilian restaurant in the street she'd sent a postcard from. If she had sent it, of course, and he'd still got no proof of that.

'OK, right. Now listen,' he said. 'You speak a bit of the dago lingo, yeah?'

'If, by which, you mean do I speak Spanish, then yes. But only to GCSE standard and I'd be lying if I didn't tell you that it's probably rusty as fuck.'

'There's something else I need you to do then, but first I need you to go get my spare credit card from where I've hidden it under the sink.'

'The sink . . . right . . . then what?'

'I want you to book me a flight.'

31

'Is everything OK, sir?' asked the stern-looking, uniformed woman at immigration control.

No, it's bloody not. The provinces of my body are bloody revolting: heart thumping, liver swelling, kidneys aching, lungs wheezing, stomach churning, brain pounding, eye throbbing, breath stinking. Oh yes, I have indeed had better days.

'Yeah, fine,' Frankie said out loud. No point bitching here of all places. It never got you anywhere at airports, messing with the man. Or woman, as it were.

'And your reason for visiting?'

Oh. My. God. It had to be his black eye. Because this was hardly the bleedin' United States. When was the last time a pasty young bloke like him had been asked something like this visiting Mallorca? When the only honest answer was, *To get laid and get pissed.*

'To visit some relatives,' he said.

The woman smiled. Good enough answer, or so it seemed. She closed his passport and handed it back. 'Have a nice stay,' she said.

'Sure.' On that note, only time would tell. But one thing

was for certain, he already had his tail up, because right there in the hotel reception back in Ibiza, there'd been a phone directory. For the whole Balearics too, not just there. And in the whole of the four islands – being Ibiza, Mallorca, Minorca and Formentera, there'd been only ten listings for Vaccaro. And all of them in Mallorca, meaning just the one family? And maybe the same family his mum was related to? Well, that's what he was about to find out.

He'd debated hard about whether to call Isabella to let her know what he was about but decided against it. For one thing, he wasn't even sure if he knew what he was about himself. This hunch of his, it could be completely wrong and he might just be about to make a total tit of himself. What's more, with someone seriously *potente* and *influente*. That was the other reason he didn't want to get Isabella involved, the last thing he wanted was to get her in trouble. Certainly not with the kind of badass the boss of this Vaccaro family was likely to be.

He bought himself a pair of black Ray-Bans and ordered a cab straight from the airport. The cabby was a sports nut, an immigrant, Brazilian. He spoke good English and started banging on about how England might win the Euros, but Brazil were odds on already for the next World Cup. And how awful it was about Brazilian Ayrton Senna dying the year before last. He reckoned some local kid called Nadal was going to be the best sports star this island had ever seen, having watched him recently at a local tennis tournament.

The names and the words all blurred into one for Frankie, as they left the sprawl of Palma and the coastal resorts behind and climbed up north into the hills. He wasn't in the mood for talking, it was all he could manage not to be sick. He had his nose to the window like a dog.

Of all the days in all his life, this had to be the worst to be hungover. Snap, snap, come on. He needed his brain to be firing on all cylinders. Not stalling like this. He made himself start all over again. For the tenth time since he'd set out that morning from the hotel to the airport. Think, come on. Think this through logically. No bloody point trying to meet this Señor Vaccaro and parlay with him if he couldn't even do that.

Step one, the postcard. It had been sent to him by name. By someone who knew him. They knew where he lived and the handwriting looked like his mother's. Maybe the lipstick could have been hers too. Step two, the location the card had been sent from. It was a road with one foreign restaurant in it, a Sicilian one, with an owner who had the same surname as the relatives Frankie's mother had used to stay with. Step three, the reason the card got sent. Yeah, here's where it got blurry, where it all started falling apart. Because why would she have come here to Mallorca?

Frankie dozed on and off, with the cabby still gamely rattling off his patter of famous sights and visitors to the island, Chopin and Michael Douglas as they drove through Valldemossa, Boris Becker and Jeffrey Archer as they crested the peak of the Tramuntana mountain range. Until, finally, he found himself snagged awake again by the mention of Robert Graves, and he saw the sign for Deià out of the window at the side of the winding hillside road.

'Les Roques is quite something,' said the cabby. 'Very expensive.'

'Yeah. So I hear.'

'I have taken many famous people to it. And, look, look, right there now . . .' He started tapping frantically at the window. '. . . your Mr James Bond himself. I had the privilege of delivering him here to the hotel from the airport only three days ago.'

He pronounced 'James' so oddly, that at first Frankie didn't quite catch it. But looking out the window, as they drove past the tall guy in shorts and a pale-pink shirt with a white panama hat on who was walking into town, he recognized him right away. Pierce bloody Brosnan, no less.

'Blimey,' said Frankie.

He'd first watched him in *GoldenEye* last year. Pretty bloody good. Preferred him to that other fellah. What's his name? Dalton? None of them a patch on Connery, mind. He was still the man. And the one Frankie had always imagined himself as when him and his brother had used to play spies as kids. Though Jack had always preferred playing the bad guys like Blofeld and Goldfinger. *Quelle* bloomin' *surprise*.

'A very nice man and very generous too,' continued the cabby, fishing for a decent-sized tip.

'Yeah, I bet he was.'

The cabby smiled at him in the rear-view mirror. 'And you? You are famous British actor too also?' He grinned, so much so that Frankie wasn't sure if he was taking the piss. 'Or a well-known DJ?'

'Me, mate? Nah, I'm nobody, just a tourist.'

The cabby looked disappointed. No need. Frankie already had a bundle of readies rolled up ready to pay him with. He handed it over, asking him to wait for him back at that nice little shaded café they'd just passed in town.

They reached the spiked cast-iron hotel gates. Shit, they were locked and security cameras glared down at them from the pillars either side. Then the gates slowly slid open, revealing a long gravel driveway snaking up through the olive groves on the mountainside up ahead.

Les Roques itself came into view half a kilometre on, a large and ancient manor house, surrounded by an impressive collection of stone outbuildings and what looked like smaller accommodation blocks. The whole place was set in an oasis of luscious green gardens, with a mix of brown dirt fields, vineyards and olive groves climbing up the mountainside towards its rocky, barren summit.

The closer you got, the prettier – and posher – it all looked. All white stone arches and balconies, with bougainvillea and wisteria hanging down. Even from the back of the cab as it pulled up in the palm-tree-shaped courtyard outside reception, the views down over the rooftops of the town and the glistening blue sea beyond took Frankie's breath away. Christ, what he wouldn't give to stay here for a few days. Just to get his shit back together and charge his batteries up.

'May I take your luggage?' a young, preppy-looking geezer dressed in pressed Ralph Lauren shorts and a matching polo shirt asked, opening the door for him.

Frankie got out. Crikey, this place even smelt expensive. All roses and God knew what else. He'd read in the plane on the way over here that the islands were all starved of water, but looking round here there was no sign of that.

'Er, no. I'm just here to meet someone,' he said.

'A resident?'

OK. Right, here we go. He should have known this wasn't going to be easy. This guy wasn't just a porter, he was here to make sure that whatever other legit guests were staying here weren't getting bothered by people who weren't meant to be here at all, people like Frankie James. He wasn't the only one either: a couple of other lads dressed in the same snazzy casual kit stood either side of the entrance. More like sentries than porters was the way that it looked.

The guy was still waiting for a reply.

No, I'm here to see Señor Vaccoro. Frankie nearly said it, but didn't. Because already he instinctively knew that it wasn't going to be as easy as that. No easier than it would be to get a meeting with someone like Tommy Riley if someone connected hadn't already vouched for you.

'Yes,' Frankie said, instead. 'I'm here to meet Mr Brosnan. Mr Pierce Brosnan.' He shot the guy his most confident smile. 'I'm a journalist from England with the *Sunday Times*.'

Probably not his best move, but once a blagger, always a blagger, and it seemed to do the trick. The guy smiled and led him through the arched stone doorway into the court-yard reception beyond. He was offered a seat at an empty cast-iron table beside a tinkling fountain. Parakeets flitted between the lush leaves and branches of exotic-looking plants and shrubs. Classical music played from hidden

speakers. No, strike that. It was only an actual bloody vio-
linist, wasn't it? Perched over there in the shade of a gnarled
and ancient olive tree.

'We've put a call into his room, but he's not answering
at the moment. What time did you say your appointment
was?'

'I didn't. But it's . . .' Frankie made a show of checking
his watch, making sure the geezer saw the weight of it too
and the make. '. . . oh, actually, I'm half an hour early.
Hmm, what to do . . . ?'

'Perhaps a coffee?'

'No, it's not good for my heart,' he said. 'But I'll tell you
what. I'm only just fresh off the plane from London. Do
you mind if I stretch my legs and take a walk round the
grounds?'

'Of course not, certainly, sir.' The waiter smiled. 'And if
you're interested in botanicals, you'll find a small information guide over there with a map listing the various rare and
exotic flora we're lucky enough to have.'

'Perfect,' said Frankie, trying not to smile too hard. The
last time he'd heard the word 'botanicals' was when Spartak had rolled a big fat one for him on Christmas Eve.

Round the back of the hotel, that's what Isabella had
told him, right? Where the family lived. He grabbed a copy
of the guide and headed out. The only problem was it was
kind of hard to tell exactly where the back was. The hotel
was one of those sprawling affairs and the deeper he delved
into the maze of neat gravel garden pathways, the more
lost he got. Of course, it would have helped if he could tell
his indigenous flora from his fauna. But there'd never been

much call for those kinds of skills back home. Another thought had started bothering him too. If even the front of the hotel felt like a fortress, God knows what the geezer's family residence was going to be like.

But then – oh, yes – right there, out of nowhere, he found it. A hard concrete driveway, lined with tall, shady trees, just the other side of a fence with *No Passado, Prohibido* written on it with a red circle around. He didn't need Xandra's help to guess what that meant – keep the hell out. And, yeah, normally, on any other little sightseeing trip, botanical or otherwise, Frankie would have heeded its message. But not today.

The fence had barbed wire on the top and was well strong-looking too, some serious shit designed to keep serious people out. But Frankie's bag was plenty strong enough and wide enough to deal with that, there was no point in messing around. The more he thought about it, the more likely he reckoned he'd chicken out and he couldn't do that. It was now or bloody never. He had to find out. Not finding out wasn't an option. It would just chew at him, eat him away.

He hit the fence at a sprint, half expecting to knock it over, but it was every bit as strong as it looked. It held firm as he scrabbled and clawed his way up.

There were dogs barking somewhere over to the right, shit. He used his bag to cover the barbs and hauled himself over, dropping down into a crouch on the other side.

He peered carefully up the driveway towards another house, every bit as beautiful as the hotel itself, but probably around half the size, perched on the hillside a hundred yards to the right. Frankie stepped out onto the drive, trying to get his bearings. He could see the hotel and the town back over there further down the hillside to the left with nothing but gardens and fences in between.

OK, sod it, just do it. Time to get himself that face-to-face. He was just hoping that Señor Vaccaro was here and he didn't get intercepted first. So he set off up the driveway, with his shadow stretching out ahead of him, the sun beating down on his brow and sweat trickling down the back of his neck.

He tried to push his nerves back down. After all, this Señor Vaccaro might be really nice. Frankie forced himself to remember why he was doing this. Because that postcard, it might have been from her . . . bloody hell, she might even be here. Now, there was a thought. Christ, it all suddenly felt so immediate. So horribly real.

Up ahead the dogs were still barking and he saw them then too. Not just them. Their handlers. Three of them. Shit. Marching right towards him, being half led, half dragged. Dobermans. Great. Why was it always Dobermans?

Then one of the handlers pointed right at him and let out a shout.

32

Should he run? No, screw that, he'd look guilty. Run and they'd let these bloody crocodiles in fur off the leash and that would be that. Because no way was he outrunning them or outfighting them either. He wouldn't stand a chance.

The first of the handlers stopped about two yards from him. His dog was snarling, spitting, looking like it hadn't had a proper meal in months. Frankie willed himself to keep cool because dogs could sense fear, couldn't they?

The bloke started shouting at him in Spanish, pointing into the bushes.

'You what, mate? *No comprendo.* I do not understand.' Frankie glanced back, to where he'd been pointing and, shit, he saw it then. The CCTV cameras covering the whole area up on top of a mast. There was another one sticking up back there in the botanical gardens. Bollocks, he'd probably been watched every step of the way.

The other two blokes pulled up alongside the first, each with different haircuts – one short, one long. Same faces, they were bloody twins. Frankie stayed exactly where he was. *Please, don't let the dogs off.* Those bastards would tear him apart. More shouting followed and then the first bloke started pointing at his bag.

'Yeah, yeah, sure, mate. You can have it.' Frankie placed it carefully on the floor and stepped back. The guy moved forward and snatched it up and began rifling through it, tipping its contents out on the ground.

'See, mate,' Frankie said. 'There's nothing in there dodgy at all.' What did they think he was, a burglar?

The guy picked up the envelope and tipped that out too. Photos of Frankie's mum fluttered down onto the ground, before the bloke snatched one of them up and started shaking it at him furiously. What, did he recognize her? No, it was something else. '*Paparazzi, paparazzi,*' he said.

'What?' Oh, shit. He meant like those bastards who were always hassling Princess Di. Maybe he thought he'd come here to spy on some of the celebs. Jesus Christ, having told them back at the hotel he was a journo suddenly didn't seem like such a smart idea.

'No.' He held up both hands. 'No *paparazzi*. No even got a camera. Look.' He pointed at the bag.

The roar of an engine. The three men turned round. Only the dogs' eyes stayed locked on Frankie. A car was coming their way from the house, kicking up dust in the air. Frankie's heartbeat started racing even faster. Great, reinforcements, like the odds against him weren't already horrific enough.

'*Inglés?*' one of the twins said.

'What?'

'*Inglés?*' He pointed at him. '*Inglés?*'

'Yes. *Sí. In*-fucking-*glés.* Me. English.'

'*Inglés*,' the guy shouted back excitedly at his two mates, and then some other stuff that Frankie didn't understand. The other guys started pissing themselves, in fact.

'I fuck your sister,' the first guy said, turning back to Frankie.

'Huh?'

'I fuck your sister, motherfucker,' he said, his smile stretching into a grin.

'You what?' Frankie couldn't believe he was hearing this right.

The twin with the buzzcut laughed even louder and said something to the others in Spanish, who both started laughing again. The open-backed four by four was getting closer by the second, fifty yards and closing. The buzzcut twin turned back to Frankie.

'I cut off your head and shit down the hole,' he said.

What the hell? Frankie didn't even know what he was meant to say to that. Cut off his head? Don't tell me these bastards were carrying knives as well? The twin said something else to him, but it got swallowed up by the noise of the engine.

Frankie gulped. A bloke on the back of the Jeep looked horribly like he had a shotgun strapped to his back. The Jeep crunched to a halt on the gravel and the engine cut.

'I've come here to kick ass and chew bubblegum – and I'm all out of bubblegum,' said the twin.'

Frankie just stared at him. 'Whuh –'

'Enough.'

The Jeep's passenger door opened and a sturdy-looking, mustachioed little bloke stepped out. Older than the handlers.

Thick grey hair swept back from a wide, furrowed brow. He marched straight up to Frankie. Right past the bastard, barking dogs. One by one they all fell silent. Worse, they even looked bloody scared. This was not good. Not good at all.

'You,' he said to Frankie. 'You do not look very happy.'

'Er . . . well, that is because,' Frankie said, 'your mate here just threatened to cut my head off and . . . well, do something pretty unspeakable, in fact . . .'

The bloke said nothing, just frowned.

'And that one,' Frankie said, 'he said something about kicking ass and chewing bubblegum . . .'

'Bubblegum? Ah,' the mustachioed guy nodded, the trace of a smile suddenly showing on his face, '*entiendo*. He and his brother, they spent a summer hiding in an old *finca* up here in the hills, where the only entertainment was American eighties action DVDs . . .'

'VHS,' the nearest twin corrected him, with an apologetic shrug.

Well, OK . . . Frankie tried to smile too, at what was clearly their idea of banter. But it was the word *hiding* not *bubblegum* that stuck with him, so to speak. Because who the hell needed to hide in a house up a mountainside unless they'd done something very, very wrong?

'What are you doing here? Why are you trespassing?' Señor Mustachio asked.

The man behind him with the shotgun slowly clambered down and came to stand by his side, the weapon now held firmly in his hands.

All right, sod it, Frankie had no choice. It was time to come clean.

'Vaccaro,' Frankie said. 'Señor Vaccaro?'

Señor Mustachio just glared. 'What of him?'

'I've come here to, well, to try and speak to him.'

'You have an appointment?'

'No.'

'You know him?'

'No.'

'And yet you decided to break into his property?'

'Because I didn't think you'd let me in if I just waltzed up and bloody knocked.'

'Waltzed?' The man looked confused. 'Like the dance?'

Frankie tried again. 'Because I know he's an important man. Because . . .' What was it Isabella had called him? '. . . because he's *influente*.' Frankie swallowed. 'And because of her . . . the woman in the pictures . . .' Frankie nodded at the twin with the buzzcut, who still had hold of one of them.

He handed it over to Señor Mustachio, who put on a pair of reading glasses and slowly studied it. Frankie spotted a tiny flicker right there below his right eye, it was enough.

'You know her . . .'

'You will wait here.'

'You do. Don't you?' Frankie took a half-step forward. Big mistake. Because the dogs were up and at him in a flash, fangs out, snarling.

'I said *wait*.' Señor Mustachio snapped something in Spanish at the nearest twin, who handed the leash of his dog over to his brother, before quickly gathering up the rest of the photos and stuffing them back into his bag.

Señor Mustachio took it and got into the Jeep, screeching it round and racing it back the way it had come. The guy with the shotgun stayed put.

'Yippee-kay-yay, motherfucker,' said the twin, kneeling on the ground beside his dog and slipping what looked like a piece of salami gently in between its glistening white teeth.

The next ten minutes didn't exactly fly by. More like limped. Sweat bled down Frankie's neck as the sun beat down. His companions kept up their insane quotations competition. It might not have exactly been improving Frankie's Spanish, but if they kept this up much longer at least he'd be fluent in Chuck Norris.

Frankie tried to stay focused. Did the bloke heading back to the house mean Vaccaro was there?

Then the pickup truck sped down the gravel path faster than before. Had his hunch been right? That his mum and this family really were somehow linked after all? That his luck had finally changed?

It took less than a second after Señor Mustachio got back out for Frankie to suss that the only change in his luck was its going from bad to worse.

Señor Mustachio started shouting at the others in Spanish. Jesus. Frankie felt his guts turn to ice. It was five against one, er, against eight, if you were counting the dogs. Which he was because already they were up and yelping for his blood again. Frankie's eyes flicked around, searching for a way out, because already he knew it – he was going to have to run.

Señor Mustachio marched up level with the three handlers. He was holding Frankie's phone and dropped it on the ground and stamped it into pieces with his heel. Reaching inside his jacket pocket, he pulled out a pistol and pointed it right between Frankie's eyes.

'Señor Vaccaro wishes to send you a message . . .'

Frankie said nothing.

'If you're lucky enough to leave this property in one piece, then you are to tell whoever sent you . . .'

Whoever sent him? 'But wait –' Frankie started to protest.

'. . . that the next person they send will end up with a bullet in their brain . . . Now run, asshole,' he said. 'I will give you a twenty-second head start. And then I release the dogs.'

33

The cabby wasn't nearly so talkative on the way back into Palma. Picking bits of gravel out of your face whilst dressed in a ripped suit and with only one shoe on will have that effect on a man.

What was it he'd asked Frankie on the way out here from the airport? If he was a film star or a famous DJ. Didn't look like either one was the first question on his mind now as he kept glancing at Frankie in the rear-view mirror. More like – what the hell happened to him to turn him into this vagrant? Just as well Frankie had given him his fare earlier, because no way would he have stopped for him now.

As well as his bag, which the boss man back there, Señor Mustachio, had nicked, Frankie had lost his plane ticket, just as he'd been scrambling over the gates at the end of that driveway, with those hounds from hell all snapping at his heels. His bundle of cash had fallen out of his pocket during his flight, and was probably halfway through being turned into Doberman shit by now.

At least he still had his passport, thank God, here in what was left of his other jacket pocket. Not that it was going to do him much good, but, still, he had another eight hours before his flight back to Ibiza and, on a day like today, who knew what might turn up? But first he'd got something else to do.

The cabby switched lanes, following the sign for the airport.

'No, mate,' said Frankie, unfolding the one crumpled photo he still had left of his mother, along with the post-card. 'Change of plan. I want you to drop me off in Palma Old Town at a little Italian restaurant there by the name of Al Duomo.'

*

'Frankie?'

'Er, yeah. Surprise, surprise.' He even said it in a Cilla Black kind of a way. Didn't exactly help clarify matters much, it had to be said.

'Oh, my God. What happened?'

'A long story.'

'But your face . . . your clothes . . . your *shoe* . . .' She reached out and touched his black eye gently with her fingertips. 'Quick. Come in. Let me clean you up.'

The restaurant was calm inside and deliciously cool. Frankie sank down at the table Isabella ushered him to in a nice dark corner. It was out of view of the few people left over from the lunchtime service, two large families chatting merrily away over coffees, and a smaller group, an old lady and a much younger woman, probably her granddaughter, he guessed. A good thing too that they couldn't see him, the

277

state he was in. He'd probably put them right off their food. Christ, he could fall asleep on a pin. Every muscle in his body ached.

'Here,' Isabella said, sitting down beside him. She'd brought a bowl of warm water and a sponge and set about cleaning him up. 'Who did this to you?'

He was still in two minds about whether to tell her the truth. Should he let on about his little trip to visit Señor Vaccaro and the only reason he'd known where to go looking for him was because of her? It would be easier not to tell her anything, to stop digging into the Vaccaros and get the hell out of here instead. Perhaps he could just bullshit and tell her he'd been mugged and needed to borrow enough money to make his way back to Ibiza and then get on with the rest of his life.

Because, yeah, that might be safer for them both. But he couldn't get Señor Mustachio's expression out of his mind. What if he really had recognized his mother? What if Frankie really was that close to finding out what had happened to her? Could he really turn back now?

'Your boss?'

'My what?'

'Señor Vaccaro?'

'He . . . he hurt you like this?'

Boom. So there it was. An easy possibility, right?

'No, or not personally,' he said. 'He ordered it . . . told his people to do it. Another guy who works for him . . . a short, squat man with a big moustache . . .'

'Giovanni.'

'That's his name?'

278

'Yes . . . he's his . . . I don't know how you say this . . . deputy?'

'*Consigliere*. Yeah, that's what I figured too.'

The last of the other two families got up and left, leaving Frankie and Isabella the only ones in the restaurant, apart from the old lady and her friend.

'But how? Where did this happen? What are you even doing back here on the island?'

He explained to her, as quickly and clearly as he could. About how he'd suddenly – he spared her the drunken, narcotic details – made the connection between the name of the man who owned this restaurant and the name of the family his mother had used to stay with in Sicily before she'd got married.

'My God. I had not yet had a chance to show him the photo you gave me. But this is what you think? That she and Señor Vaccaro are related? That you are related to him too?'

It was a crazy thought and, even crazier, it was the first time it had occurred to Frankie. He'd been so busy focusing on his mum, and whether it really was her who'd sent this card, that he'd not stopped to consider how he fitted into the jigsaw himself. He wished again he'd said something to that Giovanni about the woman in the photo being his mum, but he hadn't got the chance.

'Yes,' he said.

'But if you're wrong . . . about the card being from her, about her having a connection to this place . . . then you going there to his home, this is bad. Perhaps bad for me too.

Did you tell him that I told you where he was? Where to find him?'

'No.'

'Good. That is one thing, at least. But you should not be here. It is dangerous. Particularly dangerous now.'

'Why now?'

She lowered her voice. 'Because of her . . . that woman there . . .'

'The old one?'

'Yes. She is his . . . mother . . . the mother of Señor Vaccaro. She comes here every Sunday to eat, and often Señor Vaccaro, he will come here also . . .'

But Frankie wasn't listening. He was already up.

'No, wait, Frankie,' Isabella said.

But he was already halfway to the old lady's table.

'Excuse me. I'm sorry, but this woman,' he said. He took the crumpled photo of his mother from his pocket and held it out to her. 'Do you know her?'

Her companion was already up, staring in horror at Frankie's bloodstained shirt and bruised face. 'No, you must leave. You are not permitted to beg in here,' she said, pushing the photo away, out of the old lady's line of sight.

'No, you don't understand,' said Frankie. 'I'm not begging. I –'

But the old woman's companion wasn't listening. She shouted to the waiters behind the bar. Frankie moved past, snaking his way round her while she was distracted. He shoved the photo into the old woman's hands.

'*Qué pasa?*' a gruff voice said.

Frankie felt a firm hand grabbing his shoulder. Don't.

He just about managed to stop himself from instinctively lashing out.

'Listen, mate, I just need her to –' he said instead, starting to turn round.

'Frankie – it's you,' the gruff voice then said and Frankie found himself staring into Isabella's brother's eyes.

It all kicked off then with Isabella, her brother and the old lady's companion all talking at once. Then more voices came, followed by more movement, suddenly behind Frankie.

Bollocks. Frankie spotted Señor Mustachio at the exact same time he spotted him. He wasn't alone either, flanked by three other big lumps in suits, none of which Frankie recognized from this afternoon. So what now? Frankie had a quick look round. Running was out of the question, there was nowhere to go apart from out through the kitchen. And already half a dozen cooks were there, leering out and blocking his way.

It looked like there was nothing else for it. He was just going to have to defend himself as best he could. Giovanni's eyes were already blazing with fury as he marched towards him. He didn't look like he was afraid of getting his own hands dirty, this one.

'I'm sorry,' Frankie mouthed at Isabella. He meant it. The poor girl looked distraught and it was all his bloody fault. He pulled her quickly behind him, to make sure she didn't get hurt.

Another shout came from the oncoming pack of lads, ushering the old woman's companion and Isabella's brother out the way. Right then, here we bleedin' go. Frankie squared up to Giovanni quick – clearly he wasn't here to talk, so Frankie didn't waste his time trying. He gritted his teeth instead, the best way in his experience to stop yourself from biting off your tongue when you got hit. The least he could do was plant this bastard on his arse and teach him a lesson for ruining his suit.

He ducked the first punch, a right old haymaker, nice and easy. Good news there, then, this prick was just a street fighter. He wasn't balanced or trained and Frankie brought his knee high and hard into his gut. Then he stepped back just in time to avoid another bunch of fives thrown by the next lad in line.

All four of them were on him then, but he was sober this time and ready. Not like last night in Ibiza. Bring it on. He caught he first fellah square on the jaw, a straight right, so hard he heard the crack. Then he turned, blocked a hit from the lad to his right and a follow-up kick too. Shit, this lad knew what he was about and the bad news was the others were learning too.

Their *consigliere*, Giovanni, was back up, shouting at them, with blood trickling from his nose. They spread out then and, hell, why not? They might as well take their time about it. There was no one else here on Frankie's side and no one going to be calling the cops. Frankie took a step back, then another. Then, bollocks, he had his back against the wall. He stepped forward, feigned, drove them back a pace. Enough to give him some kick space. Right then, he had his arms up ready to block. He was planning on his first move being to the right, but, bloody hell, what was coming his way next was going to bloody hurt.

'*Lasciato!*'

Frankie braced himself, thinking it was the order to attack, but no one moved.

'Stop.'

No mistaking that one, though. Then he saw it wasn't the *consigliere* who'd spoken at all. It was Isabella's brother and with him was the old lady, the photo of Frankie's mother shaking in her hand. She was saying something, wheezing. At first Frankie couldn't quite catch it, but then he did.

'Priscilla,' she was saying.

'Yeah. Yeah, that's it,' he shouted. 'That's her. Priscilla.'

The *consigliere* was staring him down with a *yeah, so fucking what?* look on his face. Meaning he had known who she was back there on Señor Vaccaro's driveway.

'She's Priscilla James, my mother,' Frankie said. But this time it wasn't just a tiny flicker he saw underneath the *consigliere*'s right eye. It was downright shock.

The old woman started walking forward to two big lads who'd been about to introduce Frankie to the joys of Spanish hospitals.

'Mer-ther . . .' she said, her wrinkled old face crumpling even further.

'*Madre*,' Isabella told her, stepping in and taking her gently by the arm. '*Il suo nome è Frankie James di Londra*. His name is Frankie James from London,' she translated for Frankie to hear. '*E dice che questa donna è sua madre. E io lo credo*. He says this woman is his mother. And I for one believe him,' she said.

The *consigliere*, Giovanni, reached out then and, reluctantly, the old woman handed over the photograph. He looked from Frankie to it and back again, but, Christ, if it was similarities he was looking for, Frankie was screwed. She was blonde in the photo, whereas he was dark like his dad. She was petite, with him built like a brick shithouse.

But again Isabella came to the rescue. '*Gli occhi*,' she said, pointing at the photo, before again translating for Frankie. 'The eyes.'

'I asked you before, who sent you?' Giovanni said.

'No one.'

'But then . . . how?'

'Because this . . . this was sent to me.' Frankie pulled the postcard out of his pocket and held it out towards him, knowing he was screwed now if he signalled his boys to jump. He didn't even have his guard up.

The *consigliere* nodded at one of his men, who stepped warily forward and took the postcard from Frankie, but Frankie almost changed his mind. Lose this and he had nothing. Nothing left to say she might still be alive. But he did let go. Because what choice did he have? No way could he back out now.

Giovanni examined the postcard, turning it slowly over. He looked puzzled, but probably not because of the English, because of something else. What it said?

He said something to his boys, who stayed put as he then turned his back on Frankie and walked deeper into the restaurant. Frankie heard talking. First muffled, then raised voices, and he craned his neck to see, but the men still surrounding him blocked his view. Then the men parted to allow the *consigliere* back through.

284

'Very well, come,' he said to Frankie. 'I will take you to see him.'

'Who?'

'Señor Vaccaro. He's waiting for you now.'

34

Señor Vaccaro was a worn and chiselled-looking guy in his late fifties, dressed in a crisp white cotton shirt and jeans. He looked nothing like Frankie's mother, or Frankie either for that matter, not even his eyes.

He was sitting at the head of a long wooden table in the panelled private dining room at the back of the restaurant, with a plate of untouched food in front of him and a glass of red wine in his hand.

Frankie was deposited by two of Giovanni's lads in the chair furthest from him at the far end of the table, nearest the door. Señora Vaccaro, his mother, was guided to his side by her companion and sat down next to her son. Already there on the table in front of them were the postcard and the photo of Frankie's mum.

'If what you're telling us is true, then we are related,' Señor Vaccaro said. His English was every bit as flawless as his *consigliere*'s.

My God, Frankie could hardly believe what he was hearing. He wasn't crazy after all, this really *was* the same Vaccaro family his mother had used to stay with. That postcard really was from her.

'Yes.'

'If . . .' said Señor Vaccaro.

'But what reason would I have to lie?'

'That depends.'

'On what?'

'I am asking the questions.'

'Yes, I'm sorry. Anything,' Frankie said. 'Ask me anything. I swear, I've got nothing to hide.'

'How old are you?'

'Twenty-four.'

Vaccaro translated for his mother. She said nothing, nodded.

'And the name of your brother?'

'Jack. He's twenty-two.'

Another quick translation, followed by another nod.

'And your mother's full name?'

'Priscilla Maria Balistreri – which means *archer*,' Frankie said. He still remembered how his dad had always made a big joke about this, about how she'd hit the bull's-eye when she'd married him.

More translation but this time the old lady whispered something back. Her eyes locked on Frankie.

'Your childhood name . . . your *nickname*?' He said the word as though he was unfamiliar with it. 'What your mother used to call you and your brother when you were young.'

Frankie smiled. In spite of it all, the fact he was here and these bastards might still be planning on giving him a shoeing if he said the wrong thing, what his mum had used to call him way back then still brought a smile to his face.

'Laurel and Hardy,' he said.

And this time a smile crossed the old lady's face too. Just for a second, but enough for Frankie to know that whatever test this was, he'd just passed. Her look wasn't lost on Señor Vaccaro either. Frankie watched his shoulders relax. But what did it all mean? My God, he glared back out through the doorway he'd been led in through. What if she was out there right now, listening? But he couldn't see her, just Isabella and Giovanni and several of the others from next door.

'Is she here?' he said. 'Please, just tell me. Please, I've come all this way. Whatever it is . . . why ever she came here, why ever she couldn't come home . . . I don't care, I'm not here to judge her. I just want . . .'

He felt his mouth go dry then. Couldn't bring himself to say them. The kid's words dying on his tongue. *I just want my mum back . . . Please, I just want to see my mum . . .*

'She was,' Señor Vaccaro said.

'What do you mean?' Frankie felt sick. 'Has something . . . Please, has something happened to her?' But when? She'd only sent him that postcard last week.

'That I cannot tell you.'

Cannot or won't? What was this? Was Vaccaro lying to him? Adrenalin burst through Frankie and he half got up out of his chair. 'Is it you? Have you done something to her?'

'No, I assure you. She is family and we would never. It is just that we have not heard from her for a very long time.'

'But how? How is that possible?' Frankie said. 'That

postcard . . . she sent it to me from here.' He pointed at it. 'Look, see for yourself, the picture on the front . . .'

'Yes,' said Señor Vaccaro. 'But this postcard is not new. It is old. The street . . . it has changed a lot, many of these businesses are no longer here.'

'So what?' That didn't mean anything, the pictures on plenty of postcards were surely out of date. Only, yeah, Frankie remembered it now. Sky's dad at the yacht club, when he'd shown him the postcard, hadn't he said something like that too?

'And, look, the writing is faded,' Señor Vaccaro went on, holding the postcard up for Frankie to see. 'This postcard would have been written a long time ago. The postmark itself is smudged, but see here . . . the stamp, it is also old. I'm surprised it even reached you at all.'

'No, you're wrong. I'm telling you. I only got it last week.'

But even as he was saying it, a memory flashed into his mind. What was it Slim had said? About having had to pay extra postage when it was delivered? Christ, no. Please, no. Don't let what Señor Vaccaro was telling him be true.

The old lady hissed something at her companion then, and she hurriedly handed her a pair of glasses. Putting them slowly on, the old lady reached out and took the postcard from her son. More whispering followed and the companion was then sent out of the room, taking the postcard with her.

'Oi, that's mine,' Frankie said. 'Where's she going with it?'

'This restaurant, it has been renovated recently. Please bear with us just for one moment,' Señor Vaccaro said.

Frankie sank back into his chair and just stared at them in disbelief. Didn't know what to say. Everything was spinning round his head. Because what if they were right?

He looked back at Isabella in the doorway, who was staring grimly back. But her eyes were far from grim. There was just concern and kindness there and she knew these people. He couldn't believe she wouldn't warn him if they were somehow messing him about. He stared back up the table and noticed the old lady had tears in her eyes.

'*Fui lo. Lo hice,*' a voice then said behind him.

Frankie turned to see the old lady's companion was back. With her was another old woman, dressed in a black widow's shawl. She held a mop in her gnarled old hands.

'Say what?' said Frankie.

'She says it was her,' Isabella translated.

The cleaner fired off another set of rapid-fire sentences, which flew straight over Frankie's head. Señora Vaccaro hissed something at the end of the table. Turning, Frankie saw her throw her hands up in the air and cross herself, as if saying a prayer.

'This cleaner says she found it,' Isabella said, 'through there on the floor after the old radiators were taken down as part of the refurbishment. She says she stuck it in the postbox on the way home, thinking someone had forgotten to post it, but now she thinks it might have got lost down one of those old radiators years ago . . . She says she is sorry to have caused any trouble, and she feels very foolish now . . .'

'No,' Frankie said, 'thank her.'

But that was all he could say, as he found himself sinking even lower into his chair. Was that really what this was? He'd been chasing an illusion? A ghost? For all this time? Had the Old Man and Jack been right all along?

He wasn't having that because what they thought was that she'd just left. That or something bad had happened to her in England, something so bad they'd never heard from her again. But that wasn't the truth, was it? He knew that now. She'd left for a reason. And hidden here for a reason too with these people. Just because she wasn't hiding here any more didn't mean she wasn't still alive and hiding somewhere else.

'How long?' he said, his mouth going dry. He locked eyes with Señor Vaccaro. 'You said you hadn't heard from her for a long time. How long do you mean?'

Señor Vaccaro looked him straight in the eyes. 'Eight years,' he said softly. 'I'm so sorry, Frankie. I truly am . . .'

It was the first time he'd said his name.

'Tell me. Tell me what happened. Tell me how she came to be here,' he said.

Señor Vaccaro nodded. 'To begin at the beginning. Your mother, my second cousin, she used to come to stay with my family, when we still lived in Sicily, when I was a child.'

Frankie's mind was reeling. So what did this make Señor Vaccaro to him? A second cousin once removed? And his mother? The old lady was smiling sadly at him and wiping the tears from her eyes.

'Then my family moved here at the beginning of the eighties, following some trouble at home.'

A look between him and his *consigliere*: Frankie knew enough people like this back home to know exactly what kind of trouble that probably was. The kind that left you needing bodyguards and Dobermans on your property. Even a decade and a half later on.

'Your mother came here in 1988. It was my father who agreed to give her a place to stay.'

'Eighty-eight, the year she disappeared . . . or not disappeared . . . *left* . . .' Because she'd come here of her own volition. That's what Señor Vaccaro was saying. '. . . when she left us without a word . . .'

Señor Vaccaro translated for his mother. The old lady whispered something back.

'She says your mother loved you very much. Both you and your brother. And that leaving you both broke her heart. But she did it because she had no choice.'

'But why?' Frankie said. 'Why did she come here?' Why had she left him and Jack that way?

'I do not know exactly. Only that she was terrified and needed protection and had no place to hide.'

'But protection from what? From who?'

'Again, I don't know. I'm sorry, Frankie . . . she only ever spoke to my father about it.'

'Then can't we just –'

'He passed away last year.'

'I'm sorry,' Frankie said.

'Whatever secrets she might have told him, they're buried with him now.'

'You say she left eight years ago. How long was she here?'

292

'Six months. Maybe a little longer. She changed her name and worked here in the restaurant, which was when she must have written that card.'

'To what? She changed her name to what?'

'To Elena Toscano.'

'Toscano?'

'The postcard. Give it to me. Please.'

Señora Vaccaro said something to her companion, who then hurried forward to Frankie and placed the postcard in his hands. Turning it over, he read his mother's words again:

YOU WERE THERE FOR HIM. JUST LIKE I ALWAYS KNEW YOU WOULD BE.

But he still couldn't make any sense of them, because if Señor Vaccaro really was right about when this had been written, then that meant this wasn't his mother thanking him for being there for Jack last year. Then thanking him for being there for what? He stared down at the smudged postmark. You couldn't see the year, but the month looked like J – U – L something. Maybe Spanish for July was almost the same?

'Did she . . . did she ever mention anything about my brother . . . about him nearly drowning?' he asked. It was the only thing he could think of from back then. That time Jack had jumped off that bridge into the Regent's Canal.

More hurried whispered translations. Señora Vaccaro nodded sharply in reply.

'Yes.'

'Then that might be what this is about,' said Frankie.

'Something that happened a long time ago.' But, even then, he had no idea how she'd have known. 'And what happened then?' he asked. 'Why did she leave here? And where is she now?'

'You remember earlier I said that you might have reason to lie. And that you might have been sent here by someone?'

'Yes.'

'It was because we have reason to be wary.'

Wary. Now there was a euphemism if Frankie ever heard one. More like they'd nearly fed him to their dogs.

'People came looking for her,' Señor Vaccaro said. 'Here, to Palma. People from London came to track her down.'

'What people?'

'Bad people, very bad people. I did not meet them as I was away at the time, but my father did.' He pointed at a photo on the wall. A bunch of old boys, having a meal together in this exact same room.

'That is my father. There at the head of the table. Do you see the scar on his face?'

A nasty one too. Right across his jawline. Whatever had done that must have hurt. 'They did that to him? These people?'

'Yes. Just to find out, as you wish to now, where she is.'

'But he didn't tell them.'

'No.' A look of fierce pride on his face. 'And she got away that same day. She fled from here and she never came back. Though we do not know where and we have never heard from her since.'

Frankie felt like he was being crushed. Tears were welling up inside him and it was all he could do just to keep them inside. Because that's what this was, a disaster. The second he'd found her, she'd gone.

'Then I must thank you,' he finally managed to say. 'And your father. I must thank you all for everything that you've done.'

Señor Vaccaro stood and walked over to Frankie, and placed a hand on his shoulder. 'Do not look so depressed,' he said.

'No?' Frankie's voice sounded suddenly tiny, like a child's.

'No, because even though we do not know where she went, we do know this. She had with her money. A *lot* of English money. Enough to get herself somewhere safe. Enough to survive.'

35

Frankie ate with the Vaccaros, his new relatives, that night. It had to be the strangest meal he'd ever had – not the food, mind. That was wonderful – caprese salad, mushroom risotto and *brodetto* – through which another mystery was solved. The smell of the food here had reminded Frankie of his childhood since the first time he'd come here. That was because the fish stew base, Señora Vaccaro explained, was an old family recipe that Frankie's mum had learned as a child in Sicily and had added to the menu here, a part of her that still remained.

They quizzed him about his life in London, about the Ambassador, his father and Jack. They knew about them both and the Old Man being in prison and Jack nearly ending up the same last year – both stories had been big news in the English community over here, and Señor Vaccaro and Giovanni, being fluent speakers, had followed all the developments in the *Daily Bulletin*.

They asked Frankie about what he was doing here in the Balearics and he spun them a half-truth, deciding this wasn't the time to get into what he'd be flying back into later tonight, particularly as he still wasn't even sure himself. He told them instead that he was here with some colleagues from London on a business weekend. But he wondered if they'd know Jeremy and his family? How could they not know the ten families who appeared to control so much of Ibiza's nightlife, when they seemed to control a fair bit of the tourist industry over here?

But mainly what he kept thinking throughout the whole meal was that no sooner had he found out where his mother had gone than he'd lost her again. The name she'd taken when she'd lived here, that bothered him too. Elena Toscano. Was it a name his mum had travelled under after she'd fled Palma? Could she have? Señor Vaccaro had no idea whether she'd had new ID made or not. It was possible that his father might have arranged for that. Or possibly she'd moved on under a different name entirely. Because if she'd changed her name once to avoid detection, then surely she might well have done the same again?

*

It was Isabella, eventually, who took Frankie to the airport. Señor Vaccaro – who'd finally let slip his Christian name of Carlo, and had insisted on Frankie now addressing him as Uncle Carlo – had offered to drive Frankie himself. But Isabella had said that it was no problem and that she was going that way anyway.

Uncle Carlo did what he could to make Frankie's journey as easy as possible, like giving him back his plane ticket, for one thing. Seemed like the pooches hadn't gobbled it down after all, which wasn't true of the rest of his cash.

Apparently they'd torn that to shreds before the sweary twins had been able to stop them. But Uncle Carlo now more than made up for that too, by giving Frankie another thick wedge of pesetas to replace it. As well as some extra, to pick himself up some new clothes at the airport.

As Frankie bade Carlo and the rest of them farewell, he had to write their numbers down on a piece of paper, as his phone was still lying crushed back there on that driveway in Deià. He promised to call them and to visit again as soon as he could. When he looked back from Isabella's little red Fiat as she drove them away from the restaurant, he knew he'd made some friends here for life. Señora Vaccaro was openly crying and being comforted by her son, and even the lads Frankie had traded blows with – including that smooth old bruiser Giovanni – waved him off, albeit some of them with broken-lipped smiles.

Isabella was non-stop chitter-chatter all the way to the airport, like what had just happened was something they'd both read in *Hello!* And, yeah, Frankie got it. Because he was feeling like his life was no longer his own, and everything he thought he'd known was wrong. Nothing would surprise him any more.

She helped pick him out some new clothes at the Lacoste boutique at Palma airport. A gabardine jacket, T-shirt and jeans, as well as a new pair of trainers that certainly helped put a spring back in his heels.

Isabella seemed to approve too from the way she looked him up and down. All appraising, like, but still with a bit of a glint in her eyes. Which was kind of mutual, of course. Because where he'd found her pretty hot yesterday, he was looking at her through entirely different eyes now. She'd stuck up for him and had probably saved his arse from a right old beating. He grabbed her hand and led her along, as they followed the signs through to customs.

Yeah, wouldn't that be something? To be jetting off with her for real to some exotic destination? Instead of saying goodbye before more than likely heading back to Ibiza to get his head kicked in by a bunch of crazy Russian thugs.

'So . . .' she said.

Because here they now were . . . the cut-off point. People with tickets were heading through the gateway into the long snaking queue that led to customs control, while those without were heading home.

'So . . .' He smiled.

'What?'

'Just that . . . well, you know, we've been here before, haven't we?'

'Here?' She looked around, confused.

'No, not *here* here, actually here. I mean *here* . . . as in the idiom, as in the circumstances. I mean, what we're doing now, saying goodbye . . . it feels kind of the same as outside the restaurant yesterday . . . you know . . . awkward?'

'Meaning bad?' she said, frowning.

'No, not bad . . . more weird, me saying goodbye to you . . .'

'Ah . . . *me*.' She looked up at him. 'And what is it, exactly, you think about me?'

'That you're . . .'

'I'm . . . ?'

'Nice.'

'Nice?'

He tried again. 'Great.'

'And this great, it is better than nice?' She took his hands and he flinched. 'Or maybe worse?'

'No, definitely better.'

He saw she was smiling. 'OK . . .' She stepped in closer. 'In fact, good. Because I think you are very nice . . . as well as maybe a little great also too . . .'

'Just a little?'

'Maybe even a lot.'

'The only problem is . . .' he said.

'What?'

'I've been acting like a bit of a dick, lately.'

'A dick?'

'Yeah. That's, um, kind of a word for someone who keeps making bad decisions . . . who keeps getting things wrong.' And, boy, had he been doing plenty of that of late. Sharon . . . Sky . . . ending up out here on Tommy Riley's pay . . .

'You do not seem like a bad person to me.'

'No. And I don't want to be but there's stuff I need to sort out . . . before . . .' He looked down at their hands. '. . . this.'

He saw the rejection in her eyes.

'It's not like that,' he said, gripping her hands tightly in his. 'I really do like you. It's just . . .'

'Timing.'

'Yes. That's exactly it. All my problems . . . what's been

going on, what I'm heading into now . . . I need it all sorted, so I can get back to being who I really want to be.'

'The real Frankie James?'

'That's right. The very man.' He looked down at their hands, at their fingers intertwined. 'But I promise you this – I will come back.' As soon as he said it, he knew it was true.

'When?'

'The end of the summer?'

'To here?'

'Yes.'

She stared into his eyes for a moment, then nodded, as though coming to a decision. 'Then maybe that is what we should do,' she said. 'Agree to meet again. Or perhaps for the first time. To meet the real Frankie James.'

'Yes,' he said, 'I'd like that, I'd like that a lot.'

'But first I think I should give you something to remember me by.'

'Oh, yeah, and what's th—'

But he didn't get to finish his sentence and didn't need to. Because, as she rose up onto tiptoe and kissed him softly, briefly, on the lips, it was already obvious what she meant.

*

Back in his room in the Mandalay hotel in Ibiza Old Town, Frankie flopped down onto his bed and stared up at the ceiling, watching the fan go round and round. He couldn't sleep. What had happened to his mother?

Had someone on Mallorca grassed her up? But who? He

just couldn't believe it had been one of the Vaccaros. They'd loved her – still did. Meaning maybe it had been someone back in London that she'd kept in touch with?

Because that was another thing that was bothering him. Who'd told her about Jack nearly drowning? Someone must have, or how else would she have known to write what she had on that card?

The Old Man? He doubted that. The two of them had hardly been on speaking terms when she'd still been living there herself. It had to be someone else then. Someone who knew both her and Frankie well enough to know what he'd been up to. Someone at the club? Or affiliated to it? Kind Regards? Or even Slim? But why would they have sent anyone after her when they cared for her too?

Someone bad, then. Because that's what Uncle Carlo had said. Bad people. Bad people had come for her. But what kind of bad people? The kind ruthless enough to cut up that old man. Had he meant a gangster? Like a Hamilton or a Riley? Or even a cop? Some bastard like Snaresby? Someone who'd spent the last year hunting for her.

Frankie was now remembering something else too about what his mum had said to him that day she'd disappeared, when she'd made him promise to look after Jack. *No matter what happens*, she'd said. *To me or your dad, or to anyone else.* Like even then she'd known – that someone was coming for her . . . and maybe even the Old Man too?

But coming for *what*? Because that was the other question Frankie just couldn't shake. Whoever these bad people were, they'd gone to all the effort of tracking and hunting her down. Meaning she'd either done something to them, or knew something about them, or had something they wanted.

Which left Frankie with the issue of the money. Where the hell would she have got that kind of money from? And where was she spending it now?

36

The call came at 5 a.m. It was Grew telling Frankie he needed to be outside in ten minutes. A quick shower later and on with the new clothes – because, sod it, if he was heading into hell, he might as well at least go dressed to kill.

He checked himself out in the mirror, remembering how he'd caught Isabella eyeing him up in the Lacoste boutique the day before. He remembered her kissing him too. Kissing *this*, his mashed-up, bruised face. The thought made him smile, because if she liked him how he'd been yesterday – all hungover and knackered and bloodied and torn – then she really must like him, right?

Three cars stood waiting in line outside the hotel. Mercs, well pukka with tinted windows and shiny chrome hubs – the works. They were exactly the kind of convoy you'd expect any copper worth his salt to take an interest in. Only Frankie reckoned the filth around here had already been bought off.

The back door of the last car in line swung silently open as Frankie walked down the hotel steps. Jesús peered out, smiling up. Just like Frankie's, his face was looking well battered, this sunny morn. He stuck out his hand and him and Frankie shook. Grew had a point, the two of them might not exactly have hit it off to begin with, but after what they'd gone through at Indigo Blue, they were certainly now brothers-in-arms.

Jesús shuffled up to make room, dressed sharp in a suit too. Grew was on the other side of him, scowling, in jeans and a Paul Smith T-shirt.

'Late again, but at least I suppose you've sobered up,' he said, as Frankie climbed in.

I could say the same for you too, Frankie nearly said, but thought better of it. Grew didn't look in a bantering kind of a mood. He'd clearly had his three Shredded Wheat. Or a Colombian version, at least.

'So how far's this villa?' Frankie asked instead.

'You'll find out soon enough. And what the hell's happened to your face?'

'Nothing. Just the fight at the club. Or don't tell me, you forgot?'

'I don't forget anything,' Grew said. 'Right, let's fucking go.'

This last to the driver. Some local lad in Ray-Bans, who now flickered the headlights at the car in front, signalling the convoy to move off.

'Gummi Bear?' Jesús asked, offering Frankie the packet.

'Yeah, why fucking not?' Frankie somehow figured Grew hadn't thought to bring croissants.

'But not the yellow ones,' Jesús warned. 'Those are mine.'

'Fair enough.' Frankie took a green one instead and sucked it as they drove on in silence.

Somewhere along the line, he must have nodded off. Because the next thing he knew, the Merc was pulling up behind the others in a small tourist lay-by on a quiet, dry-walled country road. Down in the valley below, he could just about make out the tiled rooftops of a building among the trees.

Grew lit a smoke.

'Your job's the girl,' he told Frankie. 'Just get a hold of her and bring her back here to the car.'

The same, then, as what Tommy Riley had told Frankie back in London, when he'd first called in the favour, but everything had changed since then. Then he'd been told to persuade the girl to come back. But now? Shit. This sounded like something else entirely.

'*Get a hold of her?*' he mimicked. 'You're joking, right?'

'Do I look like Jimmy fucking Tarbuck?'

No, fair point. He did not. 'I'm not getting hold of anyone,' Frankie said. 'Not unless someone tries to get a hold of me first and I'm especially not getting hold of any girl.'

'You're working for Tommy, which means you're working for me. You'll do what you're bloody well told.'

'Just because I owe him a favour doesn't mean he can click his fingers and turn me into a kidnapper.'

'Actually, for the record, that's exactly what it means. But if it will ease your conscience, my young friend, then what I'm actually asking you to do isn't fucking kidnapping at all.'

'And how exactly is grabbing someone and bundling

them into a car against their will – and, trust me, I've met this girl, and this *will* be against her will – not kidnapping?'

'It's called protecting them. Because if you don't do it, there's a very good chance she might end up very badly hurt, or worse.'

Frankie just stared at him then. *Worse?* He meant dead.

'But I thought the whole point of this, the whole point of coming here, was to just persuade her to come back home and for you to find Duke. Which I'm guessing you now have.'

'Yeah, but now the Russians are involved.' Grew dug into a black Gola gym bag at his feet. 'And that means it all might kick off big time. And I don't want Gaz Landy's girl anywhere near it when it does.'

He took out a pistol. Frankie had only ever held one before, the one his Old Man had kept stashed behind the boiler. But this thing looked way more modern and power-ful than that.

'You ever used one of these before?'

'No,' Frankie said, 'and I don't want to either.'

'Want don't come into it. Safety off, safety on, point, *kersplat*,' Grew demonstrated, mimicking shooting the oblivious driver in the back of the head.

'I said no,' Frankie said.

'And *I* said *yes*.'

Grew shoved the gun into Frankie's hands. The way he looked at him . . . no way was Frankie going to be allowed not to take it. But no way was he going to use it either.

'Fine,' he said, sticking it inside his jacket pocket.

'What about me?' said Jesús. 'Why does he get a gun and not me?'

'Oh, don't you worry, love,' said Grew. 'You've not been forgotten.' He pulled another pistol out of his bag and handed it over.

Jesús grinned. 'Look,' he said, turning to Frankie, 'mine is bigger than yours.'

It was an' all, horrible-looking too.

'Remember,' Grew warned Frankie. 'Just the girl. Duke, the Russians . . . you leave them to us and the rest of the boys.'

'What boys?'

'Them.'

Frankie watched them, then, getting out of the two cars in front. Eight in total, and lookee, lookee, no surprise here. They were the same outfit who'd been bossing Jeremy's club, Kooks, the other night. The ones who'd cleared the Russians out, snagging their number plate in the process. But the way they were kitted out now, it didn't look like they were going to be so polite this time. All of them were armed. Their boss man too. The Scouser Frankie had had sense enough not to tangle with. Jimmy. From the way the other lads fanned out at a signal from his hand, Frankie was guessing they might be ex-Forces too.

Frankie followed Grew and Jesús out of the car and headed left, whereas Jimmy and his boys had gone right. It was hot already, the harsh morning sun beating down on the rough earth of the olive groves either side of the road.

'We had someone speccing it out here last night,' Grew said. 'Little T and a couple of women stayed over in that little guest house at the bottom of that field. While the Russians, Duke and some other fuckers they brought in kept to the main house.'

The three of them clambered over a gate and set off warily down the field, moving in single file now, with Jesús out front. Frankie had lost sight of Jimmy's boys – they must be halfway to the big house by now. Not that he could see much of it any more. Just a couple of chimneys and some red roof tiles along the valley over there to the right.

They reached the house less than two minutes later. Jesús raised a finger to his lips. What? Frankie looked around. He couldn't see anything, but his heart was banging in his chest. Then he saw it. Cages. For dogs? Bloody hell. Not again. He could still picture those bastards that had belonged to Uncle Carlo. He could still hear them too, snapping at his heels as he'd run for his life. Who knew? Maybe he would need this pistol after all?

Jesús edged forward, his own pistol now drawn. Then looked back and grinned and made an 'AOK' circle with his forefinger and thumb, before nodding at the cages. They were empty, thank God. Jesús hurried past the cages and through a gap in the tall hedgerow beyond. Frankie and Grew did the same.

The little guest house stood in a ring of palm trees on the other side. They edged round to the front. No one in sight. Just the steady thrum of cicadas in the air. They reached the terrace at the side of the house. Swimming costumes drying on sunbeds. A bright orange dragonfly darted across a deep-blue pool. A half-full bottle of rosé glinted on a cast-iron table with four glasses, also half full, next to four wicker armchairs and a pack of fags next to an ashtray on the floor. Winstons, the same brand Little T had been smoking at Kooks the other night.

'Quiet as the *Mary* bleedin' *Celeste*,' Grew muttered, glancing up at the windows, none of which had their shutters closed or their curtains drawn. 'I have a horrible feeling, our little love birds might have flown.'

'Wait here,' Frankie said, 'let me go inside and check.'

He didn't give a shit about Duke. But Little T, yeah, he'd rather it was him than these two who got to her first and at least tried to talk her out. Because whatever this Duke had done, it had pissed a lot of people off. Frankie reckoned they'd use her to get to him, if that's what it took. And if Frankie still knew one thing in this whole screwed-up mess that his life had become, it was that doing good by an eighteen-year-old girl he'd once known as a kid and keeping her safe was the one right thing he could do.

Grew nodded and Frankie tried the heavy wooden door set into the *finca*'s stone archway. It wasn't even closed and squeaked wide open with just a gentle push. He waited a second, listening, conscious of Jesús hovering at his back, that bloody pistol of his no doubt still out.

Hearing nothing, Frankie headed inside and looked around the sitting room and kitchen area. Someone had left travel bags, clothes, Rizlas and a baggie of grass on a black marble breakfast bar. The lights were still on but there was no one here.

'Tanya?' he called out. 'Tanya, it's Frankie. Frankie James. I know you probably don't want to see me right now, but I really need to see you.'

No reply. He called out again on the way up the steep flight of stone stairs leading to the first floor and went down a single gloomy, cool corridor. There were four rooms leading off it and he hit them one at a time. Not a thing in the first three, but there was something in the last – a bag. He looked inside and found women's clothes, a washbag, a wallet and – bingo – a passport.

He knew whose face he was going to see, even before he opened it, and he wasn't wrong. Little T. She couldn't have been more than fifteen when this picture had been taken, but this was definitely her. Looking round her room at the rest of her abandoned belongings, Frankie suddenly got a very bad feeling about her indeed.

*

All three of them were sat back in the Merc, driving away from the guest house. Grew hadn't spoken since he'd returned from hiking down to the big house. He'd been purple in the face when he'd got back. Frankie couldn't work out if it was heat exhaustion or fury. Even Jesús hadn't had the bollocks to ask him what the hell had happened in there.

Frankie glanced out the back window and noticed the other two Mercs still stood in the layby, but Jimmy and his lads were nowhere to be seen. Grew pulled out his fags and his Luger lighter and sparked one up. Buzzing down the window, he blew a fat lungful of smoke outside.

'OK . . .' he finally said. More of a sigh.

'It's OK?' Jesús looked surprised.

'No, it's fucking not,' snapped Grew. 'It's as far from fucking OK as it's possible to fucking be.'

In a series of snarls, sweary tirades and even the occasional bark, he told them what had gone down. Or, rather, what hadn't. The raid on the Russians' pad had been a failure. Because there'd been no one bloody there. No Russians, no Little T, no Duke. No nothing – apart from a note.

'What kind of note?' Frankie said.

'You really want to know?'

Yeah, he did. Riley had given him a job, to get that girl back, that girl who still wasn't here. 'Will you have to kill me if you tell me?' he said.

'Only if you ever tell anyone else.'

'I was joking.'

'I wasn't.' Grew stubbed his fag out on his Gola bag. 'Tommy gave Duke some money,' he said. 'A lot of money to go to Amsterdam and buy some merch. A lot of merch. Pills . . . coke . . . To send out here.'

'To us,' said Jesús. 'My people, my brother.'

OK, right. Frankie got it now. All that shit had been destined for Tommy's chosen distribution partners, whose network was supposed to have been dealing it on. 'Only let me guess,' Frankie said. 'Duke never delivered.'

Jesús nodded. 'Correct.'

'Our guess is the prick did a deal with these Russians instead, who clearly fancy getting a foothold out here,' Grew said.

'But who won't,' Jesús said. Not a comment, just a statement of fact.

'He obviously planned to keep the money for himself,'

Grew went on, 'and then vanish off the face of the earth. With Little T right by his side as collateral, like. A human shield. Because he probably thought her dad and godfather might not then come after him and risk her getting hurt.'

Only they already had. At least Tommy had. Clearly caring a lot less about her well-being than he did about his missing merch. Or his and Gaz's merch, leastways, seeing as how they were partnered up. Jackals. Wasn't that what Little T had called them? Even if she didn't know anything about what her boyfriend was up to – which was still a possibility – in that way at least, she'd been right.

'Only we turned up then, didn't we?' Grew said. 'Right while Duke was waiting for the merchandise to arrive from Amsterdam so he could complete his deal. Which we reckon it did last night, judging by the ripped-up baggies and testing kit Jimmy and his lads just found back there in the main house.' Grew smiled grimly. 'But, you see, I'm guessing these Russians were a little smarter than Duke had reckoned on. They kept him close, see? In sight? To see if they could trust him proper, like. And that's where I'm guessing things started to go wrong.'

'Wrong?'

'Oh, yes. Very wrong, for Duke, that is. Because no matter what bullshit he might have spun this Russian gang, probably about him being the big man and this being his gear to sell, I reckon us turning up here and tracking them down probably made them begin to suspect that this gear they'd just given him all that money for, it belonged to somebody else. Somebody well connected out here.' Grew slowly shook his head. 'Which is probably when he decided to do one.'

'A runner?' Frankie said.

'Exactly, and fast. It must have been some time last night he scarpered with their money, leaving poor Little T behind, so they wouldn't guess he was gone until it was too late. Leaving them with all our merchandise, which they've now correctly guessed we want back . . .' Grew reached into his pocket and pulled out a folded piece of paper 'And which it seems they're now prepared to give us, so long as they get back the cash they paid Duke for it . . .'

'So that's what that note is about? They want to do an exchange?'

'Duke and their cash, in return for Little T and our gear. Thereby leaving them and us even . . . and off each other's backs. And Duke . . . well, Christ knows what they're planning on doing to him. But I'm guessing it's not shaking hands.'

Frankie stared at the note and pictured Little T, not only ditched by that bastard, but kidnapped by those Russians as well. Nothing but a bargaining chip and something that would be worth sweet FA to them if the deal that they wanted went sour.

'So what now?'

'Well, that, Frankie, is the million-dollar question. Quite bloody literally, in this case. Because we don't yet know where this bugger Duke is. Trust me, I want to get my hands on him even more than they do because his recklessness has been causing us all sorts of trouble, even beyond all this. Isn't that right, Jesús?'

314

Jesús nodded.

'Not least the burgeoning shortage of gear on this beautiful white island,' Grew said. 'The shortage our gear should have been filling right now. One that the Russians started filling themselves, before realizing there were bigger boys than them already here. Forcing our good friends out here to do all kinds of running around to fill the gap, like poor Sky, having to run a shipment over from Mallorca.'

'Sky?'

'Well, you didn't think it was really *pata negra*, did you, down there in that hold? Any more than I believed you when you told me you'd been off with some bird called Cielo all day.'

Christ, Frankie felt a double idiot. He'd known about that too.

'I've no idea what you were doing over there on Mallorca, mind,' Grew said. 'Whatever that postcard was you was flashing about . . . Any more than I know why you went back there yesterday afternoon and got your face rearranged again.' He stared at Frankie evenly. 'But I do know you're not a double-crossing prick like Duke. I even quite like you, kid, or I'd have already put you in the fucking ground.'

And Frankie wasn't about to tell him what the postcard was about either. 'So what now?' he said.

'Same old, same old. We still need to find Duke.'

'Where do you think he's gone?'

'Well, Jeremy's already had some of his uniformed pals keeping a little eye on the airport and ferry port. One of the big attractions of a small island like this, you see. So easy for friends with the right connections to keep tabs.'

'But still no sign of him?'

'No, making me think he might have already done a flit on some private boat, or gone to ground. Which is a nuisance, of course. Because he's got a big bloody bag of cash. Meaning he might be able to stay hidden for months. But I'm still feeling sanguine, on account of how he doesn't know this island that well, so might not know anywhere nicely off the beaten track to hide up.'

Frankie thought about this, as the outskirts of Ibiza Old Town came into view in the distance.

'Maybe he doesn't need to,' he then said.

'Need to what?' Grew asked.

'Know the island that well. Maybe he just needs to know one really good place to go.'

37

The *Savage Monkey*'s engine growled menacingly as it turned into the secluded, half-moon-shaped cove on this ragged stretch of coastline on the north-east of the island.

The atmosphere on board was a lot less relaxed than the last time Frankie had been out. This time there was no skinny-dipping Sky, for one thing, and no Valium-hazed lie-in. This crew certainly weren't offering deck-side frolics, followed by rustic bread and cheese. Instead four geezers with weapons sat next to him, Jesús and Grew among them. Jeremy stood beside some local hard nut at the wheel, scanning the white crescent of beach through a pair of military-grade binoculars for any sign of movement.

All of them here because of Frankie, there was no getting away from it. Whatever went down today was because of him, and whoever got hurt. Either these lads here on board, or whoever the hell might be there in that shuttered-up clapboard restaurant there on the beach.

Or *chiringuito*, to be more precise, just like it said here on the matchbook in Frankie's jacket pocket that Little T had written her name down on. Restaurante Ca'n Costa, the old-school beach restaurant run by one of Duke's old mates. It was the perfect place to get away from it all, as Little T had told Frankie, and served the best seafood on the island too – not that Frankie would be sampling it today. For one thing, it was still only 9 a.m. and, apart from their good selves, it didn't seem like anyone else on the White Island had yet surfaced from whatever bacchanalian shenanigans they'd been up to last night. They'd seen a couple of windsurfers, but that was it on their way over here from Botafoch Marina. The beach ahead looked dead as a dodo as well.

Maybe he'd guessed wrong and Duke hadn't bolted here at all? In which case, things were looking bad for Little T, very bad indeed. Jeremy ordered the skipper to cut the engine while they were still 200 yards off shore. They dropped anchor, then it was over the side into the tender they'd been towing. Enough room for just five of them, which was fine, because the skipper was staying on the boat, with a rifle fitted with a telescopic sight fixed on the shore.

Jeremy and Jesús rowed in silence and perfect synchronicity, like they'd done it a million times before. How the hell could Frankie have ever thought they were anything other than brothers? What a mug.

He felt sick and not because of the sea, which was flat as a pancake, but because of the weight of the pistol here in his jacket pocket. He prayed it still had its bloody safety on. Even though he had no intention of ever using it, it was something that was here all the same.

The two brothers stepped out of the boat on either side as they hit the shallows and dragged the dinghy onto the untouched white sand. Jesús nodded at Frankie to follow him, and Grew padded after the tall figure of Jeremy, who set off fast for the right-hand side of the restaurant.

Frankie's mouth felt as dry as the hot sand beneath his bare feet. He and Jesús went round the edge of the restaurant double quick to the left side and skirted round a fire pit. Dozens of flies buzzed lazily over a fish head left in the ashes and a curl of smoke rose up. Someone had been here last night – maybe they still were? And if this place was only open on Fridays and Saturdays, then it was no regular punter. Both he and Jesús froze as they heard muffled voices. Was it a bloke and a bird's? Someone was talking – or were they? Perhaps it was a radio jingle.

Jesús pressed the forefinger of his right hand to his lips. His left was already curled around the trigger of his pistol as he edged up to the door and peered in through the greasy pane of glass. He held his forefinger up again. Signalling *what*? Wait? No, because he was already reaching for the handle. One, then? There was just one person inside?

Jesús threw himself aside as he heard the shout, just in bloody time. A gunshot roared and the pane of glass exploded. Then the door swung open and a body bundled through. Jesús went flying, taking the full force of the wooden door.

But whoever had charged through tripped right over the scorched bricks at the edge of the fire pit, landing just by Frankie's feet. A black gym bag spun ahead of him and smacked to a halt against a palm tree trunk.

Frankie caught the dark glint of a gun in the pit and whoever was next to it grabbed for it. Shit. Frankie needed to move. He stamped down hard on the tattooed hand

319

reaching out and caught it on the wrist. The guy was already flipping round to face him, but Frankie dropped down onto his knee, shoving his weight hard onto it, using his momentum to pin that wrist even tighter.

He followed up with a punch to the head. Frankie clocked it was Duke a split second before he broke the bastard's nose but didn't quite manage to knock him out. Duke spat something half garbled at him. A threat? Not much point in that. Jesús was already on him, pinning his other arm, as Frankie cocked and locked the one caught under his foot. Jeremy was on Duke next, dropping down beside Frankie and twisting the pistol from Duke's grip. They had him just in time for Grew's arrival.

'Gotcha, you slippery prick,' he grinned.

'No one else in there?' Frankie could still hear that bleedin' radio playing inside.

'No.' Grew stared down at Duke, who had the barrel of Jesús's pistol wedged in between his teeth. 'No?' he asked.

Duke made a little whimpering nose and jerked his head left and right, about the nearest he could probably get to a shake.

'Good,' said Grew.

'Please,' said Duke, as Jesús pulled the pistol out of his mouth.

'Please *what*?'

'Please . . .' Duke's eyes darted around, as though looking for help, for inspiration, for anything that might change this situation. '. . . *sir*?' he finally said.

Grew just stared at him, slack-jawed, for a second. Then

he started to laugh – before absolutely creasing up and slapping his thigh until tears ran down his cheeks.

'*Sir?*' he said. '*Sir?* Oh no, Duke, it's gonna take a lot more than a bit of simple ingratiation to get you out of this.' He shook his head. '*Sir?* Oh, my word. I do wish Tommy had been here to hear that.'

Frankie remembered Duke, then, in charge in the club. He'd been so sure of himself, a king in the making. But now he watched tears start running from his eyes. He was fucked and he knew it.

'Tie him up,' Grew said.

Jesús and Jeremy span Duke round onto his front, rubbing his face right down in the ashes of that pit. He started to struggle, flip-flapping around like a fish that had just been pulled out onto the shore, because under those coals the ashes were still hot. Duke started grunting and squawking, but all it earned him was a crack on the back of the head with the butt of Jesús's pistol. The smell of scorched hair rose up from the embers.

'Christ, is that necessary?' Frankie said, getting up and stepping back.

'Jesús,' Jesús said, looking annoyed.

'No, not like that . . . I mean, as in . . .'

What was the point? There was nothing he could do for Duke, even if he'd wanted. Frankly, that bastard had wanted him dead, and he'd even ditched his own girlfriend, so why the hell would he want to help him anyway?

He turned his back on them and stared back out to sea. The rifle scope winked in the bright sunlight. In the distance, he saw a sail. Then, closer, on the right side of the bay, another powerboat roared into view.

'Looks like we've got company,' he called out.

'Long, sleek and white with a British flag?' Grew called back. He was hunched over the gym bag by the tree.

'Yeah.' The boat matched that description, all right.

'That'll be ours then. Here comes Balearic Bob on his shiny charger, coming in to save the day.' Grew grinned at Frankie, getting up. 'Or didn't you know we were the good guys?'

'No.'

'Oh, yes, and, truly, it appears that we have indeed won the day.' Delving inside the gym bag, Grew pulled out a fistful of cash. 'Dollars, too. My very favourite kind of criminal currency, they're always so easy to shift. Maybe old Dukey boy here's not such a dumb piece of shit after all.'

Bob's boat slewed to a halt beside the *Savage Monkey*. Even though there was more than one person on it, Bob was there at the wheel clear as day, his face glowing as orange as a jaffa even from here.

'And what are you looking at?' Grew snapped.

Turning back, Frankie saw he meant Duke, who was up on his feet now and not a pretty sight. He had his arms roped behind his back and there was blood trickling down from where Frankie had broken his nose. His hair – what was left of it – was white with ash and there were blister marks all over his face.

'Hoping it was somebody else, were you? Whatever pal it was of yours who hid you here? Hoping they might pop back and rescue you and take you off wherever you were planning on scarpering next? Well, forget it. They show up and they're dead. The only ride you're getting out of here, sunshine, is gonna have a hammer and sickle flying on its deck.'

Duke's eyes widened through the ashes.

'Oh, yes, me laddio,' Grew said. 'Or hadn't you heard? Your little Russian buddies left us a note, suggesting we do a deal. You and this here wedge – which is theirs. In return for Little T and all that gear – which is ours.'

Duke spat out ashes. 'But she's got –' he rasped.

'Nothing to do with this? They beg to differ. Oh come on, son. What? Did you really expect they were going to just let her go? Don't bullshit me, we know you abandoned her, just like the little coward you are.' He smiled flatly at him. 'But, seriously, don't worry, Duke, we're not handing you over to them.'

'Oh, my God.' Duke's knees sagged. 'Thank God.'

The bastard. Just look at the relief on his face. Grew was right, he didn't give a shit about saving Little T at all – just saving his own skin. But judging from his complexion right now, that hadn't exactly worked out either.

'No, not with you being one of ours,' Grew said.

'Jesus, thanks, Grew, and I swear, whatever it takes. I'll make it up to you. And Tommy. I swear I wi—'

Grew slapped him hard then, right across his face with the back of his hand, and fresh blood trickled fast down his chin.

'No, we're not going to hand you over to them *yet,* because first we want a little time with you on our own.'

Duke started to cry out in protest but it was no good.

Grew already had the roll of duct tape in his hands. He wrapped it fast round Duke's head, with a shriek.

'Yeah, that's right, you're fucked,' said Grew.

Duke stared back at him for a second, moaning ineffectively through the gag, but then his head lolled.

'Take him inside,' Grew said. 'I don't want any passing windsurfer seeing us paying him Tommy's regards.'

Jeremy and Jesús dragged Duke back into the restaurant.

'You want in?' Grew asked Frankie. 'After all, he has jerked you around plenty an' all.'

'No.'

'Fair enough. Not really your gig, that sort of thing, is it? I understand. Then wait here for Bob and when he gets here, tell him to radio those Russians and arrange a nice safe spot for the exchange.' He took a camera out of his pocket and waggled it at him with a grin. 'For Tommy. He wants to see for himself how truly sorry Duke is.'

38

Frankie was given the job of escorting Little T home, a dubious honour. He felt he'd played such a small part in prising her away from Duke and the only thing she said to him – from the second he got into the Merc beside her and her bodyguards outside the Mandalay, to the moment the bodyguards nodded them unsmilingly on their way through the airport departure gates – was: 'I hope you die in pain and alone.'

The comment was too thought through to have been off the cuff, that's what Frankie was thinking during the flight back to Gatwick, as he kept glancing across at her staring resolutely out the window into the darkening sky. After all, as far as she was concerned, he'd betrayed her and her boyfriend rotten. Oh yeah, Frankie reckoned he'd made himself an enemy here for life.

He still didn't know where or exactly when the trade had taken place that had been specified in the note, but the deal of Duke and the cash, in return for Little T and the gear, had been successful. Everyone had got what they'd wanted.

Apart from Duke, of course. He'd been handed over to

the Russians, who'd been none too gruntled by his double-dealing, or so Grew had explained. Duke had cost them time, effort and pride – they'd already curtailed their little operation back there on Ibiza in the face of the united opposition they'd come up against.

Christ only knew what they'd done to him, but Frankie could only hope it had been quick. Remembering the look on that bastard Sergei's face as he'd rolled up his sleeves, preparing to kick Frankie in that night in Kooks, he somehow doubted that would have been the case.

What Frankie did know was that Little T here didn't believe a word of what she'd been told about that skuzzer Duke. She didn't even believe he'd tried ripping Tommy off, quite the reverse. She'd fully bought into what Duke had told her. He'd said Tommy had ripped him off and that's why they'd had to go on the run. As for him then doing a runner on her? Forget it, she didn't believe that either. Little T thought it was just part of some wider, smarter plan of his – one that would have somehow miraculously ended up with the two of them living wild and free together, like some more fortunate incarnation of Bonnie and Clyde.

Grew thought she was a mug, but Frankie felt differently, a part of him even liked her for it, for not being so thoroughly fucking jaded as the rest of them, and for still believing in romance and a world that wasn't just full of snakes and wolves.

More heavies were waiting for them the other side of customs. Not exactly hard to spot either. Of course, she tried pulling away from them and they let her go. But not out of sight. Oh no, Little T's independence was clearly being substantially curtailed from here on in. Possibly for good, depending on how Tommy and Gaz had decided to play it next.

Frankie thought that was job done. He'd already said his goodbyes to Grew and Jesús in Ibiza. The two of them had decided to stay put until the end of the season, but as he walked off towards the rail station for the Gatwick Express that would take him back into London, a short bloke in a neat black business suit stepped into his way and told him: 'Gaz says thank you for bringing her home and here's my card, I work for him. If there's ever anything we can do.'

Frankie didn't even answer – a part of him couldn't bear the thought of getting embroiled with yet another crook. He just slipped the card into his pocket next to the little match-book with the name of the *chiringuito* on it. The ying and the bloody yang of betrayal? Yeah, he guessed that's what it came down to. Duke's loss was his gain and who was he to say no? Because who knew when he might need a favour from someone as connected as Gaz Landy?

*

It was another favour from a more familiar source that was waiting for Frankie when he got back home. A message from Grew on the answerphone.

'All right, kiddo,' he said. 'Me, Jesús and Bob here are missing you. Being just the Three Musketeers without our d'Artagnan just don't seem the same. Anyhow, I've got some news for you – though you didn't hear it from me. Those two pigs' names you wanted checking, well, I put out some feelers – never you mind who – and they've come up with some juice.'

Frankie's heart was racing. He wanted this so bad. But already alarm bells were ringing too . . . *didn't hear it from me*. Meaning he wanted nothing more to do with this? Meaning it was information that could get him into trouble if it ever got traced back to him? And *never you mind who* . . . Meaning he wasn't giving Frankie access to who-ever had done his digging for him. Meaning whatever this was, there was nothing more Frankie could find out through him.

'The first little piggy, Craig Fenwick. Snaresby was tell-ing you the truth about him, he did move to Oz – and I've got an address for him which I'll send round when I get back home – but your other little piggy, James Nicholls . . . well, you're in luck there, because he's not bloody dead at all, he's still right there in London, working as a frigging vicar, would you believe it, a copper with a conscience. I'm guessing he must have done something very naughty indeed.'

Bloody hell. As Grew read out the address, Frankie lunged for a pen and scribbled it down. But there was no phone number, Grew said, as Nicholls was ex-directory. It didn't matter. Nicholls was going to need a lot more than that to keep him from Frankie now.

*

Frankie was up early the next morning. It felt good to be back on his own turf, playing by his own rules. Xandra and

Slim seemed pleased to see him too when they variously got up and arrived to find him mopping the floors downstairs at the club.

The three of them sat down over coffee and went through the till receipts. Frankie promised them a night out together, on top of the bonus they'd agreed. They'd clearly had their work cut out without him and he was suitably grateful, not that they were done quite yet. Tomorrow was the biggest game of the year – no, sod that, the decade. England versus Germany in the semis, on Wednesday, 26 June, at 7.30 p.m. The Ambassador would be rammed.

Frankie had a few other things to do first, mind. For one thing, that copper. James Nicholls. No rush on that, maybe. He sounded like he'd settled for the quiet life and probably wouldn't be going anywhere anytime soon, and a part of Frankie wanted to make his approach nice and slow. Maybe he would tip up there at his church this Sunday and grab a pew and size the bastard up? But another part of him couldn't wait to flat out confront the prick. Scare him even. And see what fell out the woodwork.

Then there was Jack and the Old Man. Frankie needed to see them both to tell them about Mallorca. Because he had to, right? It was their business too, even if it made no difference to them. And it might still not. Because even though he'd tracked his mum down to Palma, he'd then lost her again, with everything sort of cancelling itself out. And maybe that's how they'd see it too, as nothing having changed and her still being missing. End of.

But that wasn't how it was for him, because so what if he hadn't found her? He'd proved that her trail hadn't gone dead the day she'd vanished from their lives. There was still hope that one day he might track her down again. Because the one thing he'd learned from his little Balearic escapade was that he was good at this shit – at finding people. Perhaps because he was good at never giving up.

Back up in the flat, he showered and changed into his running gear. It was a beautiful sunny day. He did a loop round Hyde Park then back into Soho. He fleetingly thought about heading up to West End Central Police Station, wondering what it would be like to accidentally-on-purpose bump into Sharon Granger, if she happened to be there standing outside. It was something he'd thought about loads this last year, but today the idea seemed to have lost its appeal. And, come to think of it, he'd hardly thought about her at all these last few days. And maybe not just because of all the other mental bollocks he'd been dealing with, but because of Isabella too? Because that kiss had stayed with him, hadn't it? What if England did win tomorrow night? He'd be one step nearer that Ladbrokes payout. And maybe one step nearer a trip back to Palma like he'd promised her too.

He'd given Jack a bell at his new flat before he'd left, but there'd been no answer. Nothing on his mobile either. Frankie cut up onto Oxford Street and along as far as Soho Square, before hanging a left. Then, bloody hell, he nearly stopped in his tracks.

The James Boys Gym. There it was in fancy red lettering on a big black sign above the doors. Tommy Riley clearly wasn't messing around. Frankie felt a big surge of pride, he'd have to come back here with a camera and get a snap of it. The Old Man, he would bloody love it. But it wasn't

330

just pride, he felt something like hope, that this really could be a new start for Jack. Maybe this would keep him safe and he'd be able to make something of his life at last.

He found Jack inside and could hardly believe his eyes again, because it wasn't just the sign that had changed – Jack had too. He was all dressed up in a tracksuit and running shoes. Frankie nearly spat his teeth. But instead he just watched him listening to GoGo JoJo, who was stood there beside him. Bugger me, Jack was even taking notes.

'He doing all right then, is he?' he asked JoJo, walking up behind them.

JoJo smiled. 'If he keeps on listening, he might one day turn out to be the smartest boss I've ever had.'

'All right, bruv?' Jack said, grinning at Frankie. He gave him a hug. 'How was your holibobs?' He pulled back a bit. 'And what the hell has happened to your face?'

'Oh, yeah, that.' He meant the bruises on his face. 'Some young lads took exception to my dancing skills,' he said, making up the first thing that sprung to mind.

'Tossers. I bet they look worse, though, yeah?'

'Yeah. You're healing up nicely, mind.' Frankie pushed back Jack's fringe and checked the stitches. 'Yeah, no more casting calls for you for *Frankenstein*, I'm afraid.'

'Hey, Frankie.'

Frankie turned at the female voice. Did a double take when he saw who it was. Tiffany. The waitress from Brasserie du Marché, decked out in sleek black running gear, looking like she was about to run a marathon. He smiled, broad and wide, he couldn't help himself, but then he remembered: it was him she was interested in. Not any more, even if she ever had been. Now it was just Jack. And just to prove it, she gave him a kiss on the cheek.

'Not interrupting anything, am I?' she asked, clocking the bruises on his face, but not saying anything.

'Nah, just checking up on him,' Frankie said. 'I mean *in*. Just checking in.'

'Good,' she said, 'because we're on a schedule.'

Jack groaned, but she just grinned.

'No whinging. We made a deal,' she warned.

'What deal?' Frankie asked.

She counted it off on her fingers. 'No fags, no drugs, and four runs a week.'

Oh, yeah. Now Frankie remembered. She was a part-time personal trainer, wasn't she, too. '*Runs?*'

'Yeah, as in running,' Jack said, cutting off the obvious joke.

'And what do you get out of this deal?' Frankie asked him.

'My company,' Tiffany answered for him with a grin.

Jack blushed long and hard. Well, here was a turn-up for the books. He was smitten, or so it seemed.

'You all right if I go?' he asked Frankie. 'We can catch up later on, or tomorrow?'

'Yeah, yeah. Tomorrow. Come round and watch the match. He is still allowed to watch footie, right?' Frankie asked Tiffany with a grin.

'Only if he doesn't keep asking me to explain the offside rule,' she smiled back.

'Fair enough. Right. I'll see you both then.'

Frankie gave Jack another hug and off they jogged.

Yeah, tomorrow would be fine. He could fill him in on all things Mum then.

Frankie shot the breeze with JoJo for five minutes, before pushing off, promising him he'd be back for a sparring session next week. And why not? His little brother only ran the bloody place now, eh?

Just as he was leaving, a movement snagged his eye and, looking up, he saw Listerman the lawyer in that glass-fronted office, gazing back down. He raised an arm in greeting, but it wasn't an invitation. Turning his back on Frankie, he returned to his desk.

Frankie glanced over at the door where he'd seen those big geezers with the black briefcases walking out the last time he was here. What was it Tam Jackson had said? *Nothing you need to concern yourself with. Got a separate entrance. Meaning it's a separate business, OK?* No, still not OK. And wouldn't be either. Not until Frankie knew that whatever was going on in there wasn't going to affect his little brother's life.

39

Frankie had always liked Kew Gardens, it was predictable, relaxing, safe. His mum had dreamed of moving here one day, and Kind Regards the same. It had always been a running joke between them all, back when Frankie had been a kid. With only the Old Man objecting. Twee Gardens, he'd called it. Fucking Surrey, not even proper London at all.

Parking his Capri in the little horseshoe-shaped road by the station, Frankie couldn't help thinking how his own luck would fare today.

He found the block of flats soon enough, though. On a cute little tree-lined road off Kew Green, with the church spire rising in the distance. Nice thing about posh places like Kew. You could just ask people and they helped, instead of looking like you were planning on mugging them, which was how most people acted back in his 'hood.

Another kind old duck even let him in through the front door of the Reverend James Nicholls's building. She told him the Reverend lived up on the second floor. Frankie just about managed a smile as he thanked her, but already he was adrenalizing. Was reminding himself how he was going to play this. Hard and fast. There'd be no actual violence, but he'd just get right up into this guy's grill and tell him who he was and what he wanted.

He'd had second thoughts about putting the proper frighteners on him. Nicholls was an ex-copper, after all. And if he'd been pals with Snaresby, he would have once been a right bastard too and wouldn't be easy to intimidate. And probably would have had no problem tracking Frankie down and getting him done for assault if he overstepped the mark.

Better to play a few mind games with him and tell him he knew that what had happened with the Old Man's case wasn't right. And tell him that the case was being looked into again, official, like. Even though this wasn't strictly true.

He hurried up the stairs and found the right flat. Gave the front door a good hard knock and open it swung – never a good sign. Frankie steeled himself and went in fists up, already clenched, expecting the bloody worst.

And he got it too. A body. A dead one. Or at least that's certainly how it looked, hanging up there from the living room light fitting.

Shitting arse bollocks. Frankie just stood there and gawped for a second. The Reverend James Nicholls's eyes were wide open. What looked like dried spit caked his chin. A tipped-over chair lay forever out of reach beneath his feet.

And it was definitely him, right? Had to be. He was in full churchy regalia. One of them long black frocks, or whatever they called them. And his face, all monged and gurny as it was, matched the same frocked fellah in a photo above the mantelpiece.

Another photo that caught his eye showed Nicholls in a bar, a little younger, and dressed in a suit, looking well smashed too, with lots of uniforms around him. Maybe it was his retirement bash from the force? Frankie's stomach lurched, because guess who was grinning right there beside him? None other than DI Snaresby. Another three blokes as well. Right at the centre of the crowd. Arms around each other's necks. A group within a group. And all of them smiling up at whoever was taking the photo, like they were somehow in on it too.

Frankie looked round, his heart pounding. *Think*. What should he do? Search the place? But look for what? Files? Folders? Computers. Anything to do with the case. Shit, it was worth a go. He hurried over to the desk. A couple of the drawers were already open. Like someone had gone through them? No computer.

Shit. He pulled his jacket sleeves down over his hands and opened the other drawers. It was just stationery and stuff. He quickly checked the other rooms too, but nothing caught his eye.

His heart was pounding like it was going to burst now, he needed to get out of here fast. He still remembered waking up last year in another flat with another dead body in it and the sound of cop sirens closing in all around. Was that what this was? Another set-up? Or just something way sadder than that?

He looked around. A half-finished meal on the table over there in front of the TV. Which was still on, but with the sound turned down. A trailer for the bleedin' *X-Files*, of all things. Bloody hell, if only Mulder and Scully were here.

He grabbed the photo – the one of Snaresby and the others – on the way out. He wasn't even quite sure why but there was just something about them. They looked like they ruled the bleedin' world. And there, on the corner of the frame, something else snagged his attention, something that could have been the smudge of a lipstick mark.

He walked as fast as he could away from the block of flats. Holy crapola, would that old lady who'd let him in downstairs remember him? No, he'd had his cap on, right? And what about CCTV? No, he didn't think he'd seen any cameras. But even if he had been spotted, would it matter anyway? He didn't know how long Nicholls had been dead. Long enough for Frankie not to be considered a suspect even if someone had seen him go in? Hours? Longer? Days?

But it wasn't just this his brain wouldn't let go of, it was the fact Nicholls was dead at all. A coincidence? Yeah, sure, that was possible. Maybe he'd got depression or God knows what. Maybe he'd been thinking about this for weeks. Or maybe it wasn't a coincidence at all, Frankie going looking for him . . . and finding him dead. Perhaps the one thing had led to the other.

What if someone had told him Frankie was coming? Did this bloke really have something to hide?

What if instead someone had just made it look like he'd topped himself? Because, yeah, that was another thing Frankie had learned last year, sometimes deaths weren't what they seemed.

Frankie reached his car and headed out sharpish across

Kew Bridge and onto the Westway and back into town. *Think harder!* Who'd known he was going there today? He'd not told anyone, had he? No. It was just something he'd decided to crack on and do after getting the club ready for tonight's match.

But that didn't mean no one had known he might be coming here some time. Because Grew . . . yeah, Grew had known about Frankie having Nicholls's address . . . and that he'd been interested in him because of the Old Man's case. And what about the people who'd helped him find it? The *never you mind who*s? Would Grew have told them why as well? And what about Riley? Would Grew have told him too? Had he got Frankie this information under his own auspices? Or because Riley had said he could?

Then there was Snaresby. Because, shit, yeah, Frankie had told him he knew Nicholls's and Fenwick's names back at the hospital, hadn't he? And Snaresby knew he'd got hold of those case files too and that he was planning on doing something about them.

Last of all, there was Lomax and Dolf too. They'd overheard Frankie talking to the Old Man in the clink and telling him he was going to try and find a way to prove his innocence again. 'Fear Lies in the Past'. Frankie pictured that bloody note again, the one he'd found on the Capri. *Had* whoever had written it been warning him off this?

Would Nicholls still be alive if he'd not tracked him down?

*

'It's coming home . . . It's coming home . . . It's coming . . . Football's coming home . . .'

Frankie heard the chant coming from the Ambassador from halfway down Poland Street, as he hurried towards it after parking the car. Spartak waved at him from where he was stationed on a chair by the door.

'Sounds busy,' Frankie said as he reached him.

The big man wrapped him up in a bear-sized hug.

'Because it *is* busy,' he said.

Frankie reached up and touched the tip of his red mohawk with a grin.

'What's that for?' asked the giant Russian.

'Luck. So as England wins. I've got a lot riding on this one, mate. And,' Frankie added, 'because the last Russian I ran into tried to kill me and I'm just making sure you're the friendly kind.'

'Where is this son of a whore?' Spartak said, looking round. 'I will teach him some manners, if you like?'

'I'll tell you all about him later, mate. But, right now, we've got us a game to watch.'

'Three Lions on a shirt . . . Juuuuules Rimet still gleaming . . . thiiiiirrrty years of hurt . . . neeeeeever stopped me dreaming . . .'

Frankie forced himself through the crowd towards the bar. The place was jammed, buzzing. It was kick-off in less than thirty seconds' time. Someone shouted out his name and he looked around, but couldn't work out who. So many people in here he knew. Slim, Xandra, Maxine, Dickie Bird, TFI Jonny, Jack, Tiffany, Festive Al, even Tam bloody Jackson and his crew.

But it was other faces he was thinking of too as the whistle blew and a roar went up and he turned round to face the big screen. Faces from the last few days. Isabella, Sky, Jeremy, Jesús, Grew, Sergei, Uncle Carlo, Duke, Little T, Balearic Bob, the Old Man and his mum too.

But most of all it was the faces of those other three cops in the framed photo he still held in his hand, squeezing it so hard now that he felt the glass crack.

Experience the complete Soho Nights series

If you enjoyed DOUBLE KISS

then you'll love listening to FRAMED

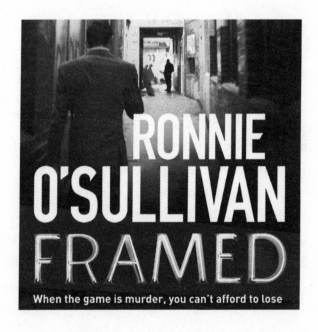

Available to download today

Read on . . .

FRAMED

Frankie hadn't so much inherited the Ambassador Club, as had it thrown at him like a ticking bomb from a speeding car. At least that's what his dad's cousin, Kind Regards, had told him five years ago – and that's how it still felt today.

Hitting the light switch in the club's main hall, Frankie breathed in the stale smell of smoke, chalk and beer, as he listened to the *tink-tink* of the strip lights flickering into life above the twelve tables.

He sighed. The hall's worn carpet was scuffed and stained and its walls and ceiling were patchy with damp. Two of the frosted plate glass windows overlooking the street had been cracked by some passing pissheads a few weeks ago and he still hadn't got round to fixing them.

Drumming his fingers along the edges of the tables as he walked to the bar, he was almost glad his dad wasn't here to see it. After his dad had been banged up and Frankie had first taken over managing the club, he'd hoped to turn its fortunes round. Easier said than done.

He'd hit the same old chicken and egg problem the old man had. The only way to make enough money to tart the place up was to bring in more punters. But the only way to bring in more punters was to tart the fucking place up.

Frankie's dad, Bernie, had taken out a thirty-year lease on the club over ten years ago, back in '84, after winning big on the horses. His plan had been to put it on the map. Make it a hub for the game here in the West End. But he'd always come up short.

End result was that Frankie and his brother Jack had hung out here pretty much full time in their teens when they weren't in school, being babysat by staff, while their mum and dad had gone out doing other jobs to make ends meet: managing brewery pubs, or running van-loads of tax-free cigarettes and booze back on the ferries from France.

Not that Frankie had minded. None of the rented houses they'd lived in at the time had ever felt as much like home as here. Frankie loved it. Soho. The club. The people. The free lemonades and crisps. And of course the snooker. He'd got the bug for it the instant he'd picked up a cue. Hadn't been a day gone by since when he hadn't fitted in a few frames.

He checked his watch. Still too early to go cap in hand to Daniel Listerman about the rent. Listerman was Tommy Riley's lawyer and Riley was the big-time gangster bastard who owned the freehold on this building along with the rest of the street.

Listerman the Lawyer was an early riser. Some said he never slept at all. But turning up this early at his swanky Beak Street office would only make Frankie look even more desperate – and skint – than he was.

Might as well make himself useful here first. He changed

out of his suit in the storeroom, coming back out in tatty blue overalls and black rubber boots, with earphones in, a Sony Discman clipped to his belt, and a bucket of warm soapy water and a mop in his fists.

He'd had to let the club's regular cleaner go a month back, not having enough money to pay her. It didn't bother him that much, to tell the truth. Apart from the khazis. Especially the gents. What the hell was wrong with blokes anyway? Why couldn't a single bloody one of them manage to piss in a straight line?

He cleaned the bogs first to get them out the way, then the bar and the ashtrays, before starting on sweeping and mopping the floor. He worked his way round the tables in the same pattern he did every day. It somehow made it go faster, like doing circuits down the gym.

He hummed as he worked. A Northern Soul compilation. Everyone was into Blur and Oasis these days, but he reckoned the old tunes were still the best. His dad had been a proper mod back in the day. There was a signed Small Faces LP up above the bar. Used to be an old Bang & Olufsen record player and a stack of Al Wilson and Jimmy Radcliffe singles back there as well. But Jack had pilfered the lot on his nineteenth birthday two years ago and flogged them down Berwick Street market to pay for a night on the razz.

Frankie still hadn't forgiven him, the little shit. Him and Jack had used to listen to those records as kids, dancing and larking about. They should have meant more to him than just some quick cash. Frankie remembered coming down here one night late when his mum and dad had still been together and seeing them slow-dancing round the empty club. He couldn't believe how fucked up his family life had got since then.

His mum had gone missing in '88, just after Frankie had turned sixteen. A year after her and his dad had started living apart, her at their rented house and him here in the flat above the club. She'd just vanished when Frankie and Jack had both been at school. No sign of a struggle. Nothing. Just gone.

Everyone else – Frankie's father, Jack and the cops – all reckoned that Priscilla James wasn't just missing, she was dead. Why else wouldn't she have come back? Or at least contacted them? But Frankie didn't believe it. He felt it in his guts. He just fucking *knew* that one day he'd see her again.

He checked his watch. Ten to ten. Nearly time to open up already. Nearly time to go see Listerman too, just as soon as Slim the barman got here to do his shift. Frankie headed back to the storeroom to get changed. The red light on the answerphone winked at him from the bar. He took his earphones out and hit 'Play'.

'Frankie?' It was Jack, sounding well stressed. 'For fuck's sake, Frankie, pick up.' Was he wasted? He was slurring. 'I'm coming over . . . Fuck. I need you. I need help . . .' A whisper, a hiss. 'I'm coming over. *Now*.'

Frankie groaned. Hell's tits, not again. How many fucking times already this year? Jack doing too much gear. Getting himself in a paranoid mess. Jack needing a lift back from some godforsaken club in the middle of piggin' Essex. Jack running out of dosh and expecting Frankie to bail him

345

out. Jack making the same stupid bloody mistakes over and over again.

Frankie's heart thundered. Just pretend you're not here. Don't answer the door. Fuck off back upstairs and turn up the radio and get in the shower.

But all he saw in his head was his mum. That last morning he'd seen her, as she'd handed him his packed lunch in the shitty little driveway of that rented Shepherd's Bush house.

'Go catch him up and make up,' she'd said.

She'd been talking about Jack. He'd just cycled off in a strop over some football sticker he'd nicked off Frankie the night before and which Frankie had just wrestled back off him.

'He thinks he can take care of himself, but he can't,' she'd said. 'You know that. And promise me, *promise me*,' she'd said, squeezing his wrist so hard he'd winced, 'you'll always be there for him. No matter what happens. To me or your dad, or to anyone else.'

Even then, it had sounded off. Had she known? He'd asked himself the same question a million times since. Had she known that by teatime she'd be gone?

Crack.

What the fuck?

He turned to face the club's front door. Someone had just given it an almighty smack.